Death in the ARCTIC

Also by Tom Hindle

A Fatal Crossing
The Murder Game
Murder on Lake Garda

TOM HINDLE

Death in the ARCTIC

C
CENTURY

1 3 5 7 9 10 8 6 4 2

Century
One Embassy Gardens
8 Viaduct Gardens
London SW11 7BW

Century is part of the Penguin Random House group of companies
whose addresses can be found at global.penguinrandomhouse.com.

Penguin Random House UK

First published by Century in 2025

www.penguin.co.uk

A CIP catalogue record for this book is available from the British Library.

ISBN: 9781529927221 (hardback)
ISBN: 9781529927245 (trade paperback)

Typeset in 13.5/17 pt Fournier MT Std by Jouve (UK), Milton Keynes
Printed and bound in Great Britain by Clays Ltd, Elcograf S.p.A.

The authorised representative in the EEA is Penguin Random House Ireland, Morrison Chambers, 32 Nassau Street, Dublin D02 YH68

www.greenpenguin.co.uk

MIX
Paper | Supporting responsible forestry
FSC® C018179
FSC www.fsc.org

Penguin Random House is committed to a sustainable future for our business, our readers and our planet. This book is made from Forest Stewardship Council® certified paper.

For Erica.
Now and always.

Author's Note

Death in the Arctic is a book that I've wanted to write for a little while, having decided in the summer of 2021 that an airship would make a fantastic location for a whodunnit.

Given my admiration for the technology, I've worked hard to ensure that the book represents as accurately as possible the history and sensation of airship travel, employing a mixture of desk research and my own personal experience of working with – and indeed of flying aboard – these incredible machines. That said, there are instances where I've taken creative liberties, particularly with regard to some of the finer technical workings of my airship, in order to devise a compelling murder mystery. I hope you'll understand why I have made these decisions, and that it won't detract from your enjoyment.

Likewise, as there are various organisations working towards the tremendously exciting goal of returning airships to our skies, I wanted to take this opportunity to say that this is a piece of pure fiction, written solely to entertain. Any resemblance a reader may notice to real individuals or organisations is unintended.

With all of that said, thank you for reading, and I hope you'll enjoy the story.

Passenger manifest for the *Osprey*, departing on Saturday 13 September 2025:

PASSENGERS

Ezra Day
Howard Barnes
Devon Sharpe
Jasper Berry
Madison Brooke
Mia Whiley
Astrid Hahn
Ben Rhodes
Chloé Campbell

CREW

Captain Fritz Schäfer
First officer Freja Nilsen
Second officer Jakob Wisting
Chef Gwyn Thomas
Chief steward Niamh Connelly
Steward Liam Mackey
Steward Jade Lycett
Steward Ivy Redmond

'At Skyline Voyages we're resurrecting a form of transport that has been absent from our skies for decades.'

Devon Sharpe had heard these words so many times that, as they were recited to him through his AirPods, he suspected he could repeat them verbatim. Not that this stopped him, as he sat in Oslo Airport's departure lounge, from listening to them again. Phone in his hand, he paid no notice to the people who bustled past on the way to their gates, wheeling suitcases and clutching boarding passes. Instead his eyes were glued to the polished promotional video that filled his screen, the image of an airship coming into view.

It was a breathtaking sight. The length of a football field and almost as wide, the craft hovered above a shimmering glacier, brilliant white against a blue sky. A series of small propellers were mounted on either side, large fins protruding from the rear. Across its belly, rows of dark windows promised spectacular views of the frozen landscape below.

'Airships do still exist . . .' The video moved swiftly

along, displaying a new image of a much smaller craft towing a banner over a NASCAR track. 'But they're a novelty. Sports events, advertising campaigns . . . They're no longer used for actual transport. At Skyline Voyages we intend to change that. And after two decades of intense research and development, we're now just months away from the official launch of our first aircraft, the *Osprey*.'

The image changed again, two men coming into view. Easily in his sixties, the man on the right had a squat appearance, with a receding hairline and a pair of slender glasses balancing on a pinched nose. He seemed considerably less comfortable than his younger companion, who was looking straight into the camera with an easy smile. Devon knew, because they were the same age, that the second man was thirty-seven years old. He was a foot taller than his co-presenter, his wavy hair carefully styled, with the sleeves of an open-collar shirt rolled back over his spindly forearms. At the bottom of the screen the words *Howard Barnes, Founder* came into view beneath the older man. And beneath his younger, smiling counterpart came *Ezra Day, Chief Operating Officer*.

No matter how many times he watched this video, as Devon looked into the face of his old school friend he struggled to take it in. It had been twenty years since they'd last seen one another, but he could still vividly remember the day Ezra had learned of Skyline Voyages at the age of seventeen. After all, Devon had been there, too.

It had happened just four months after the death of Ezra's father. A pilot by profession and a keen adventurer,

Isaac Day had been skiing with Howard to the North Pole when a sheet of ice gave way beneath him. The safety line tethering him to the rest of the group had failed, and the weight of his gear had dragged him down into the freezing water. According to Howard's eye-witness account, it had been over in seconds.

Ezra had been inconsolable. He barely ate, barely slept, barely even left his room. But then came the revelation that Howard and Isaac had conceived an idea in the days before he disappeared beneath the ice. Together, they had begun planning to return airships to the sky, starting with a luxury sightseeing tour over the North Pole.

They had even agreed on a name. Skyline Voyages.

The change in Ezra had been instantaneous. Gone was the grief, replaced by a relentlessness unlike anything Devon had ever seen.

'Howard's going to set up this company,' he had said. 'And I'm going to join him. I'm going to do it for my dad. In his place.'

Devon remembered Howard trying to tell the young Ezra that he shouldn't be hasty. 'Follow your passions,' he had urged. 'Study something sensible at university. Take some time to decide what you want to do. If the answer is still Skyline, I'm sure there'll be a job for you.'

But Ezra wouldn't be moved. Devon knew that Ezra's greatest ambition had been to make Isaac proud. To live up to his legend. Helping Howard bring Skyline Voyages to life became all that mattered.

Returning his attention to the video, Devon saw that it

was now Howard's turn to speak. 'Next spring,' he said, 'we'll offer regular sightseeing flights over the North Pole. We're already investigating other routes, too. The Amazon rainforest. The Sahara Desert. Our goal is to reach the most remote locations in the world, and to do so in style and comfort.'

As he spoke, concept images appeared of the same white airship over a lush jungle canopy, then miles of rolling sand dunes. A moment later, Devon saw the craft's interior, photographs scrolling past of a gleaming ice-themed bar area. Compact cabins with sumptuous beds. Enormous windows offering rolling views of snowy landscapes.

'But tourism is only the beginning,' Ezra took over again. 'Looking to more practical applications, we have huge ambitions. An airship may be slower than a plane, but it can stay airborne for days and, with the lift provided by helium, rather than colossal jet engines, is considerably greener. Imagine descending from the sky into an area affected by war or environmental crisis with more supplies than a helicopter could ever carry. Imagine the locations that could be reached and the green space that could be saved without the need for a runway. These are real possibilities. More than that, they are our ambitions. And it all starts here.'

The image changed again, now displaying a shark-tooth-shaped cluster of islands. Some distance below it, separated by a vast body of blue ocean, lay the very top of mainland Norway.

'For now,' Ezra continued, 'our journey begins in

Longyearbyen, on the Arctic archipelago of Svalbard. Situated just eight hundred miles from the North Pole, not only is Longyearbyen the world's northernmost permanent settlement, but its history is deeply intertwined with that of airship travel. Flying out of Svalbard, the airship *Norge* completed the first successful expedition to the Pole in 1926. Next year, when the *Osprey* officially takes flight, we will do so on the hundredth anniversary of that historic expedition, tracing its iconic route with a two-day sightseeing journey to the very top of the world. Along the way we'll travel directly over the nature reserves and national parks that make up this Arctic wonderland. We'll fly low and slow, doing our best to spot some of the polar bears and reindeer herds that make this place their home. If we're lucky, we may even see whales in the fjords and along the coastline. And from there we continue to—'

Feeling a light tap on his shoulder, Devon took out his AirPods. All around him, he heard suitcase wheels rattling, children squabbling and monotone Tannoy announcements that gates were now open.

Smiling down on him, an elderly gentleman said, '*Sitter det noen her?*' Then, seeing the confusion on Devon's face, he nodded towards the neighbouring seat and asked in a Norwegian accent, 'May I sit?'

Devon removed his coat and rucksack from the seat, thinking about returning to the video once the man had sat down. But having already watched it several times that morning alone, he put the AirPods in his pocket.

He struggled to articulate how it felt to be back in touch

with Ezra. Having shared a boarding-school dormitory for most of their teenage years, there had been a time when they were as close as brothers. But when adulthood came calling, they had lost touch. Ezra had gone to study business and finance, his heart set on joining Howard at Skyline Voyages, while Devon had built a life working in the Alps, taking wealthy tourists on bespoke expeditions into the mountains. Their schooldays now felt like another age. Another life altogether. And as for Skyline Voyages, Devon had almost completely forgotten Ezra's teenage promise to his fallen father. So to receive a phone call out of the blue – let alone a call to inform him that they had succeeded – had been one hell of a shock.

'We're trying to appeal to the same sort of tourist you take on your trips in the Alps,' Ezra had explained. 'High-net-worth, adventure-obsessed types. They want to go off the map, but they want to do it in style. We've got a little under a year before we launch, and we need to use that time ensuring everything's perfect. I was hoping you might spend a weekend with us, point out anything that could be improved.'

Devon had been flattered. 'I'd love to, Ezra. And it really is great to hear from you. But I'm not sure I can come away at the moment—'

'Please, mate,' Ezra had urged. 'It would be so good to see you again, and your experience with this kind of customer would be incredibly valuable. If it helps, I can pay for your time. We can bring you in as a consultant, write it off as a business expense.'

That stung. Not because Ezra had offered, but because he had given Devon no choice but to say yes. The proposed fee wasn't much. It certainly wasn't enough to lift Devon out of the financial quandaries with which he was grappling. But as he'd looked at the paperwork building up on his desk – letters from his accountant, his solicitor and, crucially, the solicitor of the client who was suing him – he found that he simply couldn't say no.

Across the departure hall, Devon saw a teenager sit at a piano and begin to play a tune. The kid must have been around the same age he and Ezra had been when they last saw each other. Seventeen, maybe.

He glanced down at his phone, where the video remained paused. Looking at him now, with his angular jaw and perfect hair, it was impossible to tell that Ezra had been the runt of their group. There was no sign of the kid who came last in every cross-country race or who'd been pummelled within minutes of setting foot on the rugby pitch. No trace of the scrappy underdog who'd needed Devon to save him from all the fights he would start, but could never hope to win.

'Come on, Dev,' Ezra had said over the phone. 'It's been far too long. We deserve a proper catch-up.'

It had been eerie to hear his voice again. It was deeper, of course. But the inflections and rhythm were completely unchanged. He sounded just as sure of himself as he had always been. Just as eager.

Devon supposed his own circumstances made Ezra's success more difficult to accept. Of the two of them, one had taken an impossible dream and somehow made it a reality. The other had tried only to carve an honest living. A living that, through no fault of his own, was crumbling around him.

'Ladies and gentlemen,' a voice called out over the Tannoy, 'flight SA2308 to Longyearbyen is now ready to board.'

Stuffing the phone into his pocket, Devon rose and slung his bag over his shoulder. As he did so, he realised, with a start, what he was struggling to articulate. He was resentful. Somewhere, deep inside, lay a burning, pulsing resentment of Ezra Day.

It was a frightening thought. He should be pleased for his old friend to have achieved such a feat. And if not pleased for Ezra, he should at least be looking forward to the journey ahead. A two-day flight on what had been pitched to him as an airborne challenger to the Ritz. What was there not to look forward to?

But as he hurried towards the gate, working hard to tell himself that he did indeed feel these things, for a fleeting moment Devon wanted nothing more than for his old friend to drop down dead.

Seven hundred miles north, in an aircraft hangar outside the city of Tromsø, Niamh Connelly looked up at the *Osprey*, trying to convince herself that she wasn't making the greatest mistake of her life.

Nine years had passed since, on her twenty-first birthday, she had signed up with an agency that recruited crew members for superyachts. For someone so hard-working and so eager to travel, it had seemed perfect. Working as a steward aboard an array of eye-wateringly impressive vessels, all great gleaming craft owned by finance magnates and energy tycoons, she had experienced some incredible things. But the *Osprey* was a different beast entirely.

She had seen pictures before accepting the role. Plenty of them. But no photograph could have prepared her for the sheer size of it, tethered in place as it bobbed above the ground. She was reminded of a visit to London's Natural History Museum, where the skeleton of a blue whale had been suspended from the ceiling. It was the best comparison she could think of, but it still didn't do the *Osprey* justice. The airship could have swallowed the whale several times over.

Niamh wanted to be excited. Just as she had been when the news came through that a chief steward was required for a brand-new luxury airship, or when she first saw the concept pictures of the *Osprey* hovering over a gleaming Arctic landscape, or when she received the call offering her the role. As a member of the ground crew in a black Skyline Voyages jacket led her aboard, giving her a guided tour of the two decks, she had done her best to look enthused. More than that, she had done her best to *feel* it. She had marvelled at the sparkling glassware behind the bar and had breathed in the designer scent that had been concocted for the lounge. But the entire time, a single thought filled her mind.

This was wrong.

It was a feeling she had been grappling with for weeks, as a growing number of small irritations gradually became serious issues. First there was the three-year contract that she had been required to sign upon accepting the role. Strange, she had thought, but worth it. She had already been passed over for a chief-steward role aboard three different yachts, with the positions instead going to colleagues who were that little bit older or had an extra year or two's experience. Any sacrifice was worth it, to finally make the leap. And to do it aboard this aircraft – the first of its kind – had seemed like the chance of a lifetime.

Next had come the nervous looks from her former crewmates at the agency, when she shared the news. 'An

Arctic placement isn't for everyone,' one had said. 'That environment can mess with your head. For most people, it doesn't do any good to spend weeks at a time seeing absolutely nothing in every direction.'

Then there was the team who would be working beneath her. When she'd been in talks over the role, Ezra Day had assured Niamh that she would have the chance to appoint her own stewards. But when the time came, he had sat in on all her interviews, and while he had listened to her recommendations, he had overruled her on every single one. By the time he was done, she had a cocky bartender, a budding climate activist and the owner's niece.

Even the little cabins for the crew made her uneasy. They were virtually identical to those in which she had spent hundreds of nights aboard her superyachts. But on a yacht it was easy to convince yourself that the cramped conditions below deck were worth it. She had spent countless evenings sleeping in the knowledge that it was the Mediterranean Sea lapping against the other side of her wall. Her time working had been spent with the sun on her skin, and her days off spent either on the water with her friends or shopping in nearby harbours.

But as she looked at her quarters aboard the *Osprey*, all she saw were tiny grey cupboards. There would be no shopping trips or days in the sun during her time with Skyline Voyages. After the warnings she had received from her former crewmates, Niamh found it impossible not to think of the vast expanse that would soon be looming beneath them.

For the most part she had succeeded in quelling – or at least ignoring – these reservations. But as she stood in the cavernous Norwegian air hangar, looking at the airship in person for the first time, the sight of the *Osprey* made her so nervous she thought she might be sick.

Three years, she thought to herself. *Three years* aboard this thing. What had she been *thinking*? When she had first applied for the job, the photographs of the Arctic landscape had been enchanting. It had been all polar bears and narwhals, glistening fjords and blinding sunshine. But now . . .

She had desperately racked her brain for a way to escape. But the contract with Skyline Voyages was iron-clad. The only way would be to give in her notice, and she wouldn't lower herself as easily as that. It would take years to recover from such a blight on her CV. If she were to tarnish her reputation by quitting a job before giving it a proper chance, especially after so vehemently pursuing the promotion, she could wave goodbye to another shot at becoming chief steward.

Eyes still fixed on the *Osprey*, she forced herself to stand up straight. It might not be so bad. Once they were over that cold desert she might find it just as beautiful as in the photographs. Perhaps they really would see all the incredible things Ezra had promised: polar bears and whales. Perhaps it wouldn't even matter that she hadn't chosen her own team. The three stewards under her command could be every bit the attentive professionals she'd hoped for.

She would soon find out. In the morning they would lift off, first travelling six hundred miles north to Longyearbyen, where they would collect their passengers. From there, they would continue to the top of the world.

The North Pole.

Four miles west, in the centre of Tromsø, Howard Barnes, the founder and CEO of Skyline Voyages, stood at the window of his apartment.

It was a modest little place, a single bedroom with an open-plan kitchen and lounge. But it boasted quite the view. Looking out across the traditional Norwegian rooftops, Howard could see the pointed silhouette of the Arctic Cathedral, the Tromsø Bridge that connected the city to the mainland and, beyond the fjord, a snow-covered mountain range.

Not that he was enjoying it. Instead he was working on his breathing, trying to quell a familiar, stress-induced twitch that had begun to flare up in the corner of his eye.

As far back as he could remember, Howard had always been a nervous person. Most nights when he went to bed he worried about whether he'd locked the front door. Most days when he went to the office he worried about whether he'd left the lights on. His younger sister would sometimes say that she never understood how he'd once been an airline pilot. He'd tried a few times to explain it to her: small worries, large worries . . . it was simply a state of being. One that, over the years, he'd had no choice but to learn to deal with.

But the flight that they would soon be setting out on – an unofficial test flight, as he had come to think of it – was particularly troubling. As far as Howard was concerned, this flight had been bad news from the beginning. And, as the weeks passed, it had only grown worse.

When Ezra first proposed it, Howard hadn't seen the need. They'd done their research. They had consulted experts. The *Osprey* was perfect. And even if it weren't, how much could realistically be achieved in the eight months they had left before they launched? They couldn't change the suppliers they had contracts with. Nor could they implement any major redesign work in such a short space of time.

But Ezra wouldn't be dissuaded. 'Do you really want the first people testing what we've created to be paying customers?' he had demanded. 'We need honest opinions from people we can trust. And *we* need to experience it, too.'

In the end, Howard had relented. A small part of him suspected that this insistence on gathering 'honest opinions' was actually a cover story. An excuse for Ezra to show off the *Osprey* to his old school friends. Devon, Jasper and Alec had all been there when Ezra first learned of Skyline Voyages – when he'd sworn that he would realise his father's unfulfilled dream. With his mother having died the previous year and no other close family to speak of, it made all the sense in the world that he would want his friends to see that he had succeeded.

Either way, Howard had concluded that it would be best to go along with it. He didn't think they would receive any genuinely useful advice from Ezra's friends, but he could just about see the merit in the two of them experiencing the *Osprey* for themselves. Likewise, when Alec, who since his schooldays with Ezra had risen to become an editor at *Condé Nast Traveller*, promised to run a glossy feature in the magazine after the trip, Howard couldn't deny the advertising value that such an offer would hold. Get it out of the way, he thought, and then they could return to focusing on the launch.

But during the weeks leading up to their departure, he found himself increasingly worried about the expanding list of guests. To bring Alec, Devon and Jasper was one thing. But the discovery that there would be strangers in their midst was troubling.

First there had been Alec's photographer, Ben. Howard had been willing to let this one slide, agreeing that to produce the magazine feature Alec had promised would require beautiful photos of the *Osprey* amid the Arctic scenery. He was less thrilled by the inclusion of Jasper's girlfriend, Madison. Ezra had offered a few justifications for this addition, making the case that, as both a model and the daughter of a wealthy American oil baron, Madison was precisely the kind of customer they were hoping to entice. She was well accustomed to the finer things in life, meaning that if they were to understand whether the luxuries offered aboard the *Osprey* were up to standard, hers would be a valuable opinion. Madison's father was also a prominent investor in Skyline Voyages. It was unlikely to go down well if he heard that his daughter had been invited aboard an early flight, only to be told she wasn't welcome.

Fine, Howard supposed. He didn't like it, but he could accept it. Madison could join them. The third addition to their party, however, he had been even less certain of: a blogger and social-media influencer who specialised in sustainability.

'We need an environmental endorsement,' Ezra had insisted. 'Mia can provide that. If we're flying anyway and we have a spare cabin, why wouldn't we invite her along?'

By this point Howard was growing distinctly uncomfortable, his only source of relief being the knowledge that there couldn't be any more strangers. With Astrid, the office assistant that he and Ezra shared, coming along too, all of the *Osprey*'s eight cabins were now occupied.

It seemed he'd been wrong about that as well. Just two hours ago, Ezra had told him that Alec's young son had been rushed into hospital for an appendectomy, forcing him to pull out of the trip. Not wanting to disappoint them by calling off the feature, he was sending a freelancer in his place. A young woman from London.

With the twitch in his eye refusing to let up, Howard turned away from the window and went to the kitchen. Ordinarily he would have poured a glass of wine to help calm his nerves, but his anxiety had reached such a point that he recently found himself turning to one of his more extreme coping mechanisms. Pouring himself a glass of water instead, he opened a cupboard and fetched out a bottle of sleeping pills.

He tried to tell himself that he was fretting over nothing, as he so often did. But it was no good. These strangers would have questions. Questions about Isaac and the origins of Skyline Voyages. Questions that would look unusual if Howard chose not to answer them.

Tipping a couple of the pills into his hand, he sighed. Twenty years had passed since he and Isaac embarked on their fateful journey to the North Pole. Twenty years since he told the bereaved Ezra that, in the days before the accident that claimed his father's life, they had drawn up plans to return airships to the skies.

Howard could still remember the look on Isaac's face as he'd disappeared beneath the ice. Remember the flicker of surprise as he began to sink, and the terror just before he disappeared into the water. He doubted he would ever forget it. But he didn't want to discuss it. There were some things that didn't need to be relived; certainly not with a group of strangers, stranded aboard the *Osprey* in one of the most remote places on Earth.

Knocking back the pills, he returned to the window.

After Isaac's death Howard had been determined that he would build Skyline Voyages on his own. But the first few years had been tough, peppered with doubt and insecurity. Isaac had always been the ideas man. Without him, the task had often seemed far too great. It was only when Ezra came aboard that the burgeoning organisation had started to make progress.

Freshly graduated with a degree in business and finance, Ezra hadn't even bothered to call ahead. He simply came to the office – at that point in a cramped London basement – and asked what Howard wanted him to do. He'd rolled up his sleeves within minutes, hitting the phone to potential investors and spending countless late hours poring over pages and pages of government schemes and engineer's designs. The way Skyline Voyages had accelerated after Ezra's arrival, Howard had had no choice but to quickly appoint him chief operating officer. He himself might be the founder of the company, but Ezra had brought it to life.

Looking across the town, Howard watched as people walked home from their offices or disappeared into restaurants for an evening meal. An island city, nestled among the mountains and fjords for which Norway was so beloved, Tromsø was the gateway to the Arctic, one of the last glimpses of civilisation for those planning to push on towards the Pole. He could never have imagined, when he and Isaac had spent a night here during their own journey north, that it would one day be his home. That he would have an apartment, with an office and an aircraft hangar only a few miles away.

Twenty years . . . In all that time, he and Ezra had barely spoken about the accident. There was nothing to be said; they both knew why they were doing this. And together they had created something so good from the horror of that trip. Something that would leave a lasting impression on the entire world. But now, just months before Skyline Voyages took flight, an inquisitive stranger with one badly placed question could open up wounds that Howard had fought for years to keep closed.

He heaved a sigh. He had already considered trying to duck out, pretending that he'd come down with a bug of some kind. But Ezra would never allow it.

Howard almost laughed. He saw so much of Isaac in Ezra sometimes. There was the physical resemblance, of course. Ezra looked more and more like his father with each passing year. But it was his temperament, too. Isaac would never have let him cry off, either. It had been the defining characteristic of their friendship; whenever Howard had advised caution, Isaac had insisted they go charging in.

Closing the curtains, Howard slumped onto the sofa.

Isaac was going to be spoken about that weekend. There would be no getting around it. All he could do was answer politely and try to move the conversation on. He knew what to say. He'd spent years rehearsing his answers. Right now, he just needed to sleep. That was all. A good night's sleep and, once they were in the air, everything would be fine.

Lying back into the cushions, he hoped the pills would take effect soon.

Saturday 13 September 2025

The day of the flight

1

LONGYEARBYEN: HUSKIES AND HOT CHOCOLATE IN THE WORLD'S NORTHERNMOST TOWN

OK, fellow nomads. Let's deal with some housekeeping first.

Followers of the blog will know that I was expecting to write my next post within the sun-soaked walls of Dubrovnik. But as the title of this piece might suggest, I've made something of a detour.

Rest assured, the Croatian content is still coming. I'll be there in a couple of weeks, so if there's anything you'd like to see, be sure to tell me in the comments. But for the time being I'm in a little place called Longyearbyen.

To those of you asking, '*Where on Earth . . .* ?'

Don't worry. Until recently – *very recently* – I hadn't heard of it, either.

Nestled in the Arctic Circle, Longyearbyen has a population of two thousand, a history of coal-mining and – at this time of year, at least – twenty-four-hour daylight. Oh, and with a trifling eight hundred miles to the North Pole, it also boasts the impressive accolade of being the northernmost permanent settlement in the world.

First impressions? Honestly, for a place so close to the edge of the map, it's delightful. I had a drink last night in the world's northernmost pub, and the best hot chocolate of my life this morning in an actual bona-fide husky café. (Readers of my Budapest post will know how much I love a cat café. But a *husky café*? Come on!)

A few fun facts I've picked up since I arrived. I've learned that no one is born here, because the local hospital is too small. Turns out any expectant mothers go to the mainland during their eighth month of pregnancy and come back once their baby has been born. No one dies here, either, as the permafrost prevents bodies from decomposing. (Slightly morbid, I know, but interesting nonetheless!) And then there are the polar bears. I haven't seen one yet, but the locals waste no time in letting you know that you might – there's a stuffed specimen watching over the baggage carousel in the airport, so a bear is literally one of the first things you see on arrival. The chance of an encounter outside the town is so real that residents genuinely aren't permitted to leave without a firearm for protection.

As for *why* I've come here, let me tell you that—

Before Chloé Campbell could type the rest of her sentence, there was a knock on the door of her hotel room.

Stepping away from the desk, she found Ben waiting in the corridor, with his backpack slung across one shoulder and his camera hanging from his neck. She could feel the anticipation radiating from him, a broad grin plastered across his face.

'Ready to go?'

'Just a sec.'

Hurrying back into the room, Chloé snapped her laptop shut, its lid plastered with stickers from various monuments and national parks, and slid it into her rucksack. She also picked up her own camera and strapped her GoPro to her forehead. She knew that Ben would take the pictures appearing alongside her feature in *Condé Nast Traveller*. But Alec Lewis, the magazine's editor, had said that she was free to shoot whatever she liked for her blog and Instagram – an offer she intended to make the absolute most of.

Her feature. Even now, the best part of forty-eight hours since Alec had given her the assignment, the thought of it made her want to stamp her feet with excitement.

She recalled the moment her phone had rung, a number she didn't recognise lighting up the screen. She had been feeling low. Nearing the end of a fourth week living in her friend Ellie's spare room, she had spent the morning drafting feature pitches that she knew would probably go unanswered, and the afternoon wrestling with the news that her best-paying freelance copywriting client was undergoing budget cuts and could no longer keep her on. Rubbing salt into the wound, her bank of carefully rationed

Instagram material from her recent trips to Paris and Dublin was running precariously low, and while her upcoming visit to Dubrovnik was paid for, the day's developments had left her wondering how she was going to afford *rent*, let alone fund another adventure for the blog.

So when the phone rang, she had expected two possible contenders. It would either be an estate agent, following up on one of the half-hearted enquiries she had made about a series of uninspiring rooms listed on Rightmove, or it would be her parents, making one of their endearing, if not increasingly insistent, daily check-ins. Had she found somewhere to live yet? Could they send her a little money, to help with a deposit on a room? Was she sure she shouldn't be looking for some steadier work?

They had, at least, stopped asking about whether it was worth trying to patch things up with Nate. While Chloé suspected that her mum had never cared for him, it had taken more than a fortnight to convince her dad that the break-up had been months in the making.

Three years earlier, when Chloé had given up a steady wage at a public-relations agency to focus on her travel-writing ambitions, Nate had been supportive. But as he climbed the ranks of a Chelsea accountancy firm and became keen to invest his blossoming salary in a home of their own, Chloé knew that her meagre income was causing him to see her as more of a burden than a partner. Things had finally reached a head when yet another difficult conversation about their finances – the third in a month – had culminated in Nate demanding to know how much more of her life she planned to waste on writing.

'You've been trying for three years,' he had said, 'and you've got nowhere. No sponsorship deals through the blog, and no commissions from any magazines. When will you accept it just isn't going to happen?'

The moment the words had left his mouth she could see in his eyes that he regretted them. But she could also see that he had meant it, the frustration in his voice undeniably real. And so they had reached the painful decision to bring their five-year relationship to an end.

There had been tears and, to his credit, Nate had offered her the flat. But Chloé insisted that she be the one to move out. She had no friends at that time who might move in and share the rent. And whereas Nate could afford to cover it all himself, most months she barely managed to scrape together her *half*. By the end of the week she had found herself in the Clapham flat that her old university housemate Ellie owned with her fiancé, living in their boxroom while she tried to figure out what to do with her life.

So when the phone rang and Chloé decided, from the unknown number, that it was more likely to be an estate agent than her parents, she had been so despondent that she considered letting the call ring out. She shuddered now at the thought. Because when she did answer, it most certainly hadn't been an agent. Far from it. Instead it had been Alec.

When he told her his name, his voice bounding over the line as if they were old friends, her heart had leapt into her mouth. She had sent so many pitches and features ideas to the email address Alec listed on the magazine's website – none of which had ever received a reply – that she often wondered if they even got through. As she sat bolt upright at her desk, her first thought was that she must finally have suggested something that interested him; that she was at long last about to receive a commission. As it happened, she was, although not for one of the many ideas that she had sent to Alec's inbox. Never in her wildest dreams would Chloé have imagined receiving the offer he made her instead.

Believe me, he had concluded, *this isn't how I would typically give out an assignment, especially to someone I haven't worked with before. But I can't go on this trip while my son's having surgery, and at such short notice none of my regulars can take my place. I've seen all of the pitches you've sent me. I know how keen you are to write for us and I can see from your blog that you can tell a good story. If you're up for it, I'm happy to send you. And if it helps make the decision easier, consider this a trial. Do a good job and I'll have more work to send your way.*

Chloé, who had listened to all of this with her jaw hanging wide open, was so utterly dumbfounded that when Alec finished speaking, she could barely find the words to reply. After a pause, she breathlessly accepted, the words suddenly tumbling from her mouth as she told him not to worry. She would do it. And she fully intended to do a good job.

God knows she meant it. Three years she had been

waiting for a chance like this. Three years of pitching and blogging, and hoping beyond hope that if she was persistent enough an opportunity would eventually come her way. She would have been lying if she'd said that over the past few weeks she hadn't begun to give up hope. But now? With an actual assignment to a far-flung part of the world, for a magazine she admired, and the promise of more if all went well . . .

She imagined her name printed on the pages of *Condé Nast Traveller*. She imagined not having to rely on dull pieces of corporate copywriting work to fund her travels and pay her rent. She imagined the badly veiled expressions of sympathy on her friends' faces – friends who all seemed to be spending *their* twenties getting married or promoted or buying their first houses – turning to looks of admiration as she described the distant locations she was being commissioned to visit.

So no. It didn't matter that Alec had sent her in his place because he was desperate. All that mattered was that Chloé was there. This was her feature now. Her assignment. There wasn't a thing in the world that would keep her from seizing it.

Her excitement building, she joined Ben in the corridor, wheeling a small suitcase behind her.

'Hey,' he said, showing her his camera as they walked, 'take a look at this.'

Glancing at the little screen, Chloé saw a row of traditional Norwegian cabins, beautifully framed with a fjord and mountain range in the background. There was a thin layer of snow on the ground; patchy, but enough to make the clear blue sky and pastel-coloured buildings pop even more vividly.

'Got that half an hour ago,' he said proudly. 'I found the shot yesterday, but the light was no good. Saw out of my window that it was looking better today, so I ran out to take it again.'

'It's beautiful,' Chloé replied, prompting him to smile even more widely.

She had a good feeling about Ben. When Alec had told her that he was sending a photographer, she had wondered if he might resent working with a writer on her first assignment. But within minutes of Ben meeting her at Svalbard airport the previous afternoon Chloé knew she would have no such problem.

He was around her age – certainly not much older than thirty – although, with his broad shoulders, thick beard and yellow beanie, he looked more like a lumberjack than a photographer. In the twenty-four hours they had known each other, he'd been nothing but welcoming. With a couple of months to prepare for this trip, against the meagre two days Chloé had been given, Ben had taken her to a bar in Longyearbyen, bought them each a beer and answered as many questions as he could about Skyline Voyages, the *Osprey* and the group of people they were about to travel with.

As they made their way now to the hotel lobby, Chloé looked around for the others. While from the outside the hotel resembled some kind of gleaming research facility, lifted straight from the set of a sci-fi movie, the interior was all luxury. The reception area was softly lit, furnished with comfortable chairs and a flickering fireplace, while an enormous screen behind the check-in desk showcased a range of local tourist excursions. Every few seconds, the image rolled between that of a RIB floating beside a gleaming glacier, huskies pulling sleds and a humpback whale breaking the surface of a fjord. Towards the back, Chloé saw a gift shop selling woolly hats and cuddly walruses and, beyond that, the elegant restaurant where she and Ben had eaten breakfast earlier that morning.

'Ah!'

A voice drew Chloé's eye across the lobby, and she turned to see that Astrid was seated in a nearby armchair, working on a tablet. Ezra Day's assistant at Skyline Voyages and a native of Tromsø, she had introduced herself upon Chloé's arrival the previous afternoon, speaking at length about how excited she was to be visiting the Pole. During that first meeting she wore a sweater bearing a waving seal with enormous, cartoon-like eyes. For their departure that morning, in contrast to Chloé and Ben's cold-weather gear, she had opted for a knee-length puffer jacket, a high-necked pink jumper and a knitted headband.

'You're here,' she said brightly, tucking the tablet under her arm as she hurried over to greet them. 'The others are gathering outside, if you'd like to join them. The coach should arrive soon. Did you see the helicopter?'

Chloé frowned at her.

'Yes!' Astrid continued, her Norwegian accent ringing out. 'It was flying over the valley an hour ago. Someone spotted a polar bear, and the helicopter went up to shoo it away from the town.' She looked as if she might go on, but broke off to fetch a phone from the pocket of her jacket. 'It's Ezra,' she said. 'He and Howard must have landed. You go ahead and join the others, I'll be there in a minute.'

She hurried off, leaving Ben looking pained.

'Bloody typical,' he said, shaking his head. 'I flew out here three days early, just to get a shot of a bear in the national parks. Not a whiff. And now, on the morning we leave, one turns up on our doorstep.'

Chloé offered an encouraging smile. 'You never know. We'll only be gone two days. It might still be in the area when we get back.'

'Maybe.' He forced a smile, but she could hear in his voice that he wasn't holding out hope.

As they headed out into the hotel car park, snow and gravel crunching beneath their feet, a stiff breeze enveloped them. Chloé breathed it in. The air coming off the fjord was cold, but it was also crisp and clean. It was a pleasing contrast to the soupy humidity she had become so used to in London.

A short way off, she saw Jasper Berry chatting with Devon Sharpe. Both approaching forty, the two men were easily recognisable from the photos on their respective websites, Jasper with a goatee, pursed lips and dark hair that sat on his shoulders. Taller and a little broader, Devon sported designer stubble on angular cheekbones, with his own hair so short it must only have been a grade or two above a buzz cut.

Chloé cast her mind back to the previous afternoon, when Ben had briefed her in the bar. 'And these guys know each other already,' she had said. 'They were at school together, right?'

'That's right. Alec, Ezra, Jasper and Devon.' Ben had paused at that point to take a swig of his beer. 'These days Devon owns an adventure company in the Alps, taking wealthy tourists on bespoke trips into the mountains. Skiing, hiking, high-altitude climbing – that sort of thing. Ezra wants to appeal to the same kind of customer, so he's asked Devon to point out any part of the Skyline Voyages experience that they wouldn't feel is up to scratch. Jasper, meanwhile, owns a couple of swish restaurants in Surrey. His old man had a reputation as one of the most ruthless restaurant critics in Europe. Seems Jasper's trying to follow in his footsteps. This weekend he's going to be giving notes on what Alec assures me is a pretty spectacular in-flight menu.'

A few feet away from Devon and Jasper were two women, one of whom Chloé recognised as Mia Whiley.

'She's some kind of activist-stroke-influencer,' Ben had told her in the bar. 'Heads up a website and a huge Instagram channel, covering sustainable initiatives from all around the world. I gather Ezra's hoping she'll give an official endorsement to the trip. One of the major selling points for the airship – and, frankly, one of the reasons Skyline Voyages can charge so much to fly on it – is how much better it is for the environment than your typical aircraft.'

The two women couldn't look more different. Whereas Mia was pale, with thick glasses and a shock of electric-blue hair, the woman she was speaking with was blonde and heavily tanned, dressed in a white coat with a fur-trimmed hood.

'Who's she?' Chloé asked.

Ben's eyes narrowed. 'I think that's Madison. Alec mentioned that Jasper was bringing his girlfriend, so I guess that'll be her. It's their first anniversary, so Ezra invited her to come, too. She's a model, apparently. American, if Alec's got his facts straight.'

If Madison was pleased to be spending her anniversary in the Arctic, she certainly didn't look it. She was listening to Mia with an expression close to a grimace, her eyes flicking around the car park as if some rogue piece of gravel might spring to life and attack her.

Looking at the group assembled before her, Chloé felt her first glimmer of doubt. It had all happened so quickly – Alec's call, the journey to Svalbard – and she had been so giddy with excitement to receive an assignment that there had barely been time for imposter syndrome. But now she was starting to feel it.

Alec's words from two days ago echoed in her mind. *Your role*, he had said, *yours and Ben's, that is, will be to put together a feature that really sells the luxury of it all. Ezra's a good friend, and we need to show our readers that a weekend aboard his airship is worth every one of the many pennies it'll cost to enjoy it.*

Forcing her fears back down, Chloé imagined the feature that she would soon be sitting down to write. She had waited years for this opportunity. For all she knew, she might never get one like it again. There wasn't time for doubt.

Beside her, Astrid appeared, wearing a toothy, wide-eyed grin. 'Howard and Ezra left the airport a few minutes ago,' she said. 'They should be . . . Ah!'

As if on cue, a white minibus rolled into the car park. Coming to a halt in front of the group, the door opened and Ezra Day leapt out, his gleaming smile on display.

'Ladies and gentlemen,' he announced, 'if you'd like to join us, our airship awaits.'

2

With everyone seated, the minibus turned in a wide arc and rumbled out of the hotel car park.

As they bounced along the uneven road – Longyearbyen didn't seem to contain an inch of flat terrain – Chloé observed that nearly all the hotels, cafés and stores were at least partially constructed on wooden stilts. The cars that passed them were noticeably older models, windows and number plates dusty with grit, and wherever she looked there were snowmobiles. They were parked on the side of the road, outside buildings, on top of wooden pallets or on patches of rough lawn. Ben had mentioned that more snow was forecast while they were aboard the *Osprey*, enough that the snowmobiles would probably be in use by the time they returned. She felt a small thrill at the thought of them whizzing around the town, wondering if there would be a chance for her to try one herself before she travelled home.

At the front of the bus, Ezra Day was typing furiously on his smartphone. 'If you need to make any phone calls or send any last-minute text messages, now's the time. There'll be Wi-Fi on the *Osprey*, but once we're out of Longyearbyen you won't have a phone signal until we're back here on Monday.'

With no interest at that moment in sending any messages, Chloé kept her eyes on the window instead. They passed a small timber building with a model of the *Norge* and the words 'North Pole Expedition Museum' mounted over the door. Chloé peered at it as they drove by, thinking of the chance to conduct research for her feature, and making a mental note to visit after the *Osprey* had returned to Longyearbyen. A moment later the museum was behind them, and as they neared the edge of town they passed a large pen, in which twenty huskies were chained to wooden huts. They howled and yapped as the bus moved along, eager to get out on their first run of the day.

'God, it's so bleak . . .' Turning her head, Chloé saw Madison wrinkle her nose in the seat behind her. 'When you said we were going on an Arctic cruise, this isn't what I pictured.'

Jasper patted her on the leg. 'It's fine, baby. It'll be all luxury once we're on the airship.'

Though she tried not to judge, with his Home Counties accent and his eighties rock-star hair it took Chloé a tremendous effort not to cringe at the restaurateur calling his younger girlfriend 'baby'.

Madison turned to Mia. 'Do you *really* like it here?'

'I think it's beautiful.' Mia pointed towards a crater of ice, nestled in one of the mountain ranges that surrounded the town. 'Some of these glaciers are thousands of years old. *Thousands*. Think of all the lives that have been lived. The civilisations that have risen and fallen. And for all that time they've stayed exactly as they are.'

Chloé could see how Mia had apparently amassed such a large social-media following. Turning her attention to the glacier, she couldn't help but feel buoyed. This place was wild, certainly. But 'bleak' was the last word she would use.

Madison, however, gave a short laugh. 'Honey, I think you and I have a very different idea of beauty.'

As they left Longyearbyen behind and trundled into the countryside, the fjord gave way to a sprawling valley, clear blue sky looming over the bare landscape. Having been born in the Highlands, the daughter of a Glaswegian father and a French mother, Chloé couldn't help but be reminded of the Scottish countryside in which she had spent her childhood, the sweeping snow-dusted vistas putting her in mind of winter in Glencoe. She reminisced for a moment on sledging and snowball fights with her dad, the thought warming her heart.

They were a tight family unit, Chloé and her parents – a fact she put down to the number of different countries in which they had lived while she was a teenager. At the age of twelve they had gone to live in the rural French town her mum had once called home. Two years later her dad's work had taken them to Germany and then to Singapore, before returning to Scotland just in time for Chloé to start university. It was during this time that she had started her blog, as a way of documenting their adventures. Her parents had been delighted with it, and for the most part they had since supported her ambition to make a living out of travel-writing. They understood how badly she wanted it, offering encouragement and enthusiasm whenever they could. But of course they worried, as all parents do. And when Chloé told them about her invitation to board the *Osprey*, they had immediately been nervous.

'Two days?' her mum had demanded over the phone. 'Two days' notice for something like *this*? It cannot be right, *ma fifille*. Have they asked you for money?'

Chloé had expected this reaction. Her mother was fiercely loyal to her family, with the only quality that could match her generosity being her unwavering scepticism of anything remotely unexpected. She had often insisted over the years that this was a trait found in all French people, regularly telling her husband and daughter that they could do with being more cynical themselves from time to time. In any case, an expression that regularly punctuated Chloé's teenage years – to the extent that it had become an in-joke between her and her dad – was *C'est trop beau pour être vrai*: it's too good to be true. And upon telling her parents about Alec's offer, her mum's first reaction had indeed been, *C'est trop beau pour être vrai*.

In the end it had taken Chloé's dad – a cheerful software engineer who was considerably more trusting than his wife – to convince her mum that all would be well. And as she looked through the window of the coach, breathing in the landscape around her, Chloé felt more convinced than ever that he was right. This was good. It was real. Meeting Ben's eye across the aisle, she was pleased to see that, like her, he was struggling to contain his excitement.

In the seat ahead, Ezra slipped his phone into the pocket of a thick black puffer jacket emblazoned with the Skyline Voyages logo, before turning and fixing Chloé with a grin.

'I'm so sorry,' he said, putting out a hand. 'We haven't properly met. You must be Chloé.' He shook his head, adopting an incredulous expression. 'Two days' notice . . . You know, I honestly didn't think Alec was going to find someone to take his place. Of all the times for his son's appendix to play up. Lucky for you, though, of course. He's filled me in on your background. Says you have an impressive travel blog, but this is your first assignment for the mag.'

Chloé beamed. 'Something like that.'

'Well, we really are so grateful to you for coming all this way. Howard and I, that is. This feature is going to be vital to our publicity efforts. To cancel would have been a real blow.'

He nodded towards the back of the bus, where a much older man, whom Chloé recognised from the Skyline Voyages website as Howard Barnes, was deep in conversation with Mia. Noticing that he was being talked about, he gave Chloé a quick, thin-lipped smile.

Moving the conversation along, Ezra quizzed Chloé on how she expected her feature to take shape, suggesting tours of the airship and interviews with various members of the crew. He also spent a few minutes describing how the beginning of their trip would be slightly different from that which would be undertaken by paying guests the following spring. A hangar and a small terminal were in the process of being built across the island, but despite Ezra's best hopes, the site wasn't ready for them to visit that weekend.

'You've seen the promotional video, right? On the Skyline website?' He waited for her to nod before continuing. 'The facility's being built at a place called Ny-Ålesund, the exact spot where the *Norge's* fateful expedition began in 1926. When we start operating next year, guests will be flown there by helicopter, and it'll be from there that they come aboard the *Osprey*. I'm afraid this morning is going to be a little more . . . let's say *rudimentary*.'

'Why not have us board in Tromsø?' asked Ben. 'You already have a hangar there. That's where the *Osprey*'s flying out from this morning to pick us up, isn't it?'

'A few reasons. First, there's the fact that the hangar in Tromsø isn't half as comfortable as the one we're building in Ny-Ålesund. It really isn't intended as a customer-facing facility. Second is that the *Osprey* hasn't just set out this morning. We're currently six hundred miles north of Tromsø. It's taken the crew the best part of a day to get up here.'

'The *Osprey*'s been in the air for a day already?'

'It has indeed. That's why Howard and I had to come over this morning by plane. I was hoping to ride over with the crew, but we were held up yesterday morning in an investors' meeting and I didn't want to delay their departure.'

Seeing the surprise on Ben's face, Ezra grinned. 'Don't forget – the *Osprey* is lifted entirely by helium. The only engines required are for propulsion, so it could stay in the air for weeks, if needed. A day to get up here and collect us hardly matters. But more than anything, I thought you should board here because I wanted you to have the most *authentic* experience possible. Svalbard is where the *Norge* set out from in 1926, and it's where our guests will begin their journeys when we start operating next year. So this is where I wanted you to come aboard.'

Fetching out his phone, he began scrolling through a series of photographs of the construction work taking place in Ny-Ålesund. Chloé saw the bones of a stadium-sized hangar, scaffolding standing tall around it. Connected to it by a tunnel was a squat building, which she took to be the terminal, that was also nearing completion.

'Ezra . . .' she said. 'I hope you don't mind me asking, but I read on the Skyline Voyages website that it's been twenty years since Howard founded the company. What's—'

'What's taken us so long?' Ezra laughed. 'It's a fair question. Well, for the first few years I wasn't involved at all. While Howard was setting up the company, I was finishing at school and then earning a degree in business. I joined straight out of uni, though. Came to Howard the week I graduated and told him I was helping. I wouldn't accept any argument. And from there . . . You have to understand this is a form of air travel that barely exists any more. And the one thing most people remember from the time it did is the footage of the *Hindenburg* going up in flames. It was always going to take time and, believe me, it has. We spent years in R&D, and the fundraising efforts never stop – case in point, yesterday's meeting. You wouldn't believe the amount of money it's cost to get this thing off the ground. We've made mistakes along the way, too. There have been months – several, if I'm honest – when Howard and I haven't taken home any kind of a wage. There have even been a couple of occasions when it looked as if the company might go under. But we're here now, and that's all that matters.'

'Sounds like you were very keen to join up.'

'Well, yeah.' Ezra's eyes narrowed slightly. 'How much has Alec told you about how Skyline Voyages started? Not the company itself, but the concept?'

Chloé floundered. Alec hadn't told her *anything* about how the concept for Skyline Voyages had originated. Amid the details of her travel arrangements and the requirements for her feature, all he'd told her about Ezra was that he was an old school friend who had spent two decades getting the company to the point of launch. She'd seen for herself on the website that Howard was the founder, with Ezra as his chief operating officer. She'd assumed there wasn't much more to it than that. But from the way Ezra was looking at her, it seemed she must be mistaken.

Before she could answer, the road came to a complete stop, the coach falling silent as the driver killed the engine. Looking out of the window, Chloé saw a grassy plain, contained within a basin of yet more craggy mountains. A stream trickled past a smattering of lonely mining buildings, while a small group of reindeer foraged a little way off for tufts of grass among the light covering of snow. A couple of four-by-four vehicles were there already, a dozen men and women bustling around in the same Skyline Voyages puffer jackets that Ezra wore. Three of them, she noticed, had rifles slung over their shoulders.

She felt her heart begin to beat quicker at the sight of the guns. She knew there was a chance of seeing a polar bear. In every bar, restaurant and café she had visited in Longyearbyen, there had been some kind of notice declaring *YOU MUST BE PREPARED TO ENCOUNTER BEARS ANYWHERE ON SVALBARD*. But to see these measures in action suddenly brought home the reality of it.

'This is us,' Ezra called out. 'Everyone off!'

As he sprang from the coach, Chloé turned to Ben, now feeling thoroughly confused. 'What did he mean? About the *concept* for Skyline Voyages?'

Ben shook his head. 'No idea. Sounds like Alec's told me as much about that as he has you.' He gave a little shrug. 'We'll have the whole weekend for you to ask about it. I'm sure there'll be plenty of opportunity.'

Following the others off the coach, Chloé watched as one of the reindeer raised its head, inspecting the group with soft eyes. Ben brought up his camera, prompting her to check her GoPro as the animal returned lazily to its grass. She knew there would be no reason for it to have stopped recording. Still, she checked. She wanted to be certain she was capturing every moment.

A few feet away, she noticed Madison approaching Astrid. 'Hey . . . how dangerous *is it* out here? Like, what would happen if a bear came along, and you *didn't* have one of those rifles?'

'You would die.' Astrid's response came so cheerily that Chloé was convinced she must have misheard.

'Sorry,' said Madison. 'You would—'

'You would die,' Astrid repeated, just as brightly as before. 'I mean, there's a small chance it might turn around and leave you alone. But more than likely . . .'

Chloé tried hard not to laugh at the horror that spread across Madison's face. As Astrid eagerly described how a polar bear could pick up the scent of prey from several miles away, she scanned the surrounding landscape, looking for any hint of the animal that had been skirting the town that morning. She didn't share Madison's sentiment. Instead her thinking was more aligned with Ben's. To glimpse a wild polar bear – albeit from a safe distance – would be an undisputed highlight of the trip.

'Everyone,' Ezra called out, approaching one of the ground crew, 'this is Nora. Please follow every instruction she gives. She's going to help us board the airship safely.' He then turned to the woman, and Chloé heard him ask in a low voice, 'How are we looking?'

'Good,' Nora replied. 'A little breezy, but the weather's holding up nicely. Should be an easy take-off.'

Ezra clapped her on the shoulder, his excitement becoming more palpable by the moment.

At that point a message came crackling through on a

radio, and Nora began to address the group. 'Ladies and gentlemen, if I could have your attention, you'll be boarding very soon.'

The group fell silent. Nora, however, didn't continue. Instead she cast a disapproving look at Ben, who was still taking pictures of the reindeer. Chloé nudged him in the ribs and he quickly lowered the camera, so excited that he was almost vibrating.

'When the airship arrives,' Nora went on, 'the pilots will bring it down and stabilise it as much as possible. However, this is a helium-filled craft and it won't be tethered. With that in mind, it will not be completely still. When the pilots have signalled that it's safe to do so, you'll follow me calmly and in single file. You will then step aboard only when I instruct you. Once aboard, make your way straight to the lounge at the front of the aircraft. Please don't linger in the corridor, as the next passenger may be coming right behind you. Leave your luggage on the coach. The ground crew will bring it aboard. Are there any questions?'

It seemed there were none, only nods of understanding and murmurs of anticipation. Ezra put an arm around Howard's shoulder, grinning as if he might be about to board a rollercoaster. Chloé noticed that Howard barely managed to return even a small smile, the corners of his mouth giving just a cursory twitch.

Then, as if on cue, the *Osprey* made its entrance.

Chloé heard it before she saw it. A slight whirring, a little way off. A moment later, as she realised where the sound was coming from, she tilted her head just in time to catch the *Osprey* soaring over the top of one of the nearby mountains.

The group gave a collective gasp. It was enormous. Longer, broader and much taller than the planes on which Chloé had flown to Longyearbyen, it descended slowly – gracefully – casting the entire group in shadow as it passed overhead. The reindeer scampered, fleeing from the great white whale that had appeared in the sky. Ben, meanwhile, threw up his camera, furiously taking picture after picture as the airship turned in a broad arc and touched down gently in the middle of the valley.

Once on the ground, Chloé watched as all four propellers began to move, constantly adjusting as the pilots worked to keep the craft down. It soon became a good deal steadier. Even so, Nora had been right – it wasn't perfectly still. It quivered, rebelling as the pilots forced it into submission. Again Chloé checked her GoPro, eager not to miss a second.

After a minute or so the craft stabilised and an instruction crackled over Nora's radio. Raising her voice to be heard over the propellers, she called out for the group to follow her and, with boots crunching, they walked in single file towards the airship.

With every step, Chloé marvelled at the sheer size of it, until they were close enough that it blotted out the sky itself. Her heart pounded in her ears. She was no stranger to air travel. She flew regularly, with her blog taking her to as many far-away places as she could afford to visit. But this was different. Quite simply she had never seen anything like it.

At the back of the airship, a door was thrown open and a young man in a dark Skyline Voyages uniform lowered a small flight of steps. Still standing at the front of the procession, Nora raised a hand, holding each passenger back until she was satisfied the *Osprey* was steady enough for them to board. Mia went first, followed by Madison and then Jasper. Ben came next, camera raised as he scrambled to capture every moment.

Finally it was Chloé's turn. Stepping forward, she watched as Nora did exactly for her as she had done for the others, hand raised and eyes glued to the steps. But as she was about to wave Chloé aboard, a gust of wind swept across the plain, catching the *Osprey* and causing the steps to lurch a few feet into the air.

The breeze passed almost as quickly as it had arrived, the propellers shifting as the pilots recovered their footing. Once Nora was satisfied that the *Osprey* was under control, she motioned for Chloé to climb aboard.

Looking at the steps, Chloé hesitated. In her mind, she heard Alec's words from two days ago. *Consider this a trial. Do a good job and I'll have more work to send your way.* She imagined her feature in the pages of *Condé Nast Traveller*, her own words alongside Ben's photographs. If she climbed this ladder, life would never be the same again. Aboard this airship, in the space of a weekend, she would find her future.

She took a deep breath. Then she grasped the handrail and put her foot on the first step.

3

The hour that followed passed in something of a blur.

Upon boarding the *Osprey*, Chloé found herself in a snug corridor that could have been lifted straight from a high-end hotel. Running like a spine up the middle of the airship, a navy-blue carpet lined the floor, with four snow-white doors on the left-hand wall and four more on the right. The passengers' cabins, she realised, noticing how a small plaque beside each door bore a different Norwegian word.

The beautifully furnished hallway was such a stark contrast to the wilderness outside that she wanted to stop for a second and take it all in. But, conscious that Ezra would be boarding straight behind her, and that while the corridor was glamorous it wasn't spacious, Chloé hurried to the end, where a pair of glass doors slid open to reveal the *Osprey*'s lounge. She stopped dead in her tracks. Despite knowing full-well that she had to keep moving, she couldn't help but stand motionless in the doorway, mouth falling open at the spectacle before her.

The lounge was divided into two spaces – a sitting area first, and then a dining area beyond it, in the *Osprey*'s nose. Everything was white, from the leather couches and the coffee tables that occupied the sitting area, to the bar and table that made up the dining space. A soft cream carpet covered the floor, while lights that resembled icicles hung from the ceiling. Tall windows adorned every inch of the walls, turning the space into a panoramic observation deck.

During her PR agency days, before she committed full-time to making it as a travel writer, Chloé had spent four years arranging for journalists and influencers to visit some of the most glamorous hotels she had ever seen. They had all been incredible – often luxurious beyond belief – but, at a single glance, the *Osprey* immediately ranked among the most spectacular of any of the resorts she had worked with.

Before she could stop herself, she murmured, '*C'est trop beau pour être vrai . . .*'

Take-off, once all the passengers were aboard, was so instantaneous that Chloé felt the exact second when the pilots relinquished their grip, granting the *Osprey* permission to take to the skies. Sitting beside Ben on one of the leather couches, she felt her stomach drop and her knees go weak, soaring towards the mountain tops at such a pace that an involuntary note of surprise burst from her lips.

As the snowy landscape rapidly disappeared beneath them, she held her GoPro to the window, hoping the footage would convey just how quickly they were climbing.

Within seconds, the ground crew in the valley became matchstick figures, the old mining buildings like wooden toys. Sweeping the GoPro around the lounge, she locked eyes with Ben. He wore an expression of sheer delight. Seeing the glee in his eyes, Chloé couldn't help but laugh.

After a minute or so the *Osprey* levelled off, nose pointing towards the top of the valley, and Ezra announced that they were free to walk around. He also took a moment while they were still seated to introduce the four stewards by name. A young man called Liam took up a post behind the bar, popping bottles of champagne, which he poured into crystal flutes. Ivy and Jade, two women who were in their early twenties, drifted around with trays of canapés, which they fetched from a dumbwaiter concealed somewhere behind the bar. The fourth member of their team, a slightly older woman called Niamh, coordinated the service. Standing to attention in the corner of the lounge, Chloé watched as her eyes twitched between the three members of her team, a serious expression on her face.

As they drifted onward, the mountain peaks just a short way below, Chloé raised herself from the couch. Cautiously, as if worried that the *Osprey* might trick her and give a sudden lurch, she took a tentative step. She was amazed by how still the aircraft felt, and how quiet it was, too. She knew, of course, that it had no jet engines. But she wondered if it might have been soundproofed, as she could barely even hear the hum of the propellers outside.

She had wanted to speak to Ben – to share her giddiness with someone – but he was scurrying around the lounge with his camera poised, capturing everything in sight. Instead, as gentle jazz began to play from unseen speakers, she accepted a glass of champagne and went to join Howard, Jasper and Devon by the bar. Ezra was holding court, describing how, beneath the luxurious fabrics, the *Osprey*'s furniture had all been made using lightweight aluminium, specially designed to carry as little weight as possible. He then went on to explain how a bespoke fragrance had been created for the lounge.

'We had a specialist in Paris working on it for months,' he said, 'using fir trees as a starting point.'

He was enjoying this, Chloé realised, as he encouraged them all to breathe in the designer scent. She was watching a showman relishing the drama of his creation. As well he might. The scent inside the lounge reminded her of freshly fallen snow, crisp and clean, with a slight hint of pine. It was a beautiful touch.

'Did you have an expert consulting on the decor, too?' Devon asked, casting a look across the bar.

'We had a few consultants lend us their opinions,' said Ezra, 'but we both put our mark on it, didn't we, Howard?'

'Your mark more than mine.' Howard looked Chloé in the eye, waving a hand towards the lounge. 'This is Ezra's creation. Everything you see in here – everything you smell, hear and touch – he's been involved in the decision to put it there.'

'So you'll be responsible for these.' Jasper raised his champagne flute.

Chloé hadn't given the glasses much thought, the lounge so far demanding all of her attention. But now that she looked at them properly, she saw that they were translucent, and for a moment she thought they had been so thoroughly pre-chilled that she was observing condensation. Looking more closely, she realised that the glass was frosted. With the pale liquid swirling inside, the misty surface gave the impression of a thin sheet of ice over a cold lake.

Ezra beamed. 'Yes, that's one of mine. Frosted glasses for a frosty place.'

As Jasper steered the conversation towards Ezra's lodgings in Tromsø, Chloé collected a keycard from Astrid and slipped away to her cabin, where she planned to leave her coat and rucksack. She only meant to be there for a short time, eager not to appear antisocial. But her room, much like the lounge, was such a spectacle that she had to spend several minutes taking it all in.

Most of the available floor space was taken by a large double bed, made up with pristine white sheets. A framed photograph of an Arctic landscape hung above the headboard, and she saw that her suitcase had been placed at the foot of the bed by the ground crew. But it was the view from the window that ultimately drew her eye.

A single pane of glass occupied the entire width of the far wall, stretching from the carpeted floor to the ceiling. Following the shape of the *Osprey*'s belly, the window curved outwards, giving the sensation of being inside a gigantic glass bottle that was tipped on its side. As far as she could see, Chloé looked out over snow-topped mountain ranges, sparkling glaciers and perfect blue fjords.

She could have watched the view for hours, but with an effort she turned her attention back to the cabin itself. Everything was designed to be as compact as possible. A smart wooden door hid a narrow wardrobe, just large enough for a weekend's worth of clothes. Behind another she found a bathroom, barely larger than the kind that might be encountered on an aeroplane. Not that Chloé was complaining. It had been tastefully decorated in shades of white and grey, with a shower that looked as sophisticated as any in the hotels that she had represented during her PR days.

Stepping back out of the bathroom, she ran her fingers over a soft white dressing gown that hung from a hook on the cabin door, emblazoned with the Skyline Voyages logo. Then she spread her arms and tipped backwards onto the bed. She landed with a satisfying flump, sinking into a duvet so soft that she was unable to hold back a sigh of contentment. Turning her head, she saw a small table was built into the wall. On top was a laminated *Housekeeping, please* card to hang on her door in the morning. There was also a tall glass – frosted, like the champagne flutes – a bottle of mineral water and a remote control, about the size of her phone.

Reaching for the remote, she examined the buttons one by one. A couple controlled the temperature, but as the cabin was already comfortable she didn't touch those.

Instead, she tried another marked *Blackout*, watching as a blind began to slide down across the curved window from somewhere inside the *Osprey*'s hull. It didn't get far, though, shuddering to a stop after covering only half of the window.

Frowning, Chloé sat up on the bed and pushed the button again. The blind trembled some more, a grinding noise coming from an unseen set of gears, but after a moment's struggle it remained defiantly in place.

Panicking over the thought that she had somehow broken it, Chloé felt an immense swell of relief when the blind at least obeyed her command to retract, retreating into the *Osprey*'s hull. Heart thumping against her ribs, she set the remote back down on her bedside table, swapped her hiking boots for a pair of sneakers and hurried to rejoin the others.

As the glass doors to the lounge closed behind her, she thought about striking up a conversation with Madison. The American was sitting alone on one of the leather couches, but Chloé decided she looked perfectly happy taking pictures of her champagne glass on her phone. Instead she found herself drawn to the front of the airship, where Mia and Astrid were looking down on the Arctic landscape. As she approached them, tracing her fingertips lightly on the dining table, Astrid's toothy smile stretched a little wider. She was still clutching the tablet she had carried in the hotel, as if it had been glued to her hand. On closer inspection, Chloé noticed that there were little penguins painted on each of her nails.

'So,' Astrid said eagerly, 'what do you think?'

Looking at the ground below, the landscape a swirling carpet of rising peaks and frozen craters, it took Chloé a moment to answer. 'I think I might be dreaming.'

Astrid laughed. 'Ezra's asked me to give you and Ben a tour of the upper deck,' she said. 'Show you the cockpit and the crew's quarters. We can go any time you like, but for now I would suggest enjoying the view. That's the Spitsbergen National Park beneath us, the wildlife capital of the Arctic. If we're going to see bears at any point this weekend, this is where it's most likely to happen.'

'We should make sure Ben knows that.' Chloé looked across the lounge, to where Ben was taking a picture of Liam pouring more champagne. 'He was gutted not to have seen the one that was near the town this morning.'

'Ah,' Astrid said knowingly. 'Well, better to see them from up here than down there. Less chance of being eaten.'

Again Chloé couldn't tell whether Astrid was joking. With her perpetual grin and sing-song voice, it was impossible to know. The Norwegian excused herself a moment later, leaving a curious smile playing on Mia's lips.

'An odd fish, that one. She's lovely, but she doesn't half come out with some dark things. If you'd come over a minute earlier, you'd have seen the selfies she took beside the stuffed bear in the airport.'

'Selfies?'

'Oh, yeah. Seems she's something of a budding taxidermist, so I think she was a little starstruck. Apparently she has a stoat in her flat.' Mia sighed, before putting out a hand for Chloé to shake. 'But that's enough talk of dead things. You must be the one writing the *Condé Nast* feature.'

'That's right.' Chloé took the proffered hand. 'And Ben says you're an influencer.'

Mia laughed to herself. 'Is that what they're calling me?'

'Is it not true?'

'I suppose it is. But it's not a term I've ever used myself. I started *Green World* as a blog. The Instagram stuff didn't come until much later on.'

Chloé eyes widened. 'You're a blogger?'

'I am. Or, rather, I was. As I say, these days it's more of a fully-fledged organisation. But it started small. Growing up in London, my parents would take me to see all these inner-city green initiatives. Urban farms, allotments, organised litter-pickings . . . I can remember being a teenager, and my mum saying that she wished more people would get involved. So I set up the blog as a way of letting people know about some of the things that were going on.'

'But you never planned to expand? To go into the sort of work you're doing now?'

Taking a sip of champagne, Mia shook her head. 'I had friends in other cities,' she explained, 'letting me know what was going on in their areas, so I started writing about those, too. Then, when I was in my early twenties, I went travelling around Europe, and as I went I wrote about the various bits of good work I came across. That was when Instagram was just taking off. And *that* was when *Green World* really came into its own.'

She looked off into the distance, and Chloé could see the pride behind her small smile.

'When I started, it was only ever meant to be an online noticeboard. Now we have nearly half a million followers on Instagram and even a small team, all working to cover sustainability efforts around the world.'

They paused for a moment to admire a group of around twenty reindeer, grazing in a valley below them. A few looked up as the *Osprey* passed overhead, before quickly returning their heads to the ground.

'What about Ezra?' Chloé asked, as the airship continued on its way. 'You must be pretty close, for him to invite you on this trip. Have you known each other a long time?'

'We met a few years ago,' said Mia. 'At a sustainability conference in Belgium. Ezra was giving a talk on airship technology, as part of his endless mission to raise funds for Skyline Voyages, and I was moderating a panel on some interesting projects that are being worked on in Europe.' She shrugged. 'We got chatting in the green room. I was interested in potentially covering his work, and he was keen to get some kind of sustainability endorsement before Skyline starts operating, so he asked if I would take a look once he was ready to fly. He emailed me a couple of months ago to say that they were running this flight. If I wanted to join them, they had a cabin going spare.'

'You must have leapt on it.'

Mia hesitated. 'If I'm honest, the luxury of it all is a little much. This . . .' She raised her champagne glass. 'This is not the world I grew up in. And given how heavily Ezra's pushing the sustainability angle, I'm not entirely comfortable with the fact that it takes three flights just to get up here from the UK.'

'Could people not take a train?'

'They could. I did it myself, or at least I did it as far as Tromsø. From there, of course, you've no choice but to either take a flight or a ferry to Longyearbyen. I'm hoping I might convince Ezra to encourage his guests to do it that way. Maybe even talk him into offering some kind of sustainable travel package that gets passengers to go as far as they can without flying. But it's a long journey. London to Tromsø took two days by rail.'

She shook her head. 'Either way, the technology's too interesting not to come and see it. With the amount of damage the aviation industry causes, the possibility of a genuinely clean alternative needs to be explored. And, if I'm completely frank, the content will do amazingly well on our channels. Much as it pains me, *Green World* can't thrive on goodwill alone. We have to turn a profit. Mostly that comes through advertising – ethical sponsors, I should add – but to deliver on those ads requires an engaged audience, and we've had a bit of a rocky year. This . . .' She cast a look around the lounge. 'Well, this will pull in some serious views. Views that, right now, we really need.'

Intrigued, Chloé had to restrain herself from asking about *Green World*'s rocky year. Instead, as they spoke, Mia took a pleasing amount of interest in her own blog. Any fears that Chloé might have harboured about fitting in among the group had faded away. She doubted she would succeed in making a friend for life in Madison or Jasper. But between Ben, Mia and Astrid, she was confident that she was in good company.

One of the stewards, Jade, interrupted their discussion with the offer of a fresh glass of champagne. She seemed noticeably less enthusiastic than Ivy, meeting their eyes for only a fraction of a second as she held her tray aloft. Chloé wondered if she was nervous. Though there wasn't much in it, up close Jade definitely looked younger than both Ivy and Liam.

'Actually,' said Mia, 'if you don't mind, Chloé, I might go take a look at my cabin. Maybe even see about unpacking.'

Chloé answered that she didn't mind at all, and a moment later Mia had gone, leaving her to deliberate over whether to accept another glass of champagne. She was tempted, the glass she'd had after the *Osprey* first lifted off having been delicious, but ultimately she declined. There would be time for a drink later. If she was soon going to spend the afternoon touring the upper deck with Astrid and Ben, she wanted a clear head.

As Jade moved along, Chloé looked down on the swirling landscape, a sense of complete and total satisfaction overcoming her. This was her chance, she thought to herself. The break she had been waiting for. And she was going to make the most of it.

4

Sitting alone at the bar, Devon took a sip of his pilsner.

Two hours into the flight, the group in the lounge had now dispersed. Madison and Jasper had retired to their cabin, while Howard and Ezra had gone to join a Zoom meeting with the team in Tromsø. Astrid, meanwhile, had taken Chloé and Ben on a tour of the *Osprey*'s upper deck. Mia had actually been to her cabin and come back, but sat by herself on one of the couches, happily capturing some footage on her phone of the national park drifting beneath them. Liam was there too, tending the bar, although he seemed to have sensed that Devon wasn't interested in making conversation.

In all honesty, Devon's mood was downright bleak. Having received an email from his solicitor as they'd left the hotel, he'd known it wouldn't bear good news. Just as he had known there would be nothing he could do about it while he was aboard the *Osprey*. The best course of action would be to have a comfortable couple of days, collect the consultant's fee that Ezra had promised him and deal with whatever the email contained when the weekend was over.

But despite his best efforts to ignore it, upon connecting to the onboard Wi-Fi he had found himself drawn to the message. Now, with his phone in his hand, Devon read the short correspondence again:

Dear Mr Sharpe,

I regret to inform you that your plea has been denied. The court has ruled that reparations of £150,000 are due to the plaintiff in full, in accordance with the attached payment schedule.

I attach also our firm's invoice and payment terms.

Best wishes,
Rowan Thorn

Senior Partner
Thorn and Snow Solicitors LLP

A hundred and fifty grand . . . Plus his solicitor's exorbitant fees. And all because some rich teenager had chosen the side of a cliff as a good place to ignore Devon's instructions and start showing off. Now his business was on the brink of ruin, his finances in tatters. Ezra's consultant's fee wouldn't even touch the sides. It made him wish the kid had broken his neck, rather than just his leg.

He took another sip of his beer. It was the third Liam had poured for him, having already had three glasses of champagne, and Devon could feel himself growing light-headed. He'd hoped it would help his mood. Instead, his thoughts were only becoming darker. The alcohol was clearly dulling his senses, too, because as he stared at the email, he was so enraptured that he failed to notice the sound of approaching footsteps. It wasn't until Jasper materialised beside him, settling onto the neighbouring stool, that Devon scrambled to close the email down, beer spilling over the top of the glass as he frantically shoved the phone into his pocket.

Clasping his hands on the bar, Jasper smiled to himself, making no effort to hide his amusement at having caught Devon off guard. He nodded at the beer. 'Is that the pilsner they brew in Longyearbyen?'

Devon muttered a one-syllable reply, and Jasper ordered a beer of his own.

Devon wished he had known that Jasper would be joining them. Short of offering to pay his legal expenses in full, there wasn't a consultant's fee in the world that could have tempted him aboard the *Osprey* if he had known it would mean seeing this smug bastard again. The more he thought about it, the more certain he became that this was precisely why Ezra hadn't told him. He'd been happy enough to say that Alec was coming, talking endlessly about the magazine feature he would be writing on Skyline Voyages. But he'd failed to mention even once that Jasper would be here, too.

Devon tried to recall a single moment from their schooldays when he had genuinely been pleased to see Jasper. None came to mind. He could remember befriending

Alec, bonding over their respective prowess on the rugby pitch. Alec had then taken a shine to Ezra, impressed by the scrappy boy's willingness to throw himself at opponents twice his size. Jasper, who shared a dorm with Alec, as Devon had with Ezra, had followed later, rounding out their group of four.

Devon remembered hoping they would shake Jasper loose. The son of a notoriously scathing restaurant critic, even as a teenager Jasper had taken after his old man, there being nothing and no one that he didn't treat with almost immediate disdain. Instead Devon had been dismayed to find that both Ezra and Alec were fond of him.

'Come on, Dev,' Ezra would say. 'He's a bit of an arse sometimes, but he's really not that bad.'

They'd never understood. How could they? Normanstone hadn't been the comfortable environment that most imagined, when they learned Devon had attended a boarding school. Rather than being a training ground for politicians and diplomats, it had been a place where boys were sent to become tough, where cold dorms, cold showers and cold porridge were the norm. Families from all walks of life were encouraged to send their sons, but Devon had always been keenly aware that he came from one of the least affluent, something which Jasper – usually when Alec and Ezra were out of earshot – had frequently enjoyed reminding him.

So to arrive in Longyearbyen and be greeted with the news that Alec had been forced to pull out of the trip had been a blow. But to learn in the same breath that Jasper would be joining them for their weekend over the Pole had been salt in the wound.

For a minute or two they sat at the bar in silence. Devon was determined not to speak first. It was petty, he knew, but even after all these years that was the effect Jasper's presence had. Jasper had come to sit with *him*. He could be the one to strike up a conversation. He could ask about Devon's life in the mountains, his business, whether he had any family . . .

Instead, as if oblivious to his presence, Jasper took out his phone and began to scroll. Devon knew all too well that this could be a mind-game, the sort that Jasper would have played during their schooldays to wind him up. Or it could be a genuine indication of Jasper's complete lack of interest in speaking to him. He tried to stifle the thought, unable to decide which frustrated him more.

'So Madison,' he said, after a further minute's silence. Irritated that he had been made to speak first, Devon forced as much enthusiasm as he could muster into his voice. 'She's a model. Instagram stuff, right? How'd the two of you meet?'

Jasper sighed, setting down his phone. 'She came to one of the restaurants.'

'One of *your* restaurants?'

'That's right. She complained to the manager that the vegan options weren't of a high enough standard. She didn't like the response the manager gave, so she complained again. And again. Eventually, the manager asked me for help, so I got in touch. By the end of that conversation, we'd set up a date.'

'How romantic.'

'Yeah, she's a handful. She's a good time, though. And the ex hates her, which is never a bad thing.'

Devon didn't reply. His life in the mountains had rarely accommodated any kind of serious relationship. For the most part, he had been content with that. But as he stood on the edge of his forties, with that lifestyle on the brink of ruin, he had wondered more than once if he had been short-sighted. If it wouldn't have been better to find someone. Whatever his first impression of Madison might have been, Devon wondered if Jasper knew how lucky he was to have her in his life.

'Does she get on well with your kids?' Seeing Jasper's frown, Devon explained, 'Ezra mentioned you have a couple of girls.'

'Doesn't take much of an interest, to be honest. That's fine, though. Their mother has them most of the time, and I'd rather they ignored each other than have them arguing.'

Jasper took a swig of his beer, holding it on his tongue for a moment, before humming in approval and swallowing it down. Then he turned and looked Devon in the eye, a quizzical expression on his face.

Feeling uneasy, Devon fidgeted under Jasper's curious gaze. Could he have seen the email? Devon thought he had been quick enough, locking the screen and stuffing the phone back into his pocket. Jasper surely couldn't have read it. Not properly, at least. But could he have stolen a glance?

'Boys!' Ezra's voice rang out across the lounge. '*This* is what I've really been looking forward to. The three of us finally back together. And you've already got the drinks in!' The glass doors slid shut behind him and he made his way to the bar, a grin plastered across his face. 'Arctic Collins, please, Liam.'

The young bartender began to prepare the drink, filling a gin glass with ice and fetching a lemon from beneath the bar. Exactly like the champagne flutes and the beer glasses, the martini glass was frosted, giving the appearance of having been sculpted from ice.

'He makes this so well,' said Ezra. 'Truth be told, it's just a riff on a Tom Collins. Gin, soda water, syrup and lemon juice. We'll probably call it something like a Jungle Collins or a Desert Collins, if we manage to get our next two routes up and running. All adds to the ambience, though. And don't worry, Dev.' Ezra clapped him on the shoulder. 'The staff have been briefed. They're all aware that they need to keep any citrus well away from you.'

Devon didn't reply, eyes glued to the lemon as if a hand-grenade had just been placed on the bar. Travelling with a severe allergy was always difficult. But travelling somewhere there was no chance of medical help – say, the North Pole – was something else altogether. When Ezra had assured him that measures had been taken, he'd assumed that meant any citrus fruits had been removed from the airship. He certainly hadn't expected a lemon to be whipped out just a few inches in front of him.

Oblivious to his discomfort, Ezra took a deep breath. 'It really is so good to see you both again. If only Alec had been here. Then this would have been perfect.' Liam passed him the cocktail and he took a sip. 'I don't know how you do it,' he said. 'But whatever magic you're working, I'm glad it's our bar you're doing it behind.' He took another sip, then turned his attention on Devon. 'Come on then, mate. Let's have it. Any notes for me yet?'

Devon twisted a smile into place, watching closely as Liam binned the spent lemon and wiped down the bar.

If he was honest, the lack of problems aboard the *Osprey* to critique only added to his dark mood. It would have made him feel better to hand Ezra a list of things that his high-flying clientele would feel was beneath them. But so far everything had been flawless. He could even see the rudimentary way they had boarded, which Ezra had repeatedly assured him would not be the case for paying guests, being strangely appealing to some of the thrill-seekers he took into the mountains.

'Full marks so far.'

'Well, you know I'm happy to hear that. But if you do spot anything, I want you to tell me. This experience has to be *perfect* when we launch.'

At that moment Jasper's phone buzzed. He glowered at the screen, muttering under his breath.

'Everything all right?' asked Ezra.

'Fine. Madison's in the cabin, updating her Instagram. She says it's too cold and she can't make sense of the bloody air conditioning.'

'There you are,' said Ezra. 'That's helpful. Perhaps we need to have some clearer instructions in the cabins on how to operate the air con.' He paused, frowning.

'Although I have to admit, I didn't think it needed all that much explanation.'

'It won't,' Jasper replied. 'It's probably not even true. More than likely she's bored and doesn't want to come and socialise.'

'Well, let me know if you need any help, mate. And just so you know, Astrid might give you a knock when she's finished with Chloé and Ben. We're in for a real treat for dinner. I thought she could take you up to the kitchen, show you our chef in action.'

Jasper looked considerably less enthused by this idea, but he forced a half-hearted smile. With his phone buzzing at the arrival of yet another message from Madison, he drained the rest of his beer, rose from the bar stool and disappeared into the corridor. As the glass doors closed behind him, Ezra took a deep breath.

'You know,' he said, 'I really think Dad would be pleased with what we've done here.'

Devon paused, glass suspended in mid-air.

'Do you remember the day I decided I was going to do this?' Ezra pressed. 'The day Howard told us about the idea?'

'I do.'

Ezra shook his head. 'If Dad could just see it. If I could somehow tell him that we've done it . . .'

As he heard the eagerness in Ezra's voice, Devon found himself struck by a sudden sadness. But it took him a moment to realise that it wasn't because Isaac Day would never see what his son had accomplished.

He thought back to the only time he had met Isaac. It had been the day of the Normanstone challenge, an annual event, halfway between a cross-country race and an orienteering course, in which every boy in the school was required to take part. For weeks beforehand Ezra had spoken about how Isaac was coming to watch. He might have been scrawny, but Ezra was quick and nimble. More than that, he had been training for weeks, running laps in all weathers around the school's athletics track. Every evening in their dorm he would tell Devon how he was going to make his dad proud. He was going to show the old man his worth.

Devon could vividly remember the moments after finishing the race. With all of the boys and parents gathered in the courtyard, he had looked anxiously for Ezra, eager to hear how he had done. When he did set eyes on his friend, he saw that Ezra was already speaking with Isaac. Keen to meet the great man he had heard so much about, Devon hurried over to introduce himself. But as he approached, he quickly realised that something was wrong. Not only was Ezra hanging his head, unable to look his father in the eye, but he was standing almost entirely on one leg, straining to put as little weight on the other as possible. As Devon moved closer, he saw a nasty gash on Ezra's shin, mud caked on his hands and knees.

He would later learn that Ezra had been moving at such a pace – so desperate to finish ahead of the other boys – that he had fallen halfway around the track, badly spraining his ankle. Rather than dropping out of the race, he had limped around the second half of the course to finish dead last. But in that moment, all Devon had heard were Isaac's words.

'I think,' he could still hear Isaac saying, 'it would have been better for us both if I hadn't been here to see such a shameful display.'

This would prove to be the last thing Isaac Day ever said to his son. Minutes later, he left the school grounds, and within a fortnight he had set off with Howard for their fateful journey to the North Pole.

It had been years since Devon last revisited this memory. As he looked now at Ezra, sitting beside him at the *Osprey*'s bar, he recognised the source of his own sorrow. It wasn't that Isaac would never see what his son had accomplished. It was that Ezra still cared.

'Excuse me.' Turning to face the voice, Devon saw Astrid come into the lounge, tablet in hand. 'Sorry to disturb,' she said. 'But Howard's asking for you, Ezra. He'd like to see you in his cabin.'

Ezra's smile dimmed. 'Can it wait a few minutes? Devon and I are only just catching up.'

Astrid chewed her lip. 'I think it might be best if you go now. He's getting a little . . . agitated.'

Seeing the frustration in Ezra's expression, Devon waved him away.

'Go do your thing,' he said. 'It's no trouble. We have all weekend to catch up.'

Ezra sighed, promising Astrid that he would see to Howard in a moment. As she moved along, he clapped Devon on the shoulder again.

'I'm really glad you came, mate. Having you here . . . it feels right, doesn't it?' He drained what remained of his cocktail, climbing to his feet before Devon could answer. 'Once this weekend's over with, let's not leave it another twenty years.'

After Ezra had gone, Devon thought about ordering another beer. He tried to feel happy for his old friend. He *wanted* to be happy. After all, he doubted there were many other people who knew quite how desperate Ezra had been to prove himself as his father's equal. What he and Howard had done was nothing short of incredible. But as Devon thought about the sorry state of his own business, his sympathy gave way to jealousy, and a rapidly growing sense that he shouldn't have come.

He tried to shake the thought from his head, telling himself that he was just angry with the email from his solicitor. But it was no good. In that moment, standing inside a floating monument to Ezra's immense success, the prospect of it being another twenty years before they saw each other again sounded pretty appealing.

His thoughts darkening again, he decided to leave the bar and return to the sanctuary of his cabin, where he could skulk and scowl to his heart's content.

Two days, he told himself, gritting his teeth as the glass doors opened to let him pass. Two days in the sky. Then he could collect his money and return to his mountains, where he planned to scrub all thoughts of Ezra, Isaac and Skyline Voyages from his mind.

5

Closing the door to the *Osprey*'s coffin-like office behind her, Niamh screwed her eyes shut and took a deep breath.

Three hours. It had been just three hours since they collected the passengers from Longyearbyen – a day since she and the crew had set out from Tromsø – and already she was desperate to be off this airship.

She fought to convince herself that she was being foolish. This was a job unlike any she had taken before. There was always going to be an adjustment period and it was only natural that she would feel nervous. The guests were all enjoying themselves and, to their credit, Liam, Ivy and Jade had all done well during the champagne reception. Perhaps she had been too hasty in her despair. The three young stewards were not the team she would have chosen – the team Ezra had promised her – but once they had learned each other's rhythms perhaps she would rediscover the excitement that had brought her to Skyline Voyages in the first place. She might even become accustomed to the scenery. The snow-topped mountains and twinkling fjords might become as comforting and familiar as the Mediterranean waters on which she had earned her stripes.

But it was no use. Anxiety rose within her, building with every passing minute that they travelled northwards. She felt a sudden surge of resentment for Ezra – for all of the things he had promised when he offered her the role. Her run of the ship, her own team . . . She was resentful of the stewards, too. Liam, with his endless preening and flirting. Air-headed, self-obsessed Ivy, who had been stupid enough to let Niamh catch her vaping in her cabin an hour after they'd left Tromsø. And Jade, who barely had a friendly word to say to anyone other than Gwyn, the chef. Niamh resented the captain, who seemed completely disinterested in speaking with her, let alone in treating her as an equal. She even resented her old crewmates from the agency for letting her come here. For not trying harder to show her the mistake she was making.

But most of all she was angry with herself. Taken in by the pictures of glaciers and polar bears, she had dived into this role without a second's thought, signing away three years of her life for the sake of a promotion. She yearned to go back – to be on a yacht with her friends. She pined for blue water and warm sun on her skin. If she could somehow turn back the clock, tell herself not to sign with Skyline Voyages, she would do it in a heartbeat. Instead the time that she owed to Ezra Day stretched out ahead of her, looming like the frozen wilderness that awaited them at the top of the world.

As if determined to make matters even worse, it seemed that not even the *Osprey* itself was ready for this expedition, with Howard calling her to his cabin half an hour earlier to ask why his air-conditioning unit wasn't working.

'I'm so sorry, Howard,' Ezra had said, as the three of them looked at the air vent mounted over the cabin door. 'I must have made a mistake on the room plan that I gave Niamh. I meant to put myself in here. Would you like to swap?'

Howard had looked distinctly unhappy. But before he could answer, there came a clicking sound from the vent, as cool air began flowing into the cabin.

'It's fine,' he had said, in a tone that suggested it was very much not. 'Better me than one of the guests.'

After leaving Howard in the cabin, Niamh had quietly told Ezra that nobody had informed her of a faulty air-conditioning unit.

'Not to worry,' Ezra had said. 'Astrid's working with the ground crew back in Tromsø to get it sorted. I'd hoped they would fix it before we set out, but I suppose they'll pick it up when we're back.'

Niamh had needed to fight to keep her frustration in check. 'I'm sure,' she replied. 'But, Mr Day, you've hired me as your chief steward. It's my job to run this airship for you, and if I'm going to do that, this is exactly the sort of thing I should know about. With all due respect, it's the sort of thing I should be *overseeing*. Not Astrid. What if one of the guests had been placed in there? How would I have explained it?'

'Put it out of your mind.' Ezra had smiled warmly, laying a hand on her shoulder. 'Astrid will deal with it when we're back. And please, enough of this "Mr Day". I'd much rather you call me Ezra.'

'Mr Day,' she had said, before correcting herself. 'Ezra. I hope you don't mind me asking. But why is Astrid dealing with this? Why has she even come on this trip?'

'She's here to make sure the guests are comfortable,' Ezra had explained. 'And to see that they have everything they need.'

'But, Ezra,' she had said, hoping her voice wasn't beginning to strain, 'again, that's what *I'm* here for. You understand that, sir, don't you? It's the role of the chief steward to look after the guests, not of your PA. That's precisely why you've hired me.'

She hoped this had been sufficiently diplomatic. It was a good deal gentler than what she wanted to say, which was: There is no point in me wasting three years of my life up here if you're handing that grinning idiot the very work you've hired me to do.

Ezra's smile had only become broader. 'Well, Astrid can help. Treat her as an extra pair of hands.'

Inside the office, Niamh gripped the edge of the desk. She stared at the wall, grateful there were no windows on the *Osprey*'s upper deck. Depressing as the little room might be, the office was a sanctuary. Just knowing that with every second they were drifting further into pure, endless nothing was bad enough. In that moment, watching it happen – actually *seeing* the terrain pass beneath them – would have been too much to handle.

It was only for the weekend, she told herself. Only the weekend . . . After this flight she would be dealing with paying guests, rather than Ezra and Howard. Astrid would be back in Tromsø, scheduling meetings and taking messages. She would grow used to her team and would earn the respect of the captain. She would even become accustomed to the Arctic surroundings. In time, she would have the run of this airship, exactly as she had been promised.

But even then, would that be enough? A fresh image of the azure waters on which she had spent her twenties took form in her mind. Desperate as she was to luxuriate in it, though, she pulled away, aware that if she lingered too long she might never resurface from the ensuing wave of despair.

Willing herself to return to the lower deck, she was bracing to leave when she heard the office door open behind her. Taken by surprise, she spun round, catching her shin on a canister of helium that stood beside the desk. A sharp pain exploded from the point of impact, travelling to both her knee and her ankle, and she had to screw her eyes shut as she cursed through her teeth.

She took a deep breath. Then another. When, finally, the pain had dulled, replaced by an uncomfortable throbbing, she opened her eyes. Jade stood in the doorway of the office. Beside her head bobbed a balloon shaped like a champagne bottle, with the word *CONGRATULATIONS!* emblazoned in gold font.

'Mr Sharpe says that this was in his cabin,' she explained in a monotone voice. 'I'm guessing it was meant for Mr Berry and Miss Brooke.'

Shin still throbbing, Niamh stared at her. She had brought Liam into the office that morning, where she'd asked him to inflate the balloon and put it in Jasper and Madison's cabin. With the realisation sinking in that he had failed to complete this painfully simple task, it was all she could do not to snatch up a pair of scissors from the desk and burst it on the spot.

'Did Mr Sharpe give you back the bottle of champagne as well?'

Jade shook her head. 'No champagne. Just this. His blackout blind isn't working, either.'

Bloody typical, Niamh thought. Of course he would keep the champagne.

'What's wrong with his blind?'

Jade shrugged. 'Looks like it's broken. When he pushes the button on his remote, it comes down a little bit and then sort of stops. Problem with the mechanism, I guess. Must be jammed or something.'

Niamh raised a hand to her face, pressing her thumb and forefinger against her eyelids. She doubted there was anything she could do about Devon's blackout blind. She would have to raise it with the team in Tromsø when she spoke to them about the dodgy air-con unit in Howard's cabin. The balloon needed dealing with, though. For a moment she considered having Jade deliver it to its intended cabin. Miserable as she was, of the three stewards Jade seemed to have her head screwed on the tightest. But Niamh couldn't bear the thought of it being delivered to the wrong place a second time.

She bent down to stand the helium canister upright, having knocked it over when she caught it with her shin. It was bright red, with a nozzle on the top and the words *PARTY TIME!* printed on the side in a cartoonish font. With nowhere practical in the small office to store it, she shoved it underneath the desk, beside her safe, before snatching the string from Jade's hand. She then stormed into the corridor, stopping in the kitchen to seize a fresh bottle of champagne from the walk-in fridge. With each furious step, the balloon bounced in her wake, bumping against the back of her head.

The layout of the *Osprey*'s upper level wasn't dissimilar to that of the lower, a long corridor with rooms branching off on either side. Aesthetically, however, the two decks couldn't be more different. Whereas the areas occupied by the guests were designed with luxury in mind, carpeted and gently lit, with doors made of smart pinewood, the crew's quarters had been designed for functionality. The ground beneath Niamh's feet was hard, the doors made of grey plastic, and her way was lit by bright white spotlights in the ceiling.

As she descended to the lower deck, emerging from a narrow stairwell through a door that resembled a wall panel, any hope Niamh had been harbouring of forming a bond with her team had now given way to exasperation.

She really shouldn't be surprised that Liam had managed to get the wrong cabin. She couldn't deny that he was a good bartender. But when push came to shove, he seemed interested in only two things: mixing drinks and pestering women. During the flight from Tromsø to Longyearbyen he had attempted shamelessly to flirt with Ivy. Although with no hint of reciprocation, Niamh was certain that once their guests had come aboard she saw him making eyes at Mia and Madison instead. She would need to keep an eye on him. Have words even, if it continued.

As for the balloon . . . it was ridiculous.

'Could you sort out some champagne and a balloon for Jasper and Madison's cabin?' Ezra had asked her a few days earlier. 'It's their first anniversary and he's keen for it to be special.'

Special . . . Was being among the first people in the world to fly over the North Pole on a luxury aircraft not special enough? Still, Niamh had sorted it without protest. She'd sourced a canister of helium, well aware of the irony of it being such a chore when they were spending two days suspended under such a vast quantity of the stuff. At Ezra's request, she had even bought a selection of different balloons for him to choose from. Not that he had bothered to look at them before taking off. He'd made her wait until they were in the air before making his decision, leaving her with no choice but to bring the canister with them and keep it stashed in her already-cramped office for the entire weekend. She understood that he was busy. But would it really have killed him just to pick a balloon before they left Tromsø?

Coming to a halt outside Jasper and Madison's cabin, Niamh composed herself. She rapped brightly on the door and, when Madison opened it, gave a broad, well-honed smile.

'So sorry to disturb,' she said. 'I'm afraid there's been a slight mix-up; these were meant to be waiting for you in your cabin.'

Madison squinted at the balloon. 'I don't think we want that. There isn't a whole lot of space in here.'

'Are you sure? I think Mr Berry asked for it to be waiting—'

'*Jas* . . .' Madison called over her shoulder, and a moment later Jasper appeared behind her, eyes narrowing as he saw the balloon. 'Did you really ask for this thing?'

'Bloody hell,' he murmured. 'We don't want that. Where are we going to put it?'

'That's what I just said, but she seems to think you asked for it.'

Unsure how to proceed, Niamh looked from Jasper to the balloon. 'I do apologise, sir. I think there may have been some confusion. I was told you'd requested this—'

'It's cute,' Madison cut her off, 'but there's no room. So why don't we take *this* . . .' reaching out, she seized the champagne from Niamh's hand, 'and you can get rid of that.'

Before Niamh could protest, Madison turned away, the door closing mere inches from her nose.

She couldn't say exactly how long she stood there, alone in the corridor with the balloon bobbing lightly beside her. Long enough to hear the muffled sounds of Madison giggling and the champagne cork popping.

Just the weekend, she told herself. It was just for the weekend.

She didn't believe it, though, feeling the gentle motion of the *Osprey* beneath her feet. As she turned away, willing herself to trudge back up to her office, it was all she could do not to burst into tears.

6

In the lounge Jade was setting the table for dinner.

Outside, the colours were beginning to change, the sky turning a rich orange as the late-afternoon sun crept in through the windows and glinted on the pristine crockery. The guests had all gone to get ready in their cabins, but Jade wasn't alone. Across the room Ivy was straightening cushions on the couches as she described a TikTok video she had seen about helium. Liam was there too, restocking the bar. From what Jade could tell, this was a job that involved spending a couple of minutes replenishing the fridges and giving the surfaces a cursory wipe, before propping up his elbows and scrolling on his phone.

Jade paid neither of them any notice, focusing on her work so that she could finish quickly and visit Gwyn for a coffee in the kitchen.

At the age of thirty-three, the chef was a little over ten years her senior. All the same, he was undoubtedly her favourite member of the crew. Ivy and Liam were both too self-absorbed to befriend, and Niamh too focused on her role as their superior. But Jade liked spending time with Gwyn. He was kind. When he asked her a question, she sensed that he was genuinely interested in the answer. Having him around felt akin to having an older brother aboard the *Osprey*. Someone whose presence managed, momentarily, to lessen her crippling homesickness.

Laying down one final spoon, she glanced at an iPad, consulting the seating plan that Niamh had instructed her to follow. She then reached for a basket of small wooden plaques, each engraved with the name of a guest and a delicate carving of a local animal. On one was a polar bear, on another a walrus.

She held one in her hands for a moment, inspecting an exquisitely carved ptarmigan. As she looked down at it, admiring the bird's finely inscribed body, she felt a sudden and almost overpowering urge to pocket it.

She couldn't articulate why she wanted the little item. It was pretty, but it wasn't valuable. She couldn't use it for anything and, once she had taken it, she would have to hide it until she could find a way to discreetly get rid of it. It was illogical. Pointless. And yet she could already feel the thrill of squirrelling it away. She forced herself to picture the puzzlement it would cause when the guests found it missing – the disruption to an otherwise picture-perfect evening. She hoped that the image would dissuade her. Instead she found that she wanted it even more.

With a tremendous effort, Jade thought of her home. She reminded herself of her counsellor's advice and of the clean slate she was so desperate to achieve. Then, slowly, she put the place setting down.

The moment she let it go she felt a sudden flush of shame. If it weren't for these urges, she wouldn't have found herself aboard the *Osprey*. She wouldn't be stuck here, working for months on end so far from home. She couldn't give in now. Skyline Voyages was the end of the road, a chance to prove that she wasn't the thief she had been labelled. If she crossed that line up here, where else could she go?

'I just feel like I've been lied to.'

Eager for a distraction, Jade turned her attention to Ivy's rant.

'The whole appeal of working for Skyline was that they were actually doing something for the environment. And I guess it's true that this thing doesn't need the same engines as a plane. But they're being *totally* misleading about how bad it is to use helium. Like . . . did you know that they use it to make computers? And for space exploration, too?'

'That's pretty cool, though, isn't it?'

Liam had set down his phone to answer, but the lack of enthusiasm in his voice was painfully clear. In the day between setting out from Tromsø and collecting the passengers from Longyearbyen, he had clung to Ivy like a bad smell, doing and saying all he could to impress her. During that first leg of their journey Jade expected he would have eagerly engaged her in a discussion about helium, keeping her on her toes with weak jokes and nauseating teases. But he seemed now to have given up the chase, having apparently recognised that Ivy wasn't interested.

Jade had worried that this might mean Liam's attention would turn to her. At twenty-two years old, she'd had a couple of boyfriends, neither of them particularly serious. But with his beaded bracelets and his whitened teeth, she certainly wasn't interested in the smug young bartender.

It seemed she had nothing to worry about, though. Whereas Ivy was blonde and slender, Jade knew that she was more unassuming. Shorter and in her own opinion a little plain, with dark eyes and hair that she pulled back in a sensible ponytail, she thought she might have seen Liam weighing her up once or twice. But if she was correct in those suspicions, he must have decided she wasn't worth the effort. Since they'd taken off, the only real attempt he'd made at speaking with her had been to ask if he could use her staff keycard to deliver the balloon. Having managed to leave his in Tromsø, it quickly emerged that he had already pestered Ivy so much about borrowing hers that she was at risk of becoming seriously pissed off if he asked her again.

'It's *not* cool,' Ivy snapped back at him. 'Because here's what Skyline *isn't* telling people. Helium is completely non-renewable. Once it's gone, it's gone. We're already burning through it, making computers and going to space, so what's going to happen if airships catch on? What happens when there are hundreds – maybe thousands – of these things in the sky? If we keep going, it'll be just another natural resource that we're gutting the world to dig up.'

Liam looked lost for a reply, completely out of his depth. In the silence, Ivy heaved a sigh.

'I made it *so* clear in my interview that this is why I wanted to work for them. Fine, Niamh might not have known. Working on those yachts of hers, she probably wouldn't even care. But Ezra was part of that conversation, too. *He* could have said something. Only he didn't. And now I understand why – now that I know we're serving *whale* on our menu. He puts on a good show, but he doesn't care, either. Not really.'

Liam looked confused. 'Aren't they *allowed* to serve minke whale?'

'Well, they shouldn't be. You can't claim to offer a sustainable local menu and then spring *whale* on someone. And now they've tricked Mia into coming up here, too. She's on this trip because she's been told the *Osprey* is the future of air travel. And when she gets back to the UK she's going to put it out on *Green World* and mislead even *more* people.' Ivy scowled to herself. '*Green World* has form in that, you know. It was one of the titles that got caught up in the Halo scandal last year – the sustainable fashion brand that sent out fake pictures of its factories. Mia gave them a ton of coverage, then a month later some deepfake expert revealed that everything she'd been given had been doctored. Turns out Halo has kids working in sweatshops like everyone else.' She let out a growl. 'You know what? Maybe I should just tell her. Niamh's already pissed off about my vape. I'm hardly going to make things any worse for myself by talking to Mia.'

At this, Liam's ears pricked up. 'We could get it back, if you really wanted to. The vape, I mean. I saw it yesterday. Niamh's put it in the safe.'

'I know it's in the safe,' Ivy shot back. 'I saw her put it there. But we can't get *into* the safe, can we?'

'Yes, we can. I watched her typing in the combination.'

Ivy's eyes widened, prompting Liam to lean against the bar and give an overly nonchalant shrug.

'She called me into the office,' he went on. 'On the flight over from Tromsø. She needed to get something out of the safe while I was in there, so I watched her type in the code. It's zero-eight-zero-five.'

Ivy chewed her lip, deliberating. 'Not worth it,' she said at last. 'She'd know it was me.'

Growing irritated, Jade was now hurrying to finish the table so that she could leave these two and join Gwyn in the kitchen. But before she could finish, the glass doors slid open. Immediately she saw Ivy stand to attention, adopting a broad smile. From the corner of her eye, she noticed Liam's phone fly back into his pocket. She too stood straighter, in anticipation of one of the all-important guests. But at the sight of Howard, her shoulders sagged.

They were a strange double act, dashing young Ezra and her hunched, grey-haired uncle. Jade knew it was Howard who had set up Skyline Voyages, but she couldn't help wondering how far he would really have got on his own. Ezra was charming. Funny. Energetic. He was *interesting*. All qualities that her uncle lacked. To see them side by side was like watching a movie star bring his driver to a red-carpet premiere.

Howard looked from Liam to Ivy, offering a stiff smile. 'Sorry to intrude. Would the two of you mind if I have a moment with Jade?'

The two stewards exchanged a quick, confused glance, but they didn't argue. Howard waited until the glass doors had closed behind them before taking a step towards the table. His movements were rigid, his eyes seemingly determined not to meet Jade's.

'Thought I'd come and see how you're doing.'

'I'm almost finished,' she replied, holding up one of the wooden plaques. 'Just need to set these down.'

She knew it wasn't what he had been asking. But she didn't care. It was about as much as she was willing to give him.

Howard looked down at the floor. 'You're putting them all in the right places, aren't you? Ezra drew the seating plan up himself. He'll notice if someone isn't where they should be.'

She held up the tablet in response, showing him the seating plan. Apparently recognising that niceties would get him nowhere, Howard finally met her gaze.

'Look, Jade, you need to be more cheerful this evening.'

'Cheerful?'

'Cheerful. I've done my sister a huge favour by giving

you this job. It's not her fault those hotels fired you, and it certainly isn't mine. You could show a little gratitude.'

This mention of her mum came like a blow to the gut, while the uncomfortable knowledge that Howard was right drove it home with twice the force.

I know it isn't your fault, her mum had said, tears in her eyes. *I know you don't mean to do it. But no one is ever going to give you another job. Not when there are three hotels that have sacked you for stealing. Your uncle's offering you a chance at a clean slate. A few seasons aboard his airship, to show you can do it. Show you've changed. Then you can come home.*

At first Jade had been baffled as to why her mum had turned to Howard for help. She couldn't remember him ever taking any interest in her. If anything, the handful of instances they'd met had left her thinking he must dislike her. But she supposed it made sense. Her uncle was nine years her mum's senior, and with their parents – Jade's grandparents – having died while his younger sister was still small, Howard had effectively raised her. Even after he qualified as a pilot and began flying with Isaac Day, he had sent money home after Jade's father took off. Whereas Jade saw her uncle as plain and shrewd, her mum looked up to him in a way that was almost reverential.

For a time Jade had been furious. She had never enjoyed travelling, and spending several years at the top of the world wasn't something she would ever have chosen to do. But she had promised she would try. She had meant it, too. She *wanted* to change.

Gritting her teeth, she looked down at Howard's shoes. 'More cheerful. Got it.'

She thought of telling him about the wooden place setting, revealing that she had chosen to put it down, whereas in one of her hotels she would have snuck it away without a second thought. She decided against it, though. He already watched her every move with blatant suspicion. He had even wanted to deny her a staff keycard, removing the ability to enter the guests' cabins, but had given up on that idea. Not only would it be impossible for her to carry out any housekeeping duties, but it would draw questions from the others, and he'd agreed it wouldn't do for them to know why Jade had been placed aboard the *Osprey*.

'Well,' he said stiffly, pushing his glasses up his nose, 'I'll leave you to it.'

He looked like he might say something else, his thin lips parting. But if there was anything more, it went unspoken. Instead he gave her a nod, like an old acquaintance spotted across a crowded room, before making his exit. The glass doors closed behind him and suddenly Jade was alone, with no one for company but the wooden place settings and her near-overwhelming desire to be anywhere else.

7

With the afternoon drawing to a close, and dinner due to be served in a couple of hours, Chloé returned to her cabin with her head spinning. Closing the door behind her, she lay on the bed and breathed in the pine-scented air. Could it really have been only two days since Alec had called? Between the long journey to Svalbard and her first afternoon aboard the *Osprey*, it seemed a lifetime ago.

Reaching for her GoPro, she began to whizz through the footage she had captured while touring the upper deck. Leading them past their cabins, Astrid had shown them to a narrow stairwell, hidden behind an unmarked door disguised as a wall panel. With her eyes fixed on the screen, Chloé recalled her excitement as they entered the tight space, aware that none of the paying guests would be permitted to see the area that she and Ben were about to explore.

They had spent over an hour up there, visiting Gwyn in the kitchen before inspecting the various pieces of equipment that could be deployed in the event of an emergency landing. With an upcoming assignment to a remote part of Iceland, Ben had been particularly intrigued by the inflatable survival tents, but for Chloé the most interesting part of the tour had been the cockpit. Boasting a hive of radar screens, flashing dials and complex-looking controls, each of the instruments was described to them by two pilots, a Danish woman called Freja and a young Norwegian called Jakob. It emerged that both had previously worked with Captain Schäfer, flying helicopters and passenger aircraft before he recruited them for Skyline Voyages. Neither seemed to feel this was an unusual career move, with Jakob spending several minutes describing the various ways that piloting an airship was similar to flying a plane.

Chloé had also taken an interest in the electronics bay. The footage on her GoPro jumped ahead several minutes here, with Astrid having said there were sensitive instruments that she couldn't film. Chloé remembered it well enough, though. Behind a heavy door that required a keycard to unlock it, the bay was narrow, with barely enough space for both her and Ben to move around. From the floor to the ceiling, every inch of wall space was occupied by switchboards and consoles, the dim room illuminated by countless blinking lights.

'Probably not much to look at,' Astrid had said cheerfully, 'but this is the heart of the *Osprey*. Our comms, our radar, our navigation systems. I wouldn't go so far as to say that this is what keeps us in the air. That would be the helium. But it's just as important.'

Standing inside, Chloé had had no idea what Astrid could mean by it not being much to look at. She could have spent hours in there, asking about what each switch and dial might do.

As they left the electronics bay, Astrid closing the door behind them, Chloé had asked how Skyline Voyages came to be. She was eager to know what Ezra had meant on the coach, and to understand the quizzical look he had given her when it emerged that Alec hadn't explained how the company originated. Astrid had relented, though. 'It's Ezra's story,' she had said. 'I'm sure he'd be happy for you to hear it, but I think he'll want to tell it himself.'

If anything, this only perplexed Chloé further. But before she could press Astrid for more information, she hurried them along to the crew's sleeping quarters, the final stop on their tour.

There were four cabins, each containing bunk beds and a wardrobe, plus a shared bathroom with a toilet, sink and tiny shower stall. Chloé had been surprised there wasn't a living area. At the very least she'd expected a small lounge. But Astrid explained that as each flight would last only forty-eight hours, and as there were only eight crew members – the captain, two pilots, one chef and four stewards – there wasn't enough downtime to warrant a dedicated social space. The crew was expected either to be working or sleeping, with the occasional hour of free time spent in their cabins. Astrid hastened to add that, while this might sound extreme, new recruits were briefed thoroughly on the reality of life aboard the airship before being offered a position. She also stressed that they were compensated exceptionally well in return.

'In just a few days up here, our stewards earn what they would make in a fortnight on the average yacht.'

Reaching the end of her footage, Chloé plugged the GoPro in to charge and opened her laptop, ferociously noting down observations from the tour. She didn't want a single thought to be lost, eager to have as much material as possible when it came to writing her feature. In half an hour she had typed up well over a thousand words.

Next she sorted through the pictures she had taken on her phone, updating her Instagram Stories with shots of the *Osprey* coming in to land, of the lounge and of her cabin. She had already posted a few photos of Longyearbyen, receiving an encouraging number of likes and comments from the modest following she had spent three years nurturing, but she was keen to see how the airship would be received. She didn't have to wait long to find out. Within moments of posting, she received her first like.

Finally she took a moment to check how the rest of her content was performing. A carefully crafted montage of shots from a recent trip to Paris was still doing well, as was the latest article she had published on her blog: '10 Things to Do in Paris on a Budget'.

As she looked at the numbers, she felt a flicker of

excitement. Just two days earlier they had filled her with borderline dismay. But now . . .

She was endlessly proud of her blog. Since setting it up as a teenager, to document the nomadic lifestyle she had lived with her parents, it had been a constant source of joy. Likewise, in the three years since she had set out to pursue travel-writing professionally, she had begun to see it as an invaluable portfolio. But if this trip really did mark the beginning of a steady stream of paid assignments from Alec, it would change everything.

Wary of time, she snapped the laptop shut and began getting ready for dinner. An hour later she had showered, put on a little make-up and changed into a blue designer dress that she had borrowed from Ellie. With a plunging neckline, it wasn't something she would have picked out herself, but she hadn't had the money – or, frankly, an occasion – to buy herself any expensive new clothes since leaving her PR role. She knew from Alec how luxurious the *Osprey* would be, so when Ellie offered to lend her something from her wardrobe, Chloé had felt she had no choice but to say yes. H&M wasn't going to cut it this weekend. As she checked her reflection in the mirror, it was strange to see herself so glammed up. She felt good in Ellie's dress, though, and as she crossed the corridor to call for Ben there was an undeniable spring in her step.

Knocking on his door, she heard a flurry of movement within the cabin, smiling at the thought of him bumping around inside the little room. A few moments later the door opened and, before she could stop herself, she felt her eyes widen. The yellow beanie was gone, as were the faded jeans and the plaid shirt. Ben now wore chinos and a smart knitted jumper. His hair, which was considerably shorter than his beard, had a little product in it, and he even looked to have shaved, tidying up his neckline and the straggly hairs that had strayed onto his cheeks.

'What?' Catching Chloé's expression, Ben glanced down at himself. 'Is this no good?'

'No!' she blurted out. 'No, you look great. I just . . . I think this is the first time I've seen you without your hat.'

It was a silly thing to say, but it did the trick, with Ben visibly relaxing. Feeling her cheeks begin to redden, Chloé scolded herself and turned away.

Together they made their way to the lounge, following that perfectly designed scent. They found that the table had been beautifully laid, with frosted water and wine glasses set out for each of them, and the hanging icicle-shaped lights having been dimmed. There were also little wooden plaques at each place, bearing their names. This initially struck Chloé as odd, but it quickly dawned on her that they might not be served the same dishes. She also noticed that a couple of the settings – Astrid's and Howard's – were laid for a left-handed person.

Turning away from the table, she went straight to the windows. Having left Svalbard behind, they were drifting over the Arctic Ocean, the clouds tinged pink like rippling candy floss, while the evening light bled onto the shimmering water. As she looked down on the waves, chunks of ice drifting like clusters of pale islands, Chloé found herself wondering if there might be whales dancing below the surface.

'Have you ever seen anything like it?' Ben asked.

She shook her head. 'Never.'

Side by side, they stood for a few minutes in appreciative silence, only turning their attention back to the room when Ivy appeared with a tray of champagne flutes. Ben took one eagerly, but Chloé, keen to sample everything the *Osprey* had to offer, turned hers down.

'I think I'll have something from the bar,' she said. 'A cocktail, maybe.'

Ivy moved along and, with a great effort, Chloé tore herself from the window, making her way across the lounge. The others had certainly dressed for the occasion, Ezra and Jasper both wearing open-collared shirts beneath sharp suits, while Mia had donned a flowing dress in autumnal colours. It was Madison who looked the most impressive, though. She seemed to have themed her outfit, posing beside the window in a pale-blue gown that glittered and sparkled like the glaciers in the national parks.

As Chloé approached the bar, Liam gave her an easy smile, passing her a drinks menu in a leather wallet.

'I'm loving the polar-themed cocktails,' she said. 'What would you recommend?'

Liam thought for a moment. 'Well, there's the Arctic Collins. That's a good one. In fairness, they're all good. But that's Ezra's favourite, so you can be sure it's *particularly* special. Or if you're not so into gin, there's the Winter

Mojito. We use spiced rum and a darker syrup. Gives it almost a caramel flavour.'

Intrigued by the mojito, Chloé handed back the menu and Liam set about mixing the ingredients in a glass. As he chopped the mint, she could see that he wasn't simply a confident bartender, but a talented one, every movement being made with a flourish. He was putting on a show as much as he was preparing a drink.

She held up her GoPro while he worked. 'Do you mind if I set this up somewhere on the bar? I thought it might be fun to have it filming while we're eating dinner. Get some ambient footage for an Instagram Reel.'

'Go right ahead. If you're planning to point it at the table, I'd recommend setting it up on this corner here. Put it anywhere else and you'll just get me passing drinks across the bar.'

She did as instructed, setting up the tripod on the spot he had pointed out. But as she checked her shot, paying closer attention to the room itself, she couldn't help but feel that, beneath the glamour of it all, the atmosphere in the lounge wasn't as tranquil as she had initially assumed. At the top of the table, Ezra was talking about flying an airship over Dubai, although his expression was stoic. He capped off his speech with a joke of some kind, giving a laugh that drew a grimace from Howard. At the same time Chloé saw that Madison, who had now seated herself with Jasper on the couches, was glaring across the lounge at Mia.

The silent tension made Chloé nervous, and she was

glad when Liam had finished mixing her drink, giving her an excuse to turn back towards the bar. Garnishing it with one last sprig of mint, he passed it to her and she took a sip. It seemed he wasn't just a showman. The cocktail was delicious, the spiced rum and the delicate caramel flavour that he had promised singing on her tastebuds.

'You're the journalist,' he said, a statement rather than a question. 'Getting lots of good material?'

'Loads. Astrid took us on an amazing tour of the upper deck earlier. And I'm hoping to interview both Ezra and Howard at some point tomorrow.'

'Will I get a mention?'

There was something in the way Liam asked this question that made Chloé uneasy. His tone was too familiar, his smile too confident. For a few seconds she looked at him, aware of how long it was taking her to answer. In the silence, he gave a small laugh. Then she saw his eyes wander downwards, lingering on the low neckline of Ellie's dress.

Beginning to feel uncomfortable, she fortified herself, taking another sip of the cocktail. As the liquid went down, pieces of chopped mint were left clinging to the inside of the frosted glass. Whereas a moment before it had been beautiful, Chloé couldn't help but suddenly think of it as ugly, like dead leaves beneath the surface of a frozen pond.

'I might mention this,' she said. 'The *drink*.'

She adopted a tone that was as matter-of-fact as possible, but Liam seemed determined not to take the hint.

'Only *might*?' He adopted a wounded expression. 'I'll have to try harder with the next one.'

Chloé didn't answer this time. With Devon pulling up beside her, distracting Liam by asking for a beer, she seized the opportunity to leave. She hoped to join Mia, with Ben busy taking pictures of the perfectly laid table. But finding that Mia had left while she was speaking to Liam, she instead made a beeline straight for Astrid. As she went, she threw a quick look over her shoulder, regretting it when Liam snagged her gaze. He gave her a nod from behind the bar, a small, playful smile at the corners of his lips.

8

Jasper was deep in thought as he sat beside Madison on one of the leather couches, arm draped loosely around her shoulders.

He had only seen Devon's phone for a moment, peaking over his shoulder as he'd approached the bar, but it had been enough. There had been an email with a large amount of money being discussed. There had been the words 'reparations' and 'court'. And there had been utter disdain on Devon's face, just before he realised Jasper was there and shoved the phone in his pocket.

Given these clues, it seemed fairly obvious that Devon was being sued. The most likely assumption, given his line of work, was that he'd got a tourist injured on one of his mountain expeditions.

Jasper stifled a laugh. He had often thought of Devon as something of a halfwit during their schooldays. The way he'd always stood up for Ezra . . . If the scrawny idiot had been so eager to lash out at anyone who looked down on him – if he really did have something so important to prove – Jasper had thought let him pay for it. Those playing-field scraps would have quickly come to an end if Devon hadn't stepped in every time Ezra started a fight with a larger boy. With a glimmer of amusement, Jasper looked around the lounge, pondering Devon's financial quandaries. Would he be hoping now for Ezra to bail him out, in return for rushing to his defence all those years ago? Jasper hoped he would. More than that, he hoped that *he* could be there to see it.

'I don't like the way she looks at me.'

For the past several minutes Madison had been updating her Instagram with a selection of pouting selfies taken by the windows. But without warning she abruptly broke what Jasper had thought was an enjoyable silence, eyes shooting up from her screen.

'Who are we talking about?'

Madison looked at him as if he'd asked the most absurd question imaginable. 'Are you kidding? *Mia*. I mean, I don't much like the way that reporter looks at me, either. But that Mia seems a real piece of work.'

Jasper heaved a sigh. Madison was forever insisting that someone had a problem with her. At least once a week he would have to hear about how people thought she was too pretty or too successful, or were resentful of her wealthy family. All communicated, of course, through small gestures and fleeting looks that he apparently never paid enough attention to notice.

'You shouldn't have drunk so much of that champagne,' he said, thinking of the bottle that Niamh had delivered to their cabin.

'What else was I meant to do with it? I was hardly going to send it back with the balloon, was I?' She dropped her voice. 'I think Mia knows about Dad.'

'What about him?'

'What do you think? I think she knows he gave Ezra money.'

Jasper considered this for a moment. A proud Texan, over several decades Madison's father had carved a successful career in oil. He was also a keen player of the stock market, and when Jasper had suggested Skyline Voyages as an investment opportunity, the old man had leapt on it. Within a few weeks he'd encouraged several of his former colleagues to do the same. Mia seemed like a reasonable woman. But if she were to know that, through Madison, Skyline Voyages had received an influx of funding from big oil, then he could certainly see her being unhappy about it. He couldn't imagine, though, how she would know. He couldn't see how she would uncover this information herself, nor how it would be in Ezra's interests to share it with her. More than likely this was just another of Maddie's imagined slights.

He ushered the thought from his mind, putting on a smile as he saw Ezra making his way towards them.

'Jas,' Ezra said brightly. 'I'm just dashing up to the cockpit. Apparently the captain wants a quick word. I wondered if you might like to come for that visit to the kitchen. See our chef in action.'

Perfectly content on the couch, Jasper feigned an uncertain look. 'He won't want me getting under his feet while he's working. Maybe tomorrow we could—'

'Don't be daft, mate. Come on. I'll show you the way, then I'll come back for you when I'm done with the captain.'

Jasper turned to Madison. 'Will you be all right without me?'

She shrugged, eyes firmly glued to her phone.

Jasper felt his lip curl. The one time he actually could have done with her making a scene . . . Forcing a smile, he set down his glass and rose to his feet, following Ezra from the lounge.

'I'm keen to hear what you think,' Ezra was saying. 'We had a real mission finding a chef willing to spend so much time up here, and of course Gwyn's excellent. But if you have any notes at all on what he's doing, I want you to tell me.'

Marching to the end of the corridor, he led Jasper up a narrow stairwell to the upper deck, where they found the kitchen directly above the lounge. Before they stepped inside, though, Jasper caught his arm.

'Listen,' he said, 'mate. You haven't mentioned anything to Mia, have you? About Maddie's old man giving you some funding?'

Ezra's brow creased. 'Of course not. Why? Has she said something?'

'Not as such. Maddie seems to think Mia's been looking at her funny. Happens a lot, to be honest. Most of the time I tell her she's just imagining it. But with the old boy's background, and Mia's eco concerns . . .'

Ezra put a hand on Jasper's shoulder. 'I haven't said a word. And, believe me, I don't plan to. If Mia knew about some of the places we've turned to for funding I doubt she would even have agreed to come, let alone give us an endorsement.' He adopted a small smile. 'I'll keep an eye on her. See if I can spot any of these looks she's apparently giving Maddie. If need be, I'll have a word.'

Satisfied, Jasper nodded and let Ezra usher him into the kitchen.

He did his best to look impressed as he took in the room. Kitchens were rarely glamorous, but this one was particularly bleak. A compact space of gleaming steel and artificial light, it reminded him of a morgue, the metal doors that adorned the walls looking like they could just as easily house corpses as fridges and ovens. Every surface was dark-grey metal, gleaming in the way that only brand-new machinery can.

'Gwyn,' Ezra announced. 'This is my friend, Jasper. He'll be giving some thoughts on the menu this weekend. I thought he might be interested in meeting you.'

Beside one of the shining surfaces, a broad-shouldered man who looked to be in his early thirties was hard at work. He was dressed in chef's whites, a serious expression on his face as he beat a vivid green sauce with a whisk. Upon hearing Ezra's voice, he immediately stopped, standing up straight to attention.

Jasper gave him a nod. 'Pleased to meet you.'

'And you, sir.'

Peeling off a pair of black nitrile gloves, Gwyn proffered a hand. Taking it, Jasper found himself impressed. He had expected that the presence of a chef would be a formality more than anything else. The menu would, presumably, have been designed to look as impressive as possible while requiring the absolute minimum amount of prep to be done in the air. In his mind he supposed he had pictured someone reheating pre-made dishes and half-heartedly plating up another chef's work. But this wasn't how Gwyn carried himself. Jasper could see how seriously he took his duties, despite performing them in a lonely metal cupboard.

'Right then.' Ezra clasped his hands together. 'Why don't you two have a chat, and I'll be back after I've spoken to the captain.' With one last grin, he moved along, leaving a slightly awkward silence in his wake.

Jasper gave Gwyn a stiff smile. 'So, everything's electric.'

'That's right, sir.' The chef had a soft Welsh accent. 'No open flames up here.'

'And how do you get the food downstairs, once you've plated it up? You surely can't take it up and down that little staircase.'

'We have a dumbwaiter.' Gwyn motioned towards a hatch on the far wall. 'It comes out behind the bar.'

Jasper made his way around the kitchen, pausing to inspect certain pieces of equipment or run his fingertips over the surfaces. As he went, he was aware of the chef watching. Gwyn seemed nervous, tongue flickering over his lips, and his eyes twitching to the door, as if watching for someone else to join them.

'So what brought you up here?' asked Jasper. 'Bit of a strange gig, isn't it?'

With one last glance at the door, Gwyn steeled himself. 'Can I be honest with you, sir? I know who you are. Ezra mentioned that you were coming, so I . . .' He tailed off, taking a deep breath. 'This isn't a job I've taken by choice. Before accepting the role with Skyline, I worked for two years at a restaurant in Sussex. Le Jardin.'

Jasper's eyebrows rose. 'That's one hell of a place. What did you screw up to find yourself here?'

'Nothing. At least *I* didn't . . .' Gwyn took a deep breath. 'We had a customer one evening with a severe crustacean allergy. It was a busy night, there were two of us monitoring the pass. And my colleague – I don't even know how he managed it, whether he got mixed up or if he just forgot, but he sent out a contaminated plate. Paramedics had to be called, all of our bookings for the rest of the night sent away. The owners, as you'd expect, wanted blood. I kept my mouth shut. Whereas he . . .'

'He pinned it on you.'

Gwyn nodded. 'We both knew that whoever went down for it would never work in a kitchen like that again. Turns out the fear of losing the job was too much for him.'

'And now you're up here,' said Jasper. 'I'm guessing there wasn't much competition for the role.'

'Virtually none. Don't get me wrong, I'm working with some beautiful ingredients. And everything you'll read in the brochure about the menu being designed by Ørjan Viestad – that's all true. I even met him once. But spending nine months of the year alone, in here.' He cast a glance around the small, windowless kitchen.

'Why are you telling me this, Gwyn?'

The chef drew another deep breath. 'As I say, sir, I know who you are. When Ezra told me that you'd be coming on this flight, I did some research.' He looked again towards the door, a sense of urgency in his voice. 'I've signed a three-year contract with Skyline. We all have. And I don't plan to break it. I take my work seriously. But everything you eat this weekend will have been prepared by me, and me alone. If you're impressed, then when that contract comes to an end I would love the opportunity to speak about working for you.'

Jasper didn't reply, his eyes narrowing. 'I hope you're aware,' he said at last, 'that this is incredibly unprofessional. Besides the fact, of course, that Ezra's an old friend.'

He could almost see Gwyn's heart sinking.

'That said,' he continued, 'I can't simply dismiss the opportunity to poach someone with Le Jardin on their CV.' He took a deep breath. 'Look, I won't make you any promises. But if I'm suitably impressed with what you produce this weekend, I'll consider a conversation when your contract's up.'

The elation on Gwyn's face was so blatant that Jasper thought he might cry out with joy. 'Thank you,' he replied, clearing his throat as he tried to compose himself. 'Thank you. I promise, you won't be disappointed.'

'Let's not say another word about it,' said Jasper. 'Now, why don't you talk me through this evening's menu?'

Struggling to withhold an enormous grin, Gwyn snapped on a fresh pair of black gloves.

9

'Would you like to sit down?'

Closing the cabin door behind her, Mia motioned towards the bed, but Ivy shook her head.

'I can't. Niamh would kick off if she knew I was in here.'

'Let's be quick then. Why don't you tell me what's on your mind?'

Mia sat, waiting for Ivy to explain why she had asked for this private chat. Although she had no idea why the young steward had come to her, she assumed it must be important. She couldn't claim to be an expert on luxury travel, but she was fairly certain it wasn't normal for a crew member to march up to a passenger before dinner, bold as brass, and ask if they could speak in private.

'I just want to say,' Ivy began, 'that I have so much respect for what you do. I like *all* of *Green World*'s Insta content, and I saw you at the Climate First march back in April. You gave a really inspiring speech.'

Mia smiled. 'That's very kind. But I don't suppose we're here to discuss how much you enjoy our Instagram Reels.'

Ivy nodded, her expression suddenly serious. 'It's the airship. If I'm honest with you, it's Skyline Voyages as a whole. I joined because I wanted to work for a company that was doing something good. And they put on a great show, selling this thing on the back of how green it is, but if you dig a little deeper they're actually being *incredibly* shady. I would hate for you to put your name to something that doesn't deserve it.'

Mia frowned at her. 'In what way are they being shady?'

'The helium! They go on about how much better for the environment an airship is than a plane, but it's a shameless lie.'

Mia listened as Ivy described a TikTok video she had seen on the impending global shortage of helium. She listened attentively, waiting for the young woman to run out of steam before grasping her chance to step in.

'I get it,' she said. 'I can totally see why you're so concerned. And it's good of you to come and speak to me. But I've had several long conversations with Ezra about this. You would need thousands of airships this size just to use a *percentage* of the world's helium.'

'But that's exactly what Ezra's trying to do. What happens when there *are* thousands of them?'

'I think that would take a long time to come about. And even if it did, the data suggests it could still be a marked improvement on having an equivocal number of jet planes in the sky.'

'But this . . .'

'This isn't perfect,' Mia agreed. She slipped a slight

edge into her voice, while still keeping it as gentle as she could. 'You're right about there being problems with helium. But Ezra isn't lying to you about these airships offering a solution. It's flawed, perhaps. But it's a step in the right direction.'

Ivy stared at her, prompting Mia to feel a sharp pang of sympathy. She had met enough young people at the various marches and conferences she attended to recognise how the steward felt. Ivy expected her to take this information and lead a revolt. To start a movement that would expose Ezra Day and Skyline Voyages as the corporate charlatans they must be.

'I understand the desire to change the world overnight,' she said, choosing her words carefully. 'I really do. Sometimes progress is slow. And difficult. It takes a lot of compromise and many small steps. But I promise you, I've done my research and I believe that what Ezra is doing here is good. Just as I believe *you* are doing a good thing by working for him.'

Ivy swallowed. In a voice laced with defeat, she asked, 'Did you know they're serving whale this evening?'

'Minke whale. I would much rather they didn't, but it's responsibly hunted. In the eyes of the law, Skyline Voyages is doing nothing wrong by serving it.'

She could see the disappointment in Ivy's eyes. But the young steward didn't protest.

'I should get back,' she said quietly.

Mia gave her an encouraging smile. 'You go ahead. I'll be there in a minute.'

As she closed the door behind her, Mia tried to quell her guilt. Perhaps in time Ivy would understand. She clearly meant well. If they had the chance to speak again, Mia could suggest a few other initiatives for her to involve herself in. But as she turned back to the cabin, the guilt quickly gave way to something else. A sense of unease.

She had meant what she'd said. If the *Osprey* performed in all the ways Ezra promised, it could mark a genuine turning point for the aviation industry – something that *Green World* should certainly be covering. But the sheer decadence of it all made her uncomfortable. She understood the vast amount of money that had been required for the *Osprey* to take flight, just as she understood that a certain level of service would be expected by those willing to pay for it. But having been brought up by a local councillor and a schoolteacher, it was difficult to feel confident in progress when that progress came with a price tag of nearly one hundred thousand pounds per head. Nor was it easy to ignore the fact that among the *Osprey*'s very first passengers was the daughter of an American oil baron.

She tried to shake the thought from her mind. People were not their parents. Just because she had followed as closely as possible in her own family's footsteps, she had no reason to believe Madison did the same. Still, as tolerant and open-minded as she willed herself to be, she was unable to forget Madison's assessment of Longyearbyen as bleak. Nor could she ignore how her first instinct upon boarding the airship had been to photograph her champagne flute, rather than stand in wide-eyed wonder at the *Osprey*'s windows. And as these images settled in Mia's mind, it became impossible to overlook the fact that, were this a paying flight, Madison's ticket aboard this miracle of sustainable engineering would have been paid for with oil.

Hovering beside the bed, Mia cast her mind back to the inner-city flat where she had grown up – to her childhood bedroom, which had been even smaller than the snug cabin in which she now stood – and wondered if she had made a mistake by coming. She belonged in the allotments and urban farms she had been taken to as a child, with dirt under her fingernails and a mug of builder's brew at the end of a litter-picking session. Not in this cabin, where she felt so out of place that she was almost too afraid to touch anything.

Forcing these thoughts from her mind, she smoothed the creases from her dress. This wasn't about her. Opulent or not, what Ezra was doing up here was *good*. More than that, she needed it.

Green World had taken such a hit after Halo. They lost followers, advertisers . . . And then there had been the awful things said after the scandal had supposedly passed. People who'd once admired them were now saying that *Green World* couldn't be trusted. That the team was foolish for having been deceived. Liars for trying to mislead their followers.

The memory of it made Mia shudder. But it looked, that afternoon, as if they might finally be about to turn a corner.

The bulk of the photos and videos she took aboard the

Osprey would be posted when she returned to the UK, the very best material having been sifted and curated. But the initial shots she had posted that afternoon were already proving to be more popular than anything they'd put on the channel in months – more popular, even, than almost anything they'd run *before* Halo. When she saw how many likes her pictures of the *Osprey*'s lounge had racked up in just an hour, she thought there must have been a mistake. Quickly checking it again now, the numbers had jumped even further.

So no. It didn't matter how uncomfortable the *Osprey*'s opulence made her feel. Nor did it matter if she thought there were flaws in the experience Ezra was offering his high-flying guests. Not when it looked like her brief stint aboard the airship might finally get *Green World* back on track.

Casting one last hesitant look at her cabin, Mia turned off the light, put on her most enthusiastic smile and made her way back to the lounge.

10

Closing the door behind him, Ezra stepped into the cockpit, trying to keep his concern from showing on his face. 'What is it, captain?'

Standing over Freja and Jakob, Captain Schäfer was inspecting the array of consoles. There was no third seat for him. They flew in pairs, working in eight-hour stints while the third took the opportunity to rest. Ezra knew that it wasn't a good sign for all three of them to be present.

The captain motioned for him to look at a particular radar screen. 'Need to update you, sir,' he said, a soft German accent wrapping itself around his words. 'There's an Arctic storm starting to blow up in our flight path.'

Ezra grimaced as he bent to take a closer look at the screen. He wasn't qualified to pilot the *Osprey* himself, but he could see the cloud that had caught the captain's attention.

'Is it going to cause us problems?'

'Difficult to say. There's a chance it might fizzle out. But if it turns nasty, we could find ourselves with a bumpy ride back to Longyearbyen.'

Ezra cursed under his breath. He knew that Schäfer was a cautious man. A former colleague of his father, he had flown for the best part of forty years, regularly championing the importance of protocol and procedure. But Ezra also knew that the old captain wasn't one to fret unnecessarily. He wouldn't be looking at this screen if Schäfer didn't think it was important.

'We really can't tell which way it's going to go?'

The captain shook his head, expression grim. 'Right now, it's impossible to say. Freja has plotted a new route; it puts us on a curve to give the storm as wide a berth as possible. But my suggestion would be that we turn back and try again in a few—'

'No,' Ezra said sharply. 'I'm sorry, but no. We can't turn back on our very first trip. Especially not for a weather warning that might ultimately come to nothing.'

The captain's frown became deeper, but he didn't argue. 'Should we tell Mr Barnes as well?' he asked. 'And the stewards? I could let Niamh know that—'

'I'll speak to Howard,' said Ezra. 'But if there's really a chance of it settling down, let's see how it develops before we tell anyone else. For now, carry on as you are.' He sighed, then forced himself to stand up straight. 'Keep me updated. And not a word to anyone else unless you've spoken with me first. We don't want to cause any unnecessary panic.'

The captain nodded, although Ezra could see the uncertainty in his expression.

'Thank you,' he said as briskly as he could manage. 'You're all doing a wonderful job.'

Stepping out of the cockpit, Ezra lingered in the corridor. He didn't feel good about lying to the captain. Schäfer wasn't just a trustworthy pilot. He was also a family friend. But he couldn't tell Howard about the storm. Not when the old man was already so on edge.

'We shouldn't be doing this, Ezra,' he had said in the days before the trip. 'Your friends are one thing. But Mia, Maddison and now whoever Alec's sending in *his* place . . . We don't know these people.'

Ezra had tried to quell Howard's concerns, hoping that once they had taken the leap and were in the air, his anxiety would ease. Instead he only seemed to be getting worse. Ezra cast his mind back to that afternoon, when Astrid had pulled him away from his drink with Devon. Upon knocking on Howard's door, the older man had ushered him into the cabin and held up his phone, showing him the 'About me' page of a blog called *Nomad Chlo*.

'Did you know that Chloé isn't a journalist? Look.' Howard had thrust his phone under Ezra's nose. 'I googled her. Nothing's been published on the *Condé Nast* website under her name, so I went further afield. Turns out she's a blogger of some kind.'

'I know.'

Howard frowned. 'What do you mean, you know?'

'Alec had only a couple of days to find someone who could take his place. None of his regular freelancers were available at such short notice, so he decided to take a chance on Chloé instead.'

'But how did he find her?'

'Apparently she's been desperate to get on his books. Pitches him a new feature idea more or less every week. He says they're all good ideas, and he's checked out her blog pretty thoroughly. He thought it was worth giving her a shot.'

'And you trust her? It sounds like Alec doesn't even *know* her—'

'If Alec was happy to send her, that's good enough for me.'

Ezra had paused at that point, his eyes straying to a small plastic bottle that sat on the bedside table. He always knew when Howard was on the sleeping pills. He would turn to them a handful of times each year, when the stresses of getting Skyline Voyages off the ground became too much. Prior to this flight, Ezra estimated he'd been taking them for the best part of a fortnight.

Following his gaze, Howard snatched up the little bottle and squirrelled it away in his suitcase. He didn't protest further, but Ezra had seen that he wasn't convinced. Now, as he stood outside the cockpit, he knew with complete certainty that he couldn't say anything about Schäfer's storm. The words would barely have a chance to leave his mouth before Howard insisted on turning back.

No, Ezra told himself. As he'd said to Schäfer, they weren't calling off this trip. Not when they had come so far.

11

Chloé prided herself on being pretty adventurous with the local cuisine in the various locations she visited for her blog. Likewise, on the rare occasion that her PR work had required her to visit one of the five-star resorts she represented, making the most of the restaurants had always been a top priority. But she had never anticipated that she might one day taste whale.

Seated between Mia and Ben, she was presented with a board on which three slices of impossibly dark meat were neatly arranged. As Jade placed it down, she explained that the other two were reindeer and seal.

'Minke whale,' Ben whispered, clocking the concern on Chloé's face. 'Responsibly hunted.'

Chloé looked around the table. Astrid was already tucking into hers, while Madison and Mia had been served a salad of some kind, dressed with a light-green foam.

Seated directly across from her, with Howard on his right and Jasper on his left, Ezra beamed as the starters were served. 'The menu has been designed with two goals in mind,' he announced. 'To spotlight Arctic cuisine and to scream sustainability. The *Osprey* is the future of sustainable air travel. The menu we serve should reflect that. And I just want to add, before we get stuck in: the chef knows that we have a couple of allergies on board. As do all of our stewards. Please be assured that all necessary safety precautions are being taken.'

Further down the table, Chloé saw Devon give a stiff nod from behind a generous glass of red wine.

When the starters were cleared, Chloé quietly hoped the charcuterie wouldn't make a repeat appearance on the second night. The three meats tasted as dark as they looked, rich and salty, each with a more curious texture than the last. She wondered if her glimpse of the reindeer as they boarded the *Osprey*, or perhaps the mental image of whales in the fjord beside Longyearbyen, made it more difficult to enjoy. Either way, she was glad when Jade took the board away, washing the taste down with a glass of what she thought was mineral water, but realised on closer inspection of the bottle was in fact glacier water. The main course was turbot, and the dessert comprised small, toffee-coloured domes served on dark plates.

By the time the final course was finished, the light had changed. The sun hadn't set – at this time of year, Chloé knew it wouldn't set at all – but the soft golden glow against which they had sat down was now gone. In its place was a colder hue that even seemed to bring the temperature down inside the lounge.

While they ate, Ezra had fielded questions about the

menu, explaining why certain ingredients had been chosen and describing how they would vary to reflect each of the regions in which Skyline Voyages planned to launch expeditions. But as the plates were cleared and he answered a final ingredient-focused question from Jasper, he turned to Chloé.

'You've asked more than enough for now, Jas. I'd like to hear from our resident reporter.' He gave her a small, cheeky smile. 'Is there anything in particular you'd like to know?'

Chloé knew exactly what she would have liked to ask about. Casting her mind back to the coach journey out of Longyearbyen, she was keen to pick up on Ezra's comment about the origin of Skyline Voyages. But she held back, reluctant to admit in front of Howard that she hadn't known what Ezra meant. She hadn't yet spoken much to Skyline Voyages' founder, but he seemed considerably less forthcoming than his young COO. Even as they ate, she was sure that on a couple of occasions she had caught Howard looking warily at her across the table. So, no. She couldn't yet ask about Ezra's curious comment. With all eyes upon her, and with Ezra himself having promised her a full interview before the weekend was out, she decided for the time being that a safer question was required.

'Well,' she said, Jasper and Mia having exhausted the best questions about the menu, 'before we sat down, I couldn't help but hear you talking about flying over Dubai. Is that where you're hoping the next Skyline route will depart from?'

'Ah.' Ezra deflated slightly. 'No. We do hope to launch a route over the Sahara, but I'm afraid you caught the tail-end of something quite different.'

He turned to Howard. The older man looked nervous, giving a tiny of shake of his head. In the end it was Jasper who spoke up.

'It's the other guys, right? Airborne Something-or-Other?'

'That's it.' Ignoring Howard's apparent discomfort, Ezra turned back to Chloé. 'I suppose there's no harm in you knowing. There's another company trying to launch a line of airships. *Airborne Expeditions*. They're based in Dubai, and they're desperate to start operating before we do.'

Chloé considered this for a moment. She was keen to know more, but she was also conscious of how proud Ezra was of the *Osprey* – just as she was aware of the disapproval now plastered across Howard's face.

'Is there . . .' She paused, deliberating over how to phrase her question. 'Are they likely to do it? To launch first, that is?'

'No,' Howard said, in a tone that invited no response.

Ezra gave her a small smile. 'Not at the moment. We had a good head-start, which has just about kept us in the lead. But believe me, they're trying. They have more people and a shedload more money, and they're closing the gap every day. If we were to delay so much as a couple of months, I expect they'd manage it.'

'And how much damage would it do if they did? I hope

it isn't a silly question, but Alec's told us about your waiting lists. You're fully booked for the first two years.'

'Nearly three,' Astrid chimed in.

'Right. So if they're flying over the desert, is the concern that potential customers might choose that over the North Pole? Or is there something I'm missing?'

Ezra hesitated, the little smile still in place. 'Do you know who the Wright Brothers were?'

'Of course. The first men to fly.'

'And who were the second?'

Chloé couldn't answer. She had absolutely no idea.

'You're right,' said Ezra. 'Financially, I don't expect it would make much difference if Airborne Expeditions took off slightly ahead of us. But you only have one chance to be first. If we let them beat us – let them plaster that across their website and their brochures and their social media for everyone to see – then all of this . . .' He cast a look around the lounge. 'Well, it's difficult to say that it would all be for nothing. But it's not . . .'

His voice swelled with emotion, and he had to pause to collect himself. Caught off guard by this reaction, Chloé swept a quick glance around the table. The others were watching just as closely, equally curious.

Ezra cleared his throat. 'I asked you this morning, Chloé, if you knew where the idea for Skyline Voyages first originated. I know we're going to have a proper interview tomorrow, but while we're on the subject I suppose it makes sense to cover that now.' He paused to take a sip of water. But as he held the glass to his lips, his eyebrows shot up, a thought occurring to him. 'Perhaps I can do better than telling you,' he said. 'Perhaps I can show you.'

He stood abruptly, leaving the lounge in such a hurry that he didn't even stop to put down his glass. The doors slid open and Chloé watched as he disappeared into the corridor, before hearing his cabin door open and shut.

In the ensuing silence, Madison spoke up, looking more irritated than curious. 'I thought the company was *your* idea. You're the founder, right?'

She looked directly at Howard, who gave a small, almost painful smile.

'I am. But it wasn't supposed to be me alone.'

Madison looked even more confused. But before she could press Howard further, Ezra returned. In one hand he still carried the water glass he had taken with him, which he set down on the table. In the other he clutched a small parcel wrapped in brown paper.

'I hadn't quite decided when to give you this,' he said, holding out the package to Howard. 'But I think now seems a good time.'

Howard took the parcel and began to unwrap it, the others watching closely as he lifted the paper away.

'What is it?' Madison asked.

'It's . . .' With the paper removed, Howard found himself holding a wooden frame. He stared at it until, words failing him, he turned it round. The photograph within showed two grinning men in a snowy landscape, their arms around each other's shoulders. Dressed in winter survival gear, one was a much younger Howard. And the other . . .

'That's my dad.'

Chloé could hear the pride in Ezra's voice. Not that the second man needed identifying. The resemblance between father and son was striking, from the straight nose to the rigid jaw. In the corner of the picture, Chloé saw that it was dated 14 August 2005.

'This was when it happened,' he said. 'This was the trip on which they had the idea for Skyline Voyages.' He turned to Howard. 'Last year, when Mum died, I came home to clear out the house. There were boxes of Dad's old things in the attic, and in one of them I found the camera he took on that trip. When he didn't come back with you, I couldn't bring myself to get the pictures developed. But when I dug it out again last year, I knew it was time.'

He refilled his water glass and took a sip. Howard, meanwhile, didn't speak. He'd gone pale, his eyes glued to the photo.

'Howard?' Looking suddenly concerned, Ezra set the water down again, putting an arm round the older man's shoulders. 'I'm sorry. If it's too much, I can—'

'It's fine.' Howard managed a smile. 'It's a kind thought, Ezra. I just . . . I wasn't expecting it.'

A silence settled on the group.

'It looks like you knew each other well,' said Chloé.

'We did,' Howard agreed. 'We flew together. Passenger

aircraft. And when Isaac set up his own cargo carrier, I went over and joined him.'

'You did more than just *fly* together,' Ezra prompted him. 'The two of you went all over the world. You climbed in the Himalayas, cycled the Silk Road!'

'We did,' Howard said again. 'But this was a big one. Skiing to the North Pole . . . Isaac had wanted to do it for a long time. A *very* long time. Took years to convince me to go with him, but he got me in the end.'

'Do you remember exactly where Skyline came from?' asked Ezra. 'We've never really spoken much about it, have we? From day one, we've just got on with the work. But now that we're here . . . Was there any particular moment when you decided you were going to do it?'

Howard shook his head, a mournful look in his eyes. 'It's difficult to say. It was such a long time ago. I think . . . I think a day or two into the expedition I might have said something about wishing we'd flown instead of skied.' He paused as a ripple of hushed laughter went around the table. 'And I think that might have prompted Isaac to bring up the airships that flew over the Pole a hundred years ago.' Howard stared at the photo. Then he cleared his throat, sitting up a little straighter in his seat. 'I do remember, once it had been brought up, that we talked about it for the next couple of days. We came up with plans, discussed how we would pull it all off. We knew it would be a major undertaking. But the more we spoke about it, the more serious it became. I don't think there was any doubt in either of our minds that once we were home, we were going to make it happen.'

Ezra patted him affectionately on the shoulder, before turning back to Chloé. 'So you see. This . . .' He waved an arm around the lounge, taking in the couches, the dining table and the bar. 'All of this, it was his ambition. It was my dad's dream to return these aircraft to the skies. One that I'm proud to have realised on his behalf. We have to be the first to start operating. We've come this far. We have to go the rest of the way. For *him*.'

Chloé was enraptured, hanging on Ezra's every word. In her mind she pictured the two friends, discussing how they would bring Skyline Voyages to life as they trekked towards the Pole. She wished she could somehow go back and hear their conversations. But more than anything, she wanted to know what had happened to Isaac. Ezra said he hadn't come back, and while she was desperate to hear why, she could think of no appropriate way to ask.

Ezra looked sharply towards the bar. 'Liam. Two Laphroaigs, please. In fact small measures for everyone, if you all don't mind. I think we should toast Dad.'

Howard forced a shaky laugh. 'Ezra . . .' he said. 'You know I'm not drinking at the moment.'

'I know, but just a small one. Look at where we are. Look at what we've done. We have to toast his memory.'

Howard looked like he might protest, but he stayed silent as Liam made up a tray of nine whisky glasses. Once they each had a measure, he clinked glasses with Ezra and took a cursory sip, turning immediately to his empty water glass. Chloé, who had never enjoyed whisky, was already in the process of pouring herself a large glass of water, having made sure to give her measure a cursory sip while Ezra was watching. Reaching across the table, she topped Howard up as well, and he nodded appreciatively before tipping it back in one go.

'I think you should be very proud,' said Mia. 'Both of you. If he were here to see it, I'm sure Isaac would be overwhelmed by what you've achieved.'

Ezra gave her a warm smile. 'I do hope so. He was . . . well, he was a great man.'

'He was a *shit*.'

At first Chloé thought she must have misheard. But as the silence dropped like a dead weight upon the table, her heart leapt into her throat. Every eye turned to Devon, all watching as he drained his whisky and heavily set his tumbler down.

'Ezra . . .' he continued. 'Come on, mate. What you've done here is amazing. This!' Slurring a little, he waved a hand around the lounge, narrowly avoiding slapping Ben in the face. 'All of this – it's amazing. But you shouldn't be doing it for Isaac. You should be doing it for yourself.'

Chloé expected Ezra to be furious. Instead, he looked hurt. Confused even.

'Dev, he was my father. Of course I'm pleased with what we've done here. But it was *his* dream.'

Devon scowled. 'What did he say to you, Ezra? After the Normanstone challenge. What did he tell you?'

Ezra's expression flickered. 'I don't remember.'

'That's funny. Because I remember word for word.' Devon turned suddenly to Chloé, looking her straight in the eye. 'There was an annual event at our school. A race. Isaac came one year to watch, and Ezra was desperate to show him what he was made of. But he took an injury halfway round and ended up being the last kid across the line. What did he say to you, Ezra, after you'd finished?'

Ezra said nothing, his eyes like stone.

'I'll tell you what he said. He told you how ashamed he was. And that it would have been better for everyone if he hadn't come.' Devon shook his head, incredulous. 'You don't *need* to make Isaac proud, Ezra. He didn't deserve it then and he doesn't deserve it now. You should be proud of *yourself*.'

Nobody spoke. For what felt to Chloé like an eternity, nobody even moved.

'If you're quite finished,' Jasper said eventually, 'I suggest you apologise.'

'Apologise?' Devon shot back at him. 'For telling the truth? For being the only one prepared to admit who Isaac *actually* was—'

'For being obscenely inappropriate. Ezra invites you on this incredible trip, and you decide to thank him by getting pissed and making a scene?'

'Jas . . .' Ezra fixed him with a pleading look. 'It's OK. This really doesn't—'

'No,' Jasper cut over him. 'Devon's been drinking since the moment we came aboard. I'm not standing for it, Ezra, and neither should you. He needs to get a hold of himself and apologise. And if he can't do that, he should get out and leave us in peace.'

A fresh silence descended, infinitely more tense than the last. Holding her breath, Chloé watched as Devon seemed to consider these two options. After a long pause, a dark glimmer of amusement spread across his face.

'Pathetic,' he murmured. 'It's just pathetic.'

He pushed himself away from the table, drained what remained in his wine glass and then tottered towards the glass doors, muttering to himself as he went. After he had gone and they had heard the door to his cabin close, Ezra heaved a sigh.

'I'm so sorry, everyone,' he said. 'Devon's clearly had a little too much to drink. I'm sure we'll hear an apology in the morning.'

There came a murmur of understanding from the others, although the fragile moment of respite didn't last long.

'Oh my God!' A cry came from the far corner of the table, and Chloé looked across to see Madison staring at her phone. 'Was there meat in my salad?' Before anyone could reply, she threw up her phone. 'Someone's just replied to my story,' she continued, her voice rising. 'He says it looks like there's *meat* at the bottom of my salad.'

Jasper snatched the phone off her, glaring at the screen. Chloé, her curiosity overcoming her, took out her own phone and found Madison's Instagram profile. Holding it under the table, she skipped through several photos of

Longyearbyen and the *Osprey*, as well as a considerable number of pouting selfies taken inside her cabin, until she came to a picture of the salad that Madison hadn't eaten. Beside her, Ben was squinting at the screen, searching for whatever her eagle-eyed follower had apparently found.

'There!' Peering over Jasper's shoulder, Madison jabbed at the screen. 'I see it. It's right there.'

Jasper's eyes narrowed. 'That looks like a bit of the whale we had on our charcuterie boards.'

Chloé saw it now, too. It was buried at the bottom of the plate, a sliver of something dark poking out from beneath a large leaf. To Madison's follower, it must have looked like a charred bit of meat. Something akin to brisket. Chloé wondered if Madison, viewing it through the lens of her camera, might have mistaken it for a particularly juicy mushroom. But having reluctantly eaten the whale herself, Chloé knew exactly what they were looking at.

'Whale?' Madison's voice climbed higher still, hysteria creeping in. 'Are you saying I nearly ate *fucking whale*?' She shot a look across the table. 'You,' she snarled, eyes settling on Mia. 'This was *you*.'

Mia recoiled. 'Me? Why would I do that? *How* would I even do it?'

'I don't care *how* you did it. I just know that you *did*. I've seen the way you look at me. You think you're subtle, but I've seen you. Looking down on me. *Judging* me.'

'Judging you . . .' Mia leaned forward in her seat. 'I understand you're upset,' she said. 'If that had been my plate, I would be, too. But no one here is *judging* you.'

'Maddie,' Jasper cut in, before she could reply. 'Be serious. How on Earth is Mia supposed to have put this on your plate without you noticing? And besides, what does it really even matter? You didn't *touch* that salad. If that *is* bit of a whale in this picture, there was never any risk of you actually eating it.'

But Madison wasn't pacified. If anything, Jasper taking Mia's side only seemed to make matters worse. For a few seconds she just pouted at him, face slowly turning red. Then she turned back to Mia.

'You *know*,' she said. 'Don't you? That's what this is about. You know my family's invested in this thing.'

Mia's face creased into a frown.

'Give me a break,' Madison chided. 'You can drop the puppy-dog eyes, honey. Nice as it would be, wind farms and solar panels aren't paying for us to go partying over the North Pole. This is the real world. And in the real world, the money comes from people like *me*.'

Mia turned to Ezra, terror in her eyes. 'Ezra,' she said, 'is this . . . ?'

He fixed her with a desperate look. 'Please, Mia. You have to understand. The amount of capital required to get Skyline off the ground – we couldn't afford to turn down offers of investment, regardless of where they might come from.'

'How many other investors in oil do you have?'

'I can hardly give you an exact figure off the top of my—'

'*How many?*'

Admitting defeat, Ezra sighed. 'Several. Madison's

father put us in touch with a number of his colleagues. When they heard about what we were doing up here, they all seemed eager to invest.'

Chloé watched as panic spread across Mia's face. 'Oh, God,' she murmured. 'My Instagram Stories . . .'

She scrambled for her phone, so desperate to delete whatever she had posted that she dropped it onto the table.

'Mia,' Ezra protested, 'I really don't think it's—'

'I can't be here,' she snapped at him. 'Do you have *any idea* how our followers would respond to me being on this thing if they found out it's funded by oil barons?'

'Only *partially* funded—'

'It doesn't matter! There's no way of explaining that to these people – it's everything or nothing. What the *fuck*, Ezra? I can't believe you would let me come here. I can't believe you didn't . . .' She tailed off, rising to her feet. 'I can't,' she said. 'I just can't.'

She hurried from the lounge. Madison watched her go, a satisfied smile on her lips.

'Fuck's sake, Maddie,' Jasper murmured.

She was on him in an instant. 'You really don't think it was her? You're meant to be on my side!'

'How can I possibly be on your side when you're coming out with *shit* like that? Of course it wasn't Mia. How the hell is she supposed to sneak a bit of whale into your salad from across the bloody table?'

Madison didn't answer. Instead she too leapt to her feet, spilling a glass of wine as she flew from the table.

'Maddie,' Jasper called after her. 'Maddie!'

But it was no good. She had disappeared into their cabin before the glass doors to the lounge even had the chance to close behind her.

Nobody moved. Then Jasper made a sound that was somewhere between a sigh and a growl, before draining what remained of his whisky.

'Jas.' Ezra looked up at him as he climbed to his feet. 'Do you really have to . . . ?'

Jasper dropped his eyes, genuinely remorseful. 'I'm sorry, mate. I know this isn't how you wanted your evening to play out. But if I don't go after her, I'll never hear the end of it.'

Ezra nodded, watching mournfully as Jasper made his way to the door. Chloé felt as if she should say something – do something – that might comfort him. Twenty years he had been working towards this, and this was how the first night had gone. But nothing came to mind that would possibly help.

Pausing at the glass doors, Jasper turned back. 'I'm sorry,' he said again. 'It'll be better tomorrow.'

He and Ezra exchanged a nod, then he went into the corridor. As he opened the door to their cabin, Chloé heard Madison's raised voice ricocheting from inside the room, insults and accusations being hurled at Jasper before he'd even had a chance to step inside. Then the door closed again, plunging those who were left in the lounge into a sombre, stony silence.

Sunday 14 September 2025

The second day of the flight

12

When Chloé woke, it was to the sudden sensation of falling.

She sat up sharply in bed, heart thumping against her ribs. She couldn't recall any nightmares. Still, she closed her eyes, taking a moment to steady herself. It was only when she opened them again, and saw that her breath was steaming in front of her, that she noticed the cold.

The cabin was freezing. Scrambling for an explanation, it occurred to her that she must have turned down the air conditioning before going to bed and failed to notice the falling temperature while she slept under the duvet. Shivering, she reached for the remote, tapping urgently at the button that would crank it back up.

It was curious, though. As she cast her mind back, she couldn't, for the life of her, remember adjusting the temperature.

After Jasper left the table, the evening had been done. Ezra had tried to get things back on track, asking Liam to fetch another bottle of wine, but Howard had departed at that point too, announcing that he was feeling strange and wanted to turn in early. Ezra had then been called away for a conversation with the captain, leaving just Chloé, Ben and Astrid. For a short while they'd sat at the bar, enjoying the view while Liam made them each another round of cocktails. But the series of sour notes that had brought dinner to a close lingered over them and, in the end, they had agreed to call it a night. As Jasper had said, things would be better in the morning.

Chloé tried to remember what she'd done upon returning to the cabin. After climbing into bed, she had browsed some of the ambient sounds that she could play while she slept, wondering if she might struggle to drift off without Clapham High Street rumbling outside Ellie's flat. Instead she'd found the *Osprey*'s near-complete silence, save for the distant whirring of the propellers, surprisingly comforting. Not even the dusky light of the midnight sun had troubled her, having been too nervous to attempt her temperamental blackout blind again. And so, between the sumptuousness of her bed, the gentle motion of the airship and the wine and cocktails she had drunk at dinner, she had slipped into a comfortable sleep.

She could remember it all so clearly. Could she really have drunk so much at dinner that she had forgotten changing the temperature? She didn't think so.

There came a click from the air vent above her door. It would soon warm up. But almost as suddenly as she had noticed it, the cold was quickly forgotten. Because as she turned her attention to the window, she saw with a start that they were no longer floating over water, but instead above a pale-white landmass.

Wrapping the duvet around her shoulders like a shroud, Chloé hurried to the window with her GoPro. Gone was the fluffy pink sky that she had admired before dinner, a grey haze having now taken its place. Fine snow was falling, powder-like flakes settling against the glass before quickly melting away. Through the mist, Chloé saw white dunes looming beneath them, rising and falling, the only way to tell one from the next being the pale-blue shadows that each cast upon the ground. It was the same in every direction, a white desert. Or an ocean, the thrashing waves frozen in place before one could crash into the other. Yet more snow came surging from the peaks, taking to the air like icing sugar. At the same time it occurred to her there was also a new sound in the cabin. One that she was certain hadn't been there the day before. It was the whistling of the wind outside. Otherwise, the place was still. Completely still. Not in any direction was there a single sign of life.

'Oh my God . . .'

She whispered it, as if the landscape might be disturbed by speaking any louder. She wanted to be awed by it, and to an extent she was. But as she stood there alone, huddled beneath her duvet, the emptiness made her nervous. Not the same nervousness that came when she thought of Alec's assignment – the kind of nerves that accompanied the desire to do a good job. Instead she was thinking about how far they were from home. From shelter. From life. As she watched the snowflakes hurling themselves at her window, she couldn't help but think that this place itself didn't want them there.

She shivered, choosing to blame it on the temperature of her room. This was the end of the season, she reminded herself. In a few short weeks polar night would descend, plunging this entire part of the world into twenty-four-hour darkness. They were bound to run into some adverse weather. The majority of Ezra's customers would be coming during the summer, when they would look out at a clear blue sky.

She held the GoPro steady, wondering how many people had ever seen the view she was seeing now. She thought of the *Norge*, following this same route a hundred years prior. And, with a cold shudder, she thought of Isaac Day. Ezra hadn't described how his father had died, but he did say at dinner that he had never come back from his trip to the North Pole. His body must be down there somewhere. Resting in the ice for all of time.

She checked the time on her phone. Almost seven o'clock. Only five hours remained until they reached the Pole – until they touched the exact point at the top of the world. Trembling now in her cold cabin, and eager to be around some other people, Chloé dumped the duvet onto the bed and reached for her jeans. But no sooner had she tugged them on than the floor beneath her gave a sudden lurch.

This time there was no question of whether she might be dreaming. Without a doubt, she had felt the *Osprey* move.

She hurried from the cabin, the whistling rising to a

howl – a scream even – as the wind wrapped itself around the airship. Growing more nervous by the second, she found that in the corridor as well it was ice-cold. What was going on?

Inside the lounge – also freezing – she found that the table had been freshly laid with glassware and cutlery, although the jolt she'd just felt had sent the knives and forks skidding out of place. Jasper and Madison were on one of the couches, gripping the underneath as if riding a rollercoaster, while Mia and Ben were seated at the table. At the bar, Devon sat alone with a steaming mug of coffee. He was dabbing his trousers with a napkin, the tremor having spilled some of his latte. All wore winter jackets. Madison had even put on a woolly hat.

'A little bumpy this morning,' Chloé said to the room, hoping she sounded brighter than she felt.

'It's been going on all bloody night,' Jasper called back. 'Got up to use the loo at four and it nearly sent me flying.'

Chloé went to Ben and Mia, dropping her voice to a murmur. She clutched her arms as she went, wishing that she, too, had thought to put on her jacket.

'What's happening?' she asked.

'No idea,' Ben replied.

'Should we be worried?'

'I don't know. Ezra was in here a few minutes ago. He says everything's fine. Only a bit of turbulence apparently, but . . . well, he's with the captain at the moment. Said he'd speak to us all properly when he knows more.'

Chloé swallowed back a lump, trying not to think of the

near eight hundred miles that loomed between them and Longyearbyen.

'What about the cold? I thought I'd done something wrong with the air con in my room, but it's freezing here, too.'

'It's all of us,' said Mia. 'Every room. Again Ezra hasn't said as much, but there's clearly something going on with however they control the onboard temperature.'

They were silent for a moment, gentle piano music fighting a losing battle with the sound of the wind. Then, as if on cue, Ezra appeared, with the captain, Niamh and Astrid falling in behind him.

He cleared his throat, tucking his hands into the pockets of the enormous Skyline Voyages puffer jacket he had worn on the coach. 'Everyone, if I could have your attention for a moment. Apologies for this morning's turbulence. I'm afraid we're on the edge of a storm that has turned nastier than we were expecting during the night.'

'Are we safe?' It was Madison who spoke, panic clear in her voice.

'Perfectly,' Ezra assured them. 'But Captain Schäfer has insisted we turn back. The storm is expanding quickly. If we continue on to the Pole, our return journey will take us right through the middle of it.'

'That doesn't *sound* safe,' Madison protested.

'We're fine,' said Ezra. 'I promise. It'll be a bumpy few hours, but the conditions shouldn't get any worse than they are now.'

As if to challenge this assessment, the airship gave

another lurch, forcing Ezra to grip the edge of the nearest sofa to keep himself upright.

'What's happening with the temperature?' Jasper demanded. 'It's bloody freezing.'

'We're looking into it,' Ezra replied. 'Our climate-control system appears to have glitched during the night, but I'm sure we'll have it resolved soon.' His expression shifted. He looked bereft. 'I'm so sorry, everyone. I know it will come as a disappointment not to reach the Pole itself, but safety must come first. If the weather lets up by the time we reach Svalbard, and if we've managed to get the heating back on, we'll spend a few extra hours over the national parks to make up for it. But as it stands, our new flight plan should see us back in Longyearbyen around three o'clock tomorrow morning.'

Chloé locked eyes with Ben. She could see that he shared her disappointment. But between the cold and the way the *Osprey* was swaying beneath their feet, she couldn't say she wasn't also a little bit relieved.

'Where's Howard?' Ezra looked around the lounge, brow furrowed, before turning to Astrid.

She shook her head. 'He must still be in bed.'

Ezra's frown intensified. He didn't press the matter, though, instead turning and heading back into the corridor.

'Ezra,' Astrid called after him, 'is everything OK?'

He brushed her away. 'The man's been so stressed these past couple of weeks he's needed sleeping pills just to get down for a few hours. There's no chance he's having a lie-in during *this*.' Chloé watched as Ezra raised his hand and knocked sharply on one of the cabin doors. 'Howard,' he called out. 'Howard, can I come in?'

When no answer came, he knocked again. 'Howard, is everything all right? Can you hear me?'

Still there was no answer.

Panic spread across Ezra's face. 'Jesus Christ,' he whispered. With a crowd now gathering, he looked frantically around. 'Keycard,' he said. 'I need a keycard.'

Niamh fumbled her keycard loose from a lanyard on her belt loop, and Ezra snatched it from her hand. When he slid it into the slot, the lock clicked and he threw open the door. Or, rather, he tried to throw it open. As if in protest, the door moved only a few inches before sticking in place.

Panic overcoming him, Ezra put his shoulder to the door, this time throwing his full weight against it. Again it moved only a few inches. He shoved it a second time and then a third, until the gap was large enough for him to squeeze into the cabin. The captain came next. Dropping to one knee, he revealed what had been keeping the door from opening. A dressing gown. It must have fallen from the hook on the back of the door, and with each determined shove from Ezra had become more firmly wedged between the door and the carpet.

With the dressing gown removed, the captain was able to open the door wide, and the nightmare began in earnest.

13

The first thing Chloé noticed, as the captain threw open Howard's door, was a sickly-sweet smell. It burst from the cabin, clashing so suddenly with the now-familiar scent of pine that for a second it was completely disorientating.

'Back!' the captain barked at them. 'Everyone, stand clear!'

He planted himself in the doorway, trying to hold them all at bay, but it was no use. Immediately the cold was forgotten. So too was the shuddering of the *Osprey* beneath their feet. They were all hooked on the morbid scene inside the cabin.

Chloé had never seen a corpse before, but it was clear the instant she laid eyes on him that Howard was dead. Beside the bed, Ezra was on his knees, gripping the older man's shoulders as if trying to rouse him. Tucked up beneath the duvet, though, Howard lay perfectly motionless. With his head tilted towards the cabin door, Chloé could see that his eyes were closed, his lips were blue and the skin around his mouth and nose had turned red.

Stunned into silence, she stood shoulder to shoulder with Ben and Mia, watching the scene unfold from the corridor. They hovered behind Jasper and Devon, all crowded so tightly around the door that every other second someone would stray into her eyeline and block her view. In the fleeting glimpses she stole between their jostling heads, she could see that the cabin hadn't been disturbed. If she'd had to guess, she would have said that Howard must have died in his sleep. All that appeared out of place about the room itself was the sweet vanilla-like scent that lingered in the air.

'Back!' the captain bellowed at them. 'Everyone back to the lounge – there is a helium leak inside this cabin!'

This, finally, caught the attention of the group. But before anyone could move, Ezra leapt to his feet, barging them out of the way as he dashed across the corridor to his own cabin. The door slammed shut behind him, and a moment later Chloé winced at the muffled sound of retching that came through the wall.

With this display awarding the captain some semblance of control, the group hurried back to the lounge. Chloé stole one last look through the open door before being ushered away, watching as Niamh crouched by the bed to take Howard's pulse.

The sight of the scattered breakfast things on the table, accompanied by the piano music and the angry wind outside, was a bizarre spectacle. Jasper and Madison sank onto the couches, while Mia stood alone by one of the windows. Devon went straight to the bar.

'He's dead,' said Madison. 'He's *actually* dead, isn't he?'

The *Osprey* gave another shudder, drawing a whimper from the frightened American. Looking back into the corridor, Chloé saw Niamh emerge from the cabin. Locking eyes with Captain Schäfer, she shook her head, expression grim. Without a second's hesitation the captain closed the door, stuffing the dressing gown against the bottom.

'What did he mean?' Madison asked those in the room. 'About there being a helium leak?'

Again, no one replied. They all watched as the captain disappeared for a few moments to the *Osprey*'s upper deck, returning with two curious items. In one hand he held a rectangular device made of grey plastic. In the other was a small tank, connected by a tube to a rubber face-mask.

'What's that?' asked Chloé.

Ben shook his head, uncertain.

'It's an oxygen mask,' said Devon. 'And the thing that looks like an old radio must be a helium detector. Looks to me like the captain's checking how much is in the cabin.'

Chloé said nothing, wondering how he had so quickly recognised the equipment. Casting her mind back to her first afternoon in Longyearbyen, when Ben had briefed her on their travelling companions, she remembered him saying that Devon took wealthy tourists on adventure holidays into the Alps. If he offered high-altitude climbing as one of his excursions, he would presumably be no stranger to an oxygen mask.

They all watched as the captain put on the mask and slipped into Howard's cabin, Astrid ensuring that the dressing gown was still in place as she closed the door behind him. While he was away, Ezra returned from his own cabin, joining Astrid and Niamh in the corridor. He had gone completely pale, eyes wide.

'Devon . . .' said Chloé, 'they're treating this as if the leak killed Howard. Is that possible?'

She had tried to keep her voice low, wary of potentially causing further panic. Even so, she noticed the others all turn to hear Devon's answer.

'Completely,' he said. 'There's no oxygen in helium. If you were to be trapped in a room full of it, as it appears poor Howard might have been, you'd die of asphyxiation in minutes.'

'But he would leave,' said Jasper. 'He wouldn't just lie there and choke. Even if he was asleep, he would wake up and leave the cabin.'

'Ezra said that he was taking sleeping pills.' It was Mia who spoke up this time, her voice trembling. 'Perhaps if they were strong enough, or if he took too many . . .'

With this assessment hanging on the air, the lounge fell silent. They all watched through the glass doors, sitting up in unison as the captain returned to the corridor. He had taken the oxygen mask off, a troubled expression on his face. Holding up the detector so that they could see, he began to speak quietly with Ezra, Niamh and Astrid.

'He took off the mask,' said Chloé. 'So . . . what? The helium's gone?'

She turned to Devon, who gave a small shrug. 'Suppose it must be.'

'And where did it go?'

'I've no idea. But the door was open for a good couple of minutes before he managed to get us all clear. If I had to guess, I'd say that whatever helium was in there escaped while we were staring at Howard and has mixed with the oxygen out here.'

Madison leapt to her feet. 'But doesn't that mean *we're* breathing it?'

'It'll be fine,' Devon assured her. 'If that *is* what's happened, then the amount of oxygen in here must have diluted it. I'm no expert, but if it was going to cause us any trouble, I suspect we would have noticed by now.'

Madison didn't look convinced. Sitting back down beside Jasper on the couch, she glared up at the ceiling, as if she might somehow see the escaped helium lurking above their heads.

'That's all well and good,' said Jasper. 'But if you ask me, what we should really be discussing is the leak itself. Because if there *was* a leak in Howard's cabin, why does it look as if there isn't one now?'

14

It was nearly twenty minutes before Ezra, Niamh, Astrid and Captain Schäfer came back to the lounge.

After the first ten, Ben had taken Chloé's keycard and fetched a jacket from her cabin. She tried to insist that she was fine, wary of the investigation that was taking place in the corridor, but he wouldn't hear it, her chattering teeth giving her away. Otherwise, very little else was said. As they sat shivering, gripping the edges of their seats every time the *Osprey* heaved and shuddered, Chloé suspected that their minds were all filled with the same two things. The image of Howard's frozen body, with his blue lips and inflamed skin, and the sheer distance between themselves and help.

In the rare, fleeting moments when Chloé did manage to turn her thoughts elsewhere, they drifted to her feature. She wasn't proud, considering that a passenger had lost his life, that this was where her mind went. But Alec was hardly going to run a magazine article on the airship that had accidentally killed its owner. For a minute or two she considered suggesting something new to him – something that didn't rely so heavily on the *Osprey*. '10 Incredible Reasons to Visit Longyearbyen', maybe. But she knew it would be no good. She had been sent there to write about an airship. About the glamour and luxury that readers could expect from a weekend over the North Pole. Much as she had been taken by it, Longyearbyen wasn't the objective.

It occurred to her next that perhaps the trip would be rescheduled. Howard's death had been an accident, after all. A *terrible* accident. Surely, once the helium leak had been fixed, there would be another press trip. Ezra had spoken on the coach about how important the feature would be to Skyline Voyages' publicity efforts. Once things had settled down again, he would presumably still want to see it through.

But even if that rang true, and another press trip really was on the cards, Chloé was certain that she wouldn't be on it. Alec had sent her as a last resort, turning to her out of desperation rather than because he wanted to work with her. She could easily imagine, a few months down the line, an email to the effect of: *Sorry, Chloé. I appreciate you filling in for us back in September, but one of the regulars can take it from here.*

Whichever way she looked at it, her big break was fizzling away.

'Ladies and gentlemen,' Captain Schäfer announced, 'for the avoidance of any doubt, I'm sorry to confirm that Mr Barnes is dead. I expect a post-mortem will need to be carried out on the mainland, but the cause appears to have been asphyxiation, resulting from a helium leak inside his cabin.'

Over the captain's shoulder, Chloé saw Ezra's eyes drop to the ground, and for a moment she wondered if he might run to his own cabin and be sick again.

'Are we safe?' asked Madison. 'Is it still . . . I mean, is there still a leak in there?'

'For the time being, the leak seems to have stopped. But we'll continue monitoring the cabin for the remainder of the flight and keep it as airtight as possible, so that any further helium is contained in the event it starts again. For now, rest assured that we've increased our speed and are travelling as quickly as possible back to Longyearbyen, with our estimated time of arrival currently around midnight. Upon disembarking, you'll be taken back to the hotel, where you'll receive further instructions.'

'What kind of instructions?' asked Ben.

Before the captain could reply, Madison chimed in with, 'Will the police be involved?'

Schäfer bristled. 'As far as we can tell, Mr Barnes's death was an accident. But yes, I expect the police will need to be informed. If there's any action they need to take, I'm sure we'll hear about it soon enough. For the time being, I encourage you all to stay in the lounge with the rest of the group. Of course if you would prefer to return to your cabins—'

'Hold on,' Jasper leapt in. 'It's all very well saying this was a horrible accident. But how has it *actually* happened?

And if there was helium in there last night, why isn't there now? I'm no expert, but when something's leaking, it doesn't tend just to plug itself back up. If there's somehow an on–off leak in Howard's cabin, what's to say there isn't one in here, too?'

'Howard's cabin is a special case.' Ezra's voice was wobbly. 'It's . . .' He tailed off, turning to the captain.

'The *Osprey* is airtight,' Schäfer explained. 'This is partly, of course, to prevent helium from escaping the envelope. But given the altitude and the extreme weather conditions, it's also so that we can control the onboard climate. Oxygen is taken in, the temperature is modified and it's distributed around the airship.' He indicated an air vent in the corner of the room.

'So helium has somehow got into the climate-control system,' said Ben, 'and come out in Howard's cabin.'

The captain nodded. 'We have safety procedures to prevent such an occurrence. There are sensors in the envelope, monitoring the amount of helium contained inside and which will sound an alert in the cockpit if ever there's a drop. If any helium were to enter the system, each of the air vents also has a filter, designed to keep it from entering a cabin or the lounge, for instance. And in the event that any does somehow get through, we've given it an artificial scent, to alert anyone who might be nearby. That was the sweet scent you'll have noticed when we opened the cabin door.'

'So why didn't Howard's filter work?' asked Mia.

'And why,' Jasper added, 'didn't your pilots know that the helium in the envelope had dropped? I appreciate that those cabins aren't huge, but if enough had escaped that it could travel through the air con and fill an entire room, surely your sensors should have picked that up.'

'Mr Barnes's cabin has a faulty climate unit.' The captain spoke these particular words through gritted teeth. 'It seems to be operating as required now, so our best guess is that it stopped working temporarily during the night. As for why the sensors failed and how the helium even entered the climate-control system in the first place, these are all questions that we're actively investigating. Although I suspect we won't have answers until the *Osprey* can be returned to Tromsø and inspected by our engineers.'

'Is this related in any way to the temperature?' asked Mia. 'Presumably it's so cold in here this morning because something's malfunctioned inside the climate-control system. Could that same malfunction have let in the helium?'

'It shouldn't be connected,' the captain replied. 'The system is set to keep the airship at a constant comfortable temperature, with the option for each of you to adjust it inside your own cabins. Something, clearly, has gone wrong during the night for that ambient temperature to have plummeted so severely. But it shouldn't be affected by the presence of helium.'

'It's surely possible, though,' said Ben. 'Doesn't it seem a little too coincidental for the system to have malfunctioned *and* for it now to be full of helium?'

'It's within the realm of possibility that the two are connected. But again, until the ground crew has run a full diagnostic of the aircraft, we simply can't say.'

'How cold is helium?' asked Madison. 'What if it's the helium that's affecting the temperature of the rooms?'

'Haven't you been bloody listening?' Jasper snapped at her. 'It doesn't matter if the helium's cold. If there was any in here with us now, we would all *smell* it.'

Madison looked at him as if he'd slapped her, the group falling into an uncomfortable silence.

'Mr Berry is right,' said Schäfer. 'If there were helium in here, we would know about it. As for the cold, we've reset the system, but it will take some time to get back up to temperature. All being well, it should warm up within the next hour or so.'

'Could it have been the storm?' asked Ben. 'If we were being bounced around all night, could something have been jostled loose?'

'I'll tell you what was jostled loose,' said Jasper. 'Howard's dressing gown. It must have fallen off the hook during the night. It covered the gap beneath the door, kept the helium sealed inside the cabin while he was dosed up on sleeping pills.'

The captain was about to reply, but before he could get any words out, Madison rounded on Ezra.

'This storm,' she said. 'You told us it had become worse than you expected. That means you knew it was coming, but you kept going anyway.'

'Our instruments told us it could go either way,' Ezra replied. 'It could just as easily have fizzled out as turned nasty. I had to make a decision, and I decided it was worth carrying on.'

'So it's *your* fault Howard's dead,' Madison pressed. 'Jas is right. That robe must have fallen down while we were being shaken about all night. And Ben's probably right, too. Something in the air con must have been damaged by the storm!' She glowered at him. 'You tell us that we're safe, but how are we supposed to believe you when you don't even know—'

'Enough!' The captain raised his voice, silencing Madison's protests in an instant.

'Ezra . . .' Mia spoke up, her voice gentle, 'how long had Howard been taking sleeping pills?'

Ezra sighed. 'He's taken them on and off for years, during periods of intense stress. For him to have slept through *this*, he must have . . . well, I suppose he must have taken too many.'

'But does that seem likely?' said Mia. 'If he's been taking them for years, surely he would know what constitutes a dangerous dose?'

Across the lounge, Jasper grimaced. 'What are you getting at, Mia?'

'I suppose I'm asking how certain we can be it was the helium that killed him. If he's really been using these pills for years, it seems odd for him to have taken too many. Could he not have died of some natural cause, before the helium filled his cabin?'

Captain Schäfer took a deep breath. 'The blue lips are a clear sign of asphyxiation. Given that anyone who was sleeping naturally would surely wake up and leave the cabin, I think we have to assume that he had indeed taken more pills than was advisable.'

'And what about the rash around his mouth?' Mia pressed. 'What does that—'

'Please,' Ezra said sharply, making Chloé jump. 'Can we just . . . Can we please all . . .' He pressed his hands to his face. 'It should have been me,' he said through his fingers. 'I was meant to be in that cabin. I should have made Howard swap. Should have insisted.'

He tailed off, the words refusing to come. Chloé tried to imagine the thoughts that must be passing through his mind. The disaster that had befallen their first flight, the loss of Howard . . . She suddenly felt ashamed for mourning her feature, trying to imagine how Ezra was meant to process his own misfortune.

'Are you sure we're safe?' asked Ben. 'I get that you need to return the *Osprey* to Tromsø before you can give us any specifics. But if we're stuck up here for another fourteen hours, I'd rather not be breathing helium the entire time.'

'Mr Barnes's climate unit is the only one that shows any sign of malfunction,' said the captain. 'And right now it seems to be working. We've been back into the cabin and tested the atmosphere – our equipment picked up no trace of helium in the air, and the scent has now almost completely gone. All the same, we're keeping the door closed and the gap plugged, in case it fails again between here and Longyearbyen. And in the meantime I'll check it regularly to ensure—'

Before the captain could finish, the *Osprey* gave a particularly stomach-churning jolt, the wind outside screeching.

'I know that none of this is ideal,' he went on, teeth gritted. 'We're all as distressed by the situation as you are. But please try to stay calm. It's going to be a rough return journey, so make yourselves comfortable, try to stay seated until we're away from the storm and if at any point you think you can smell helium, please report it to the stewards. Right now, you know as much as I do about what will happen next, but if I hear anything else that you might need to know, I promise to update you.'

Before any of them could speak, Captain Schäfer strode from the lounge, leaving a gloomy silence in his wake. For a few seconds, no one moved. Ben tried to meet Chloé's eye, but she quickly looked away, reluctant for him to see just how shaken she was. She needn't have worried. They were all feeling it. She could see it clear as day. They were afraid, bracing for the long day that loomed ahead.

15

Up in the kitchen, Gwyn was in a foul mood.

Still riding high from his conversation with Jasper, he hadn't believed it when Ezra had come to see him at the end of the evening, demanding to know how a slice of whale meat had made its way into one of the vegetarian starters.

'There must be a mistake,' he had said. 'Never in a million years would I allow something like that to happen. Honestly, sir, I don't know how I *could*.'

In the end, Ezra had needed to show him the picture from Madison's Instagram Stories before Gwyn accepted that it had happened. He had stared at the image, nose inches from the screen. But no matter how closely he looked, there was no denying the dark slither nestled at the bottom of the dish.

'I don't understand,' he had said, hearing the fear in his own voice. 'I would never . . . I couldn't.'

His expression grim, Ezra had put the phone away, declaring that they would speak properly once the weekend was over. He had then stormed out of the kitchen, leaving Gwyn in a stunned, lonely silence.

For much of that night the chef had lain awake in his bunk, replaying every moment of the evening's service in his mind. He had *not* put that piece of meat on Madison's plate. He was certain of it. The only possible explanation was that someone else had placed it there maliciously, although he had no idea why. He would need to find out, though. If he were to have any hope of holding Jasper Berry to his word, Gwyn had to determine who had done this.

And now the morning had brought a new blow.

Like the rest of the crew, Gwyn had woken up freezing, the airship weaving and rocking beneath him. Not that he had stopped to complain. The captain was investigating the temperature, and the guests, in the meantime, still needed to eat. But upon setting foot in his kitchen, he found that the heating wasn't all that had malfunctioned during the night. His walk-in fridge had also inexplicably stopped working. There was no sign of any damage and the temperature was set correctly. And yet when he opened the door it had been tepid, as if it had been off for several hours during the night.

Hurrying inside, his heart had sunk as he inspected his stock. Some of it was salvageable. But much of the meat and fish he had been saving for the second evening was spoilt.

An hour later, having taken an inventory of the consumable food he had left, he tried to rethink his menu. As he did so, he absent-mindedly carved a flower from a small piece of carrot. He needed to keep his hands busy, and the delicate task proved almost soothing. But as he applied the finishing cuts, the floor moved beneath his feet and he had to grasp the nearest work surface just to keep himself from going flying. He clenched his teeth, his pots and pans singing around him in a steel chorus. If he really had no choice but to waste his talent at the top of the world, was it too much to ask for an airship that was at least *functional*?

Swearing, he went to hurl the ruined flower into the bin. But as he stamped on the pedal and the lid swung open, he paused.

Without fail, the last thing he did every evening, after cleaning down the kitchen, was empty the bin. It had become a rhythm, honed over years of working late nights in the kitchen. He would remove the day's liner, toss his gloves inside and then tie the top, before putting in a new liner ready for the next day. It stood to reason, therefore, that the bin should be empty. And yet . . .

Setting down the flower, he reached inside and carefully withdrew a pair of black nitrile gloves.

For a long moment, Gwyn looked at them. Could he have deviated from his routine? Tossed his gloves into the new liner, as opposed to the old one? As unlikely as it seemed, he supposed he must have. Because the alternative was that, for a reason he couldn't fathom, someone had taken a pair of his gloves, only to then dispose of them in the kitchen bin.

His thoughts were interrupted by the sound of footsteps

in the corridor. None of the stewards had yet spoken to him that morning. He assumed they were giving him a wide berth, having sensed his dark mood after the incident with the salad. Not even Jade had been to say hello. But as he stuffed the gloves into his pocket, he looked up just in time to see Niamh striding into the kitchen, the stewards trailing behind her.

He frowned. 'What's this?'

No one answered him, all four of them looking forlorn. He tried to catch Jade's eye, but her expression was the grimmest of all.

'Gather round please, everyone,' said Niamh.

'What the hell's going on?' Gwyn tried again. 'This isn't a meeting room, it's my bloody kitchen.'

Niamh gave him a look that was genuinely sympathetic. 'I'm sorry, Gwyn. But this concerns you as well.'

Gwyn didn't protest this time. He didn't know Niamh well, but he could see the fear etched on her face.

'All right,' she said. 'I'm going to keep this brief, because I need the three of you back downstairs. But for the sake of complete clarity, I can confirm that one of the passengers has died during the night.'

The words hit Gwyn like a punch in the gut.

'We'll learn more once we're back in Tromsø,' Niamh continued, 'and the ground crew has been able to carry out an investigation. For now, all we know is that there's been an accident involving a helium leak inside one of the cabins.'

'Are we safe?' Ivy asked.

'Yes.' There was complete certainty in Niamh's tone. 'The leak was only present in one cabin, and for the time being it seems to be contained. We've made the room as airtight as possible, and the captain has assured me that so long as it remains that way, there's nothing to worry about.'

Ivy didn't look convinced, but Niamh continued regardless.

'Here's the situation. It's going to be somewhere in the region of fourteen hours before we make it back to Longyearbyen and, not including Ezra and Astrid, we still have six guests who are under our care until they can safely disembark. They're likely to be anxious. Frightened even. But we need them to remain calm. If they want a drink, make them a drink. If they get hungry, ask Gwyn to plate up some food. If they ask questions, assure them that they're safe and that they know as much as we do.'

She paused, her voice softening. 'This is going to be a difficult day. Look after each other. Communicate. If you need to come up here and take a minute, no one's going to judge you. But until we've returned these guests to Longyearbyen, I want at least one steward in the lounge at all times.'

She brought the briefing to a close, and a moment later the three stewards had glumly moved along. Before Niamh could follow them, Gwyn called her back.

'Niamh . . .' he said, his frustration at their intrusion now gone. 'Who is it? Which of the guests has died?'

'It's Howard.'

'Jesus. And are we definitely safe? I mean . . . I get that accidents happen. But is the captain sure? Really, genuinely sure?'

Niamh chewed her lip. She had seemed so sure of herself while the stewards were there. Now that they had left, it looked to Gwyn as if all her certainty had vanished.

She hesitated. Then she stiffened, her expression becoming stern again. 'Let me know if there's anything you need.'

Gwyn tried to call after her. But before he could find the words, Niamh had gone.

16

Closing the door to the crew members' bathroom and slamming the lock into place, Liam gripped the sink with such force his knuckles turned white.

He had barely managed to hold himself together during Niamh's speech. Now, with no one to observe him, he tried not to retch into the sink. When he was sure that he wouldn't be sick, he looked up, staring into his own eyes in the mirror.

Had he done this? Had he killed someone? The guests were meant to wake up freezing in their beds, not *dead*.

He fought back a sob, fist flying up to cover his mouth. It must be a mistake. He might not have read the *Osprey*'s handbook from cover to cover, but he was certain that his fiddling with the air conditioning shouldn't have opened the way to a lethal dose of helium. And even if it had, the climate-control system was full of gas filters. It should be near-impossible for any helium that had escaped the envelope to make it into a cabin.

Except that the air-con unit in Howard's room was on

the blink. The only person aboard who was dosing himself with sleeping pills, and *his* filter was the one not working.

Liam screwed his eyes shut, forcing the thought from his mind. It must have been the storm. With the *Osprey* jostling about in the air, something must have been damaged or shaken loose. *He* couldn't have done this. It couldn't be *his* fault.

Gripping the sink even tighter, he tried to force the thought from his mind. He thought of the money he would be paid on his return. He had done what was asked. Regardless of how it had turned out, Airborne Expeditions would surely still pay.

But as he struggled to focus on all the frivolous things he would buy to reward himself, a new question took root in his mind. What if he had been played? Adjusting the ambient temperature wouldn't, on its own, allow helium into the climate-control system. But what if something had been done on the ground? What if the way had been paved while the *Osprey* was still in Tromsø and, by adjusting the temperature, Liam had inadvertently allowed the helium through?

He had already assumed that he wasn't the only one to be contacted by Airborne Expeditions. Having someone in the *Osprey*'s ground crew was the only way they could have known so much about the airship's inner workings. So perhaps he *had* made this happen. Perhaps, unbeknownst even to himself, he had been part of a two-man job.

Before he could stop it, the thought began to snowball.

Airborne Expeditions had wanted the *Osprey* grounded, so that they could steal the lead. They only needed a few weeks. Fiddling with the climate-control system, turning off the walk-in fridge, damaging the blackout blinds in a handful of the cabins . . . they were all small acts of sabotage, but they would still have required investigating. Combined, they might just have grounded the *Osprey* long enough.

Or at least that was what he had been told. He hadn't given the reasoning a great deal of thought. For the sake of jimmying a few blinds during the flight over from Tromsø, and then fifteen minutes spent messing with the fridge and the air con during the night, he stood to make an entire year's salary aboard the *Osprey*. But now, as he reflected on his instructions in the cold light of day, he couldn't help but suspect that he had been misled. A few harmless things going wrong *might* ground Skyline for long enough. But the death of a passenger – a death caused by the airship itself – that would undoubtedly do the trick.

The more Liam thought about this theory, the more it made sense. It didn't matter how much money Airborne Expeditions offered; he wouldn't ever have done this if he had known it would cost someone's life. Wouldn't even have entertained it. But making the guests *cold*? He'd agreed to that without a second's hesitation. He couldn't even check his instructions for clues that he'd been lied to. They had come to him by text message from an unknown number, and the moment he'd completed his task he had deleted every one.

With this realisation, a new thought occurred to him. He probably wasn't even going to be paid. What was it he had been told? Follow the instructions while in the air and his payment would be wired to him after they had made it back to Tromsø. But what proof did he have that the money would come? *They* had found *him*. There had never been any names, and even if he hadn't deleted every message they had sent, they had contacted him exclusively from a withheld number. Unless there was another message – and with his tasks accomplished, he was now certain there wouldn't be – he had no way of proving that Airborne Expeditions had ever contacted him.

Before he could stop himself, Liam dropped to his knees and vomited into the sink. When he was finished, his empty stomach groaning, he climbed to his feet and washed his mouth with cold water.

He had to keep it together. Be logical. If he had, as he feared, played a role in Howard's death, then it was done now. He couldn't make amends for it, and he couldn't take it back. All that mattered was that no one found out.

He tried to calm his mind. He had acted during the night, while everyone had been asleep. The evidence was gone, and the captain was convinced that what had happened to Howard was an accident. Gwyn hadn't even heard him leave their cabin, he'd been so soundly asleep.

He could get away with this. All he had to do was keep it together.

17

During the first hour that passed after Captain Schäfer left the lounge, Chloé felt as if time were standing still.

In a way, she supposed it was. She had read during her journey to Longyearbyen that each of the world's time zones converged on the North Pole, rendering them all effectively meaningless. It had felt at the time like a harmless piece of trivia. A curious anecdote that she might include somewhere in her feature. But now it put her on edge, leaving her fighting to convince her overactive mind that she wasn't trapped in time, as well as aboard the *Osprey*.

Madison, Jasper and Mia had all gone to their cabins, while those who remained in the lounge had fallen into an uncomfortable silence. Devon was at the bar. Guzzling coffee and water, Chloé thought of the alcohol he had put away during dinner, suspecting that he must now be nursing quite the hangover. Astrid and Ezra spoke on the couches, hunched over her tablet, and the stewards were all on hand too, although they didn't seem sure of what to do. They wandered aimlessly around the lounge, eyes probing as if they were waiting for some other calamity to strike.

The stress that radiated from them all was palpable, to the extent that Chloé would have sworn she could feel it humming in the air. She put it down to the sense of confinement – knowing that the very craft that was meant to keep them safe was now responsible for the death of one of their number. She tried to imagine how Ezra must be feeling. To have lost not only his father, but now Howard, to this frozen wilderness.

Seeking an escape, but reluctant to sit alone in her cabin, Chloé had disregarded the captain's suggestion that they stay seated and had instead gone to stand by the window. She often found comfort in nature, and on their outward journey she had been in awe of the landscape. But after the morning's developments, it didn't soothe her in the way she had hoped. The snow lashed against the glass, trying to reach her – to claw its way inside. Through the blizzard, she looked down not on an Arctic wonderland, but on a cold desert, barren and lifeless. Feeling every inch of the distance between herself and home, she yearned for the sight of open water and, beyond it, the northern coast of Svalbard. Despite her jacket she shivered, clutching her arms against herself, hands buried inside her sleeves. The lounge was beginning gradually to warm up, but for the time being it was still uncomfortably cold.

'C'est trop beau pour être vrai.'

As Chloé reflected on the morning's events, her mother's

words returned to her and she once again found that she was murmuring them under her breath.

Interrupting her gloomy inner monologue, Ben came to stand beside her. 'How're you holding up?' he asked. 'You doing OK?'

'I'm all right,' she lied. They stood silently, listening to the howling wind. Then she asked, 'Have you ever . . . I mean, have you ever seen someone—'

'No,' he said quickly. 'No, that was my first time.' His eyes remained glued to the window. 'I'm really sorry,' he said. 'About the assignment. If it helps, I'm going to tell Alec how well you've done. Recommend that he gives you another chance.'

'I haven't done anything.'

'That's not true. You've carried yourself well, asked good questions. Ezra seems to have taken a shine to you. If you ask me, Alec would be making a big mistake if he didn't give you another shot. I'm going to do my best to make sure he knows that.'

Chloé had no idea how to respond. She felt a rush of gratitude, so much so that she could easily have turned to Ben and hugged him. At the same time she couldn't help but feel pessimistic. Would a few kind words from Ben really be enough to keep her at the front of Alec's mind? Wasn't it more likely that as soon as they were home she would be forgotten? Within a few days she expected that she would be back to corporate copywriting jobs, grinding out pitch after pitch in the hope that someone like Alec would take another chance on her.

The thought made tears sting at the corners of her eyes, but she quickly fought them back. Howard had died, and Ezra had lost a father figure. They were hundreds of miles from the sanctuary of Longyearbyen, itself one of the most remote places on the planet. She had occasionally run into trouble on her travels, but never had she faced a situation as bleak as this. And yet, despite all that was happening, she couldn't help but grieve for the opportunity to finally write a magazine feature. She told herself that she was being ridiculous. But no matter how she tried, it was dismay, rather than fear or sympathy, that she found herself feeling.

'Did Alec really not tell you?' she asked, wiping her eyes with the back of her hand. 'About Ezra's dad? Where the idea for Skyline came from?'

Ben shook his head. 'Didn't say a thing. All he told me was that he and Ezra were old school friends.'

'And how . . . ?' She paused, wondering if it was too morbid even to ask.

'How do I think Isaac might have died?'

Chloé nodded, and Ben heaved a sigh.

'Ezra said last night that Isaac didn't come back. I'd say that rules out hypothermia. They'd presumably have called for help and sent him back the moment he started showing symptoms. So even if that had killed him, I reckon he would have died at a base camp somewhere and the body sent home. I suppose they could have been attacked by a bear, but while it's not impossible to run into one this far north, you'd have to be *really* unlucky. My best guess is that it was an accident of some kind.'

As she looked down on the frozen plain, a shiver ran up Chloé's spine. 'You think he fell through the ice.'

'It's the only scenario I can think of that would explain why they didn't bring him back. He strays onto a patch that's too thin, isn't tethered to the rest of the group, or whatever tether they're using fails . . .' Ben grimaced and shook his head. He forced some brightness into his voice, suddenly eager to change the subject. 'Has it always been travel-writing? Is that what you've always wanted to do?'

Grateful for the distraction, Chloé did her best to shake loose the image of Isaac Day sinking beneath the ice.

'Not always,' she said. 'I started thinking about it five or six years ago, but for the first few of those it didn't ever feel like something I could actually do. I guess it probably felt like trying to become an actor or a rock star. But I've always loved travelling. We moved around a lot when I was a teenager. I was born in Scotland, but my mum's French, so we spent some time living over there when I was twelve. Then Dad got a job that required him to travel. We were in Germany at one point, then Singapore for a while . . .'

'Did you do a lot of exploring while you were out there?' asked Ben.

'As much as we could. That's when I started the blog. I was sixteen and I'd found that I loved writing, so I started journaling about all the places we were visiting. When we eventually made our way back to the UK I got a degree in

English Lit, and after uni I landed a job at a PR agency that specialised in luxury travel. For a few years I was happy. But the shine started to wear off. I started to wish that I was the one *going* to these places – the one writing about them – rather than the one booking the flights and the rooms for the people who were.'

'So you stepped away.'

Chloé nodded. 'The agency I was working for went bust. A lot of my old colleagues got snapped up by competitors. Some went in-house, but I decided it was time to take the plunge. I thought that if I didn't try it now, I never would.' She took a breath. 'That was three years ago. I've spent every penny I can spare on travelling. I've written endlessly for the blog, I've built up my Instagram following, I've pitched every idea I can think of to every travel editor I can reach. And I don't have anything to show for it. I haven't had anything published, I'm completely skint, my boyfriend and I just split up—'

'Hold on.' She heard the surprise in Ben's voice. 'You split up with your boyfriend because you want to be a writer?'

Chloé shrugged. 'He wanted to buy a flat, but when I started writing full-time I was barely making enough to cover my half of the rent, let alone save for a deposit on a place in London. It took three years, but in the end the money became too much of an issue.'

'He sounds like a dick.'

Chloé couldn't help but laugh. 'I don't think that's true. When we met I was making a steady wage. Climbing a ladder of my own at the agency. He's worked hard these past few years, bagged himself a couple of good promotions. Now he wants to take that money and live in a better place. Buy a nice car. But I wasn't interested in any of that. I just wanted to travel – give the writing a proper go.'

She stared into the hazy distance, watching the snow as it clung to the window. She was briefly reminded of the mojito Liam had made for her, the finely chopped mint clinging to the frosted glass.

'It's been a month now since we split up,' she continued. 'I've spent that time wondering how well suited we could ever really have been, if he couldn't get on board with me pursuing my dream job. But maybe he was right. Maybe I'm being naive, thinking I could make a career out of this.'

'Chloé, come on,' said Ben. 'Witnessing a freak accident over the North Pole doesn't make your ex right.' When she didn't answer, he asked, 'Are you still living together?'

Chloé winced. 'Please don't ask me where I'm living.'

Ben gave a laugh. 'It can't be that bad. Are you back with your parents?'

'If you must know, I'm living with an old uni friend and her fiancé. They're letting me crash in their spare room while I look for a place.'

Ben weighed this up for a moment. 'Could be worse,' he said. 'I once spent three months sleeping on my brother's sofa. Don't think my back's ever fully recovered.'

Chloé forced a smile, appreciative of his attempts to cheer her up. 'Well, there you have it. That's the sorry state of my life.' She looked down at the ground. 'This weekend was supposed to change things. I was going to go back to London, write my feature and get myself on Alec's books. But now . . . well, I guess there's no feature to write any more, is there? Alec's hardly going to print a write-up on the airship that killed its owner.'

Ben seemed to be searching for something he could say that might comfort her. But, having found nothing of use, he just sighed. As they settled once more into gloomy silence, Chloé swept a look around the lounge, lowering her voice to a murmur.

'Do you really think it was an accident?'

Ben frowned. 'Of course. Don't you?'

Aware of how quizzically he was now looking at her, Chloé tried to order her thoughts.

'I guess we have to take the captain at his word,' she said. 'But doesn't it seem odd? That the one night Howard happens to take too many sleeping pills is the night he's sealed inside a room full of helium?'

'You think someone might have set this up?'

'No,' Chloé said. Then, more tentatively, 'I don't know. But you can't tell me it doesn't feel strange. That Howard's cabin – Howard, the only member of our group who's effectively sedating himself – is the one with the dodgy air con unit? And that these sensors, which are supposed to pick up a helium leak, didn't report anything to the cockpit while it happened?'

Ben weighed this up. 'I get it,' he said eventually. 'It's disconcerting. Of course it is. But when they get this thing back to the mainland, there's going to be a massive investigation. The ground crew will work out exactly what's happened.'

Seeing that Chloé wasn't convinced, he took a deep breath. 'All right,' he said. 'Let's consider the possibility of this being done maliciously. How would someone go about that? Because if I've understood everything correctly, you would need to know that the gas filter in Howard's room was dodgy, and then you would have to somehow get helium flowing from the envelope into the climate-control system without triggering an alert in the cockpit. Something the captain seems to think shouldn't be possible. Then there's Howard himself. Again, if the assumption is that someone has done this intentionally, the culprit can't simply assume that Howard's going to give himself too many sleeping pills. So I guess we're also suggesting that he was given an extra dose, to make sure he wouldn't wake up while the cabin was filling with helium. Quite how you would go about that, I have no idea. And there's the dressing gown, too.'

Chloé frowned. 'The dressing gown?'

'We saw what happened when Ezra tried to open the cabin door. The dressing gown was wedged flat against the bottom. You can't rely on a storm jostling it off the hook at the exact moment you need it to. Certainly not when it's a storm that none of us knew was coming. So are we suggesting that whoever engineered the leak also put it there? If so, then how? The door opens inwardly, meaning it could only have been laid flat against the bottom from *inside* the room.'

Chloé said nothing.

'I think the biggest question, though,' Ben continued, 'is why? It would have to be done by someone up here, right? Someone aboard the *Osprey*?'

'Makes sense.'

'But why would any of us do that? None of the guests would have any reason to want Howard dead. And as for the crew, he was their boss. A boss who, presumably, they only knew from a distance. So why would anyone up here go to the effort of doing it?'

Chloé thought for a moment. 'Ezra said that he was meant to have been in that cabin. There must have been a mix-up when they were being assigned or when the ground crew brought our things aboard. What if it was supposed to have been him?'

'Doesn't work,' said Ben. 'Ezra wasn't taking sleeping pills. He would just have woken up, found that he was choking and left the cabin.'

'But if we're assuming someone planned to give whoever was in that cabin some *extra* pills . . .'

Ben frowned. 'Seems odd, doesn't it? To give extra sleeping pills to the guy who was already on them, and for that to be your *back-up plan*.'

Chloé fell silent again.

'All right,' she said, gearing up for another attempt. 'What if this wasn't about Howard? He might well have been the intended target, but what if the *who* didn't really matter. What if this was about Skyline Voyages?'

Ben's eyes narrowed. He was sceptical, she could see

that clearly enough. But he wasn't going to challenge her just yet.

'Ezra told us last night that there's another company trying to launch its own line of airships first. Well, this would do that, right? The owner of Skyline has been accidentally killed aboard his own airship. More than that – *by* his own airship. Surely that would cause enough trouble for the guys in Dubai to take the lead.'

She saw Ben withhold a sigh. 'I'm no expert on industrial espionage,' he said, 'but I can't imagine Airborne Expeditions *killing* their competitors to get ahead.'

'What if he wasn't supposed to die? Airborne might have convinced someone up here to engineer the leak, but they wouldn't have known that Howard was taking sleeping pills, and there's absolutely no way they could have predicted that a storm would jostle his dressing gown loose.' She heard the eagerness building in her own voice. 'Think about it, Ben. Ezra said that if the *Osprey* were grounded for as little as a few weeks, Airborne Expeditions would pull ahead. Even without the death of a passenger, a seemingly impossible helium leak would surely be enough to achieve that. Howard's death might have been an accident, but the leak could still have been sabotage.'

Ben released the sigh he'd managed to contain a moment before. 'Maybe,' he agreed. '*Maybe*. But how would they know how to create the leak?'

'Well, how different can Airborne's ships be to the *Osprey*? If they have the expertise and the resources that

Ezra claims, I reckon they could find a way of making it work. Maybe . . .' She tailed off, a new theory occurring to her. 'Maybe it was done before we even flew out. They might have someone on the ground to set it up and someone up here to pay it off. Someone who works on the *Osprey* and would know how to do it.'

This time Ben didn't argue. For a short while they stood together at the window, feeling the floor sway gently beneath their feet.

'Tell me something,' he said after a long pause. 'I might be reading too much into this, but the way you're speaking . . . it almost sounds as if you *want* this to have been done deliberately. Like you want someone to blame.'

Chloé stared at him, no idea how to respond.

'I get it,' he said. 'What's happening up here is frightening. And the captain not being able to explain it only makes it worse. But we'll be back in Longyearbyen tonight, and once the *Osprey* is back in Tromsø the crew will be able to work out what's happened. For now . . . I'd say try not to dwell.'

The *Osprey* jerked beneath them. As Chloé righted herself, looking down on the ice, she considered whether Ben might be right. Perhaps she did want there to be something to pursue. Someone to accuse for the loss of her big break.

'I'm gonna sit down,' he said, 'before this thing sends me flying. Are you coming?'

Chloé shook her head. 'I'm good here.'

He didn't argue. With a nod, Ben went to the couches, leaving her standing silently by the window.

18

Alone in his cabin, Devon struggled to process the morning's events.

The hangover didn't help. He'd been gulping down fluids since the early hours, trying to soothe the dull ache that was throbbing inside his skull, but the constant rocking of the airship counteracted every mug of coffee and glass of water that he tipped back.

Sitting on his bed, he sighed. When he returned to the cabin the previous evening he had bitterly regretted coming aboard the *Osprey*, his resentment towards Ezra reaching a peak. All Devon wanted was a way for his business to survive. This modest business around which he had built his entire life . . . And yet here was Ezra, having achieved the monumental feat of putting an airship in the sky – a feat that would no doubt make him rich beyond belief – and all *he* wanted was to please a long-dead man who had treated him like dirt. It was an irritating thing, admitting to being jealous. But to hear Ezra talking about Isaac had been *maddening*.

When he woke, that fury had subsided. Aside from the confusion that he shared with the others over the storm and the *Osprey*'s plummeting on-board temperature, he mostly felt despondent. With the words he'd fired over the dinner table, his consultant's fee was almost certainly off the cards. Now he just wanted this trip to be over, so that he could board the first flight out of Longyearbyen and put Ezra as far behind him as possible.

But with the discovery of Howard's body, Devon suspected the coming days would be anything but simple.

He hadn't known Howard particularly well. He remembered that, from time to time in their dorm, Ezra had mentioned him. He would speak about the exotic locations that his father and Howard were venturing to next, vowing that one day he would go with them. And he remembered crossing paths with Howard a few times after Isaac had died. In the months that followed, Devon, Alec and Jasper had all made sure to visit Ezra and his mother at the family home. Howard had done the same, checking in on a regular basis, and they had briefly met on a handful of occasions. He had always struck Devon as quiet – possibly even dull – but it had been good of him to keep such a close eye on his fallen friend's son and widow. He certainly didn't deserve the grim fate that he had suffered during the night.

And then there was Ezra. Was Devon jealous of him *now*? Ezra had waited years for this moment – his first triumphant flight over the North Pole – only for it to become the scene of his most trusted associate's death.

Even if Skyline Voyages recovered, Airborne Expeditions would surely pull ahead in the time it took to investigate how the leak had occurred. Devon struggled to imagine how Ezra could be dealt a more devastating blow.

No, he decided. In light of Howard's death, it wasn't possible to hold on to the resentment that had caused him to speak up over the dinner table. Watching Ezra's dreams fall apart came only with a sense of tragedy. A tragedy in which he wanted no part.

He felt more desperate than ever to be away, the thought of being stuck in Longyearbyen while a police investigation took place filling him with dread. He should never have come. He needed to get home. And he needed to do so as soon as possible.

Sitting on the bed, he let out a breath, a faint plume coming from his lips. He knew that he was better adapted to the cold than the other passengers. All the same, he wished they would calm down. He had met plenty of people like Schäfer during his time in the mountains. Sturdy, no-nonsense sort of people. If the captain said they were safe, Devon was happy to believe it.

As if determined to prove him wrong, the *Osprey* gave a particularly dramatic jolt, causing Devon's unsettled stomach to groan in complaint. Fighting the urge to be sick, he screwed his eyes shut until the airship steadied itself. In the darkness, his mind drifted to the image of Howard's body.

It would have been painless, he supposed. If Howard

had been so heavily dosed up on sleeping pills that he didn't even wake up, he wouldn't have had any idea it was happening. Wasn't that really the best way to go out?

There was something in that, Devon told himself. But he struggled to take any comfort in it. Because while he couldn't articulate what it was, he was certain that something about the scene in Howard's cabin hadn't been right.

He scolded himself. He was being stupid. *Nothing* was right about a room that could become a death-trap without a moment's warning. But it was no good. Growing frustrated with his throbbing skull and cloudy thoughts, he couldn't place it, but with each passing second he was increasingly certain that something in Howard's cabin shouldn't have been there.

For several minutes he turned the problem over in his mind, until at last he thought he might know what was troubling him. It was Howard's body itself. Specifically his face, with his blue lips and the red skin around his mouth.

The captain had been certain it was the helium that had killed Howard. The blue lips, he'd said, were proof. During his time in the mountains Devon had only twice been unlucky enough to see a corpse, and neither of those poor fools had died from asphyxiation. And yet, he was sure. No, he was convinced. Somewhere, at some time he couldn't pinpoint, he had seen someone with Howard's symptoms before.

19

Despite her determination that it wouldn't affect her, by the time they had flown far enough that the ice was starting to break, turning from a frozen landmass to a white mosaic, the swaying of the *Osprey* beneath Chloé's feet became too much. Feeling too sick to stand any longer by the window, she admitted defeat and made her way to the table.

'Mind if I join you?' she asked.

Wrapped up in the long puffer coat and knitted headband that she had worn during their departure from Longyearbyen, Astrid was typing on her tablet, the penguin-painted nails still on show through a pair of pink fingerless gloves. As Chloé approached, she looked up from her screen and removed an earbud. 'I'm sorry?'

'I was wondering if I could sit with you.'

'Of course. Can I get you anything? Jade made a herbal tea to help me warm up. I'm sure she could fetch one for you as well.'

'No,' Chloé said. 'No, that's not what I'm . . . To be

honest, I was just hoping for a friendly face.' She nodded towards the earbud. 'What are you listening to?'

'Some Rammstein. It's soothing. Do you know them?'

A small smile played on Chloé's lips. Nate had been a fan of Rammstein. A sonic barrage of angry guitars and bellowing German vocals, when he played their music in the flat, 'soothing' would have been the last word Chloé used to describe it. But she was quickly learning that Astrid's tastes were different from most people's.

'My ex used to like them,' she said. 'Where did Ezra go?'

'His cabin. He said he had to send some emails, but I think really he just needed a minute to process it all.'

'And what about you? How are you holding up?'

Astrid thought about this for a second, as if she were surprised to be asked. She gave a nod. 'Not so bad, all things considered. Although it looks like I might need to dust off my CV when we get home.'

'You don't think the *Osprey* will fly again?'

'I mean . . .' she gave a small shrug. 'Maybe it will. But I guess they need to prove first that this can't ever happen again. And right now we don't even know *how* it happened. The captain insists it should be impossible. And yet, here we are. So . . . yeah. CV.'

There was still a breeziness to Astrid's tone, an almost musical quality that Chloé attributed to her Norwegian accent. But she could hear the sorrow behind her words, the broad smile that had been fixed in place for the first leg of their journey unquestionably dimmed.

'How are the crew?'

'Ah,' said Astrid. 'Well, Jade looks as if she's taking it all quite badly. To be expected, I guess.'

'Why would Jade take it any worse than the others?'

'Howard was her uncle. He got her this job.'

Chloé was so blindsided that she didn't have a reply. She looked across the room, to where Jade and Ivy were standing to attention by the glass doors. They both looked unsettled, but now that Chloé paid them proper attention, she could clearly see that Jade was in worse condition.

'I don't think they had the best relationship,' Astrid continued. 'But still . . . it's a terrible thing.'

'Has anyone asked if she's OK?'

Astrid frowned. 'I know Niamh gathered them all for a briefing upstairs. Just after the captain addressed everyone down here. I suppose she'll have checked on Jade then.'

Chloé was silent, lost in thought. If Niamh had spoken to Jade, then she didn't look reassured by what had been said. But before she could ponder this any further, Astrid turned the tablet towards her.

'You're a writer,' she said. 'Could I get your opinion on something? Ezra's asked me to draft a statement that he can send to the company, letting everyone know what's happened. I know he'll want to make changes. Put it in his own voice. But English isn't my first language, and I don't want there to be any . . . any *silly* mistakes when he reads it.' Seeing the surprise in Chloé's expression, she looked suddenly sheepish. 'Sorry,' she said. 'That's probably very unprofessional.'

'No.' Before she could turn the tablet away, Chloé put a

hand on Astrid's arm. 'It's no problem. It'd be good to feel useful.'

Thanking her, Astrid slid the tablet across the table and Chloé began to read. She pointed out a handful of instances where she might use a different word, but for the most part it seemed a perfectly decent piece of corporate communication.

'I feel so sorry for Ezra,' said Chloé, handing the tablet back. 'To have lost not only his dad, but now Howard as well.'

Astrid hummed in agreement. 'He's had a rough time. To this day, I think losing Isaac still hangs over him in a big way.'

'How so?'

Astrid thought for a moment. 'We travel a lot together,' she said eventually. 'It's part of the job. If Ezra has somewhere to be, usually I'll go with him. When his mother passed away last year, he had a lot on his plate with the airship, so I went with him to the UK and helped with the funeral arrangements. There was a day when I was helping him clear out her house. Sort through all the documents and stuff. We were going through some boxes from the attic and he found this big folder full of papers. The look on his face when he saw them . . .'

'What were they?' asked Chloé.

'They were notes. Handwritten notes from Isaac. Pages and pages of them. I don't know what they were about. I guess they can't have been anything too important, to have sat up there forgotten all those years. But when Ezra looked through them – when he saw Isaac's writing – he looked like he'd seen a ghost.' Astrid cast a sad look around the lounge. 'That was the day he found Isaac's camera, too. The one with the photo he gave to Howard last night. I hope this all gets sorted out. For him, if not for anyone else. Ezra's a good person. He doesn't deserve this.'

They sat together in silence for a little while, Chloé trying her best not to think about Ben's theory – to picture Isaac Day falling through a sheet of ice. She couldn't imagine how traumatic an image it must be for Ezra. It was harrowing enough for *her*, having never even met Isaac. If that really was what had happened, and if Ezra really did admire his father as much as he seemed to, she could see why it would still affect him so many years later.

Astrid began to climb to her feet, motioning with the tablet. 'I'd better show him this,' she said. 'He asked to see it as soon as it was ready. Are you sure there's nothing I can sort for you?'

Chloé smiled at her. 'I'm fine. Honestly. You do what you have to do.'

Astrid nodded and made her way from the lounge, Chloé watching as she paused outside Ezra's cabin, knocked and stepped inside. Once she had disappeared from view, Chloé's attention strayed to the glass doors, where Jade now stood alone. She looked terrible. Not simply bereft, as might be expected, but frightened, too. Her body was rigid with tension, eyes twitching around the lounge as if looking for any hint of danger.

Chloé looked away. They were *all* frightened. Understandably so. They were trapped for another twelve hours beneath a vast container of what had proven to be deadly gas. As the youngest member of their group, and the only one who had lost a blood relative, Jade couldn't be blamed for looking rattled. If Astrid said that Niamh had spoken to her, then Chloé had to trust that she was being looked after.

She almost convinced herself. But when Jasper sneezed and Chloé saw Jade jump half a foot in the air, she knew that she had to say something.

Rising to her feet, she adopted an encouraging smile as she made her way towards the glass doors. 'Sorry,' she said, 'I hope you don't mind, but I wanted to ask . . . Are you OK?'

She kept her voice low, presuming Jade would prefer that she didn't draw attention. Even so, the panic in the young woman's eyes was immediate.

'Fine,' she said, spitting out the word as if it were burning her mouth. 'Is there anything you need?'

'No,' Chloé replied, wishing that people would stop trying to offer her things. 'I just . . . well, I hope this isn't inappropriate, but I was speaking to Astrid a minute ago. She mentioned that you and Howard were family.'

The panic in Jade's eyes turned to outright terror.

'I wanted to check that you're all right,' Chloé continued. 'I'm not trying to pry, but when I saw you across the room you looked—'

'I'm fine.' Jade cut her off, her voice barely above a

whisper. Her eyes started to dart around even more frantically than before, looking not for danger, but a way to escape.

'Are you sure? Because if you need someone to talk to—'

She didn't finish. Before she could say another word, Jade turned away, fleeing through the glass doors. Chloé could only watch as she ran to the end of the corridor, flung open the door to the stairwell and disappeared.

Sitting at the bar with a glass of water, Ben had been tinkering for a long while with his camera. Chloé assumed he was going over the pictures he'd taken of the trip thus far, but at the sound of Jade hurrying away, he looked up.

'She OK?' he called out.

Chloé shook her head. 'No,' she said. 'No, I don't think she is.'

20

Seating herself on the bed, Mia felt a sense of déjà vu as she invited Ivy to sit down beside her. But just as she had done the previous evening, the young steward declined.

'I can't,' she said. 'If Niamh knew I was in here *today*, with everything that's happening, I think she really would kill me.'

Mia nodded. There was an undeniable change in Ivy's energy. Gone was the headstrong soul who had approached her the previous afternoon, insisting on a private chat. With the steward's eyes flitting every few seconds to the door, Mia could see that she was as frightened as the rest of them.

'Ivy,' she said, keeping her voice as level as she could manage, 'before I ask this, you need to understand that I'm not trying to suggest anything. I promise I'm not. But . . . if you know anything about what's happened to Howard, you have to say something. You realise that, don't you? If you know anything – anything at all – you *have* to tell someone.'

Ivy looked confused. Then her features morphed into an expression of horror. 'You think I had something to do with this?'

'I'm not saying that.'

'You are! What else would you be saying, taking me to one side and asking about whether there's *anything I know*? You think I did this!'

Wary of Ivy's rising voice being heard from the corridor, Mia put out a hand in an attempt to soothe her.

'I'm not accusing you of anything,' she insisted. 'But try to see it from my point of view. You came to me yesterday afternoon, talking about how immoral it is for Skyline Voyages to be using helium and serving whale. Then, only a few hours after that conversation, a slice of whale turns up in Madison's salad. And this morning we wake up to find that Skyline's founder has been killed by a helium leak.'

At the mention of Madison's salad there was an undeniable spark of panic in Ivy's eyes. She looked terrified, eyes bulging.

'I can't believe this,' she stammered. 'I came to you yesterday because I admired you. Because I didn't want you to make a mistake by putting your name to this company. And now you think I would *kill* someone?'

Mia felt a stab of guilt, so powerful that she almost abandoned her suspicions. She rose from the bed, hoping to lay a comforting hand on Ivy's shoulder, but the young steward backed away before she had the chance.

'You're going to tell the others,' Ivy continued. 'You're

going to tell them I did this. And the police . . . When we get back, you'll tell them, too.'

'No,' Mia urged. 'Ivy, no. I only wanted to—'

'Stop!' Ivy retreated so far that her back pressed against the door, staring at Mia with wild eyes. 'How can I know *you* didn't do it? I saw your face last night, when you learned who was funding this thing. When you learned that Ezra had lied to get you up here. I know why, too. You can't risk another Halo scandal – can't have all your followers knowing you agreed to come aboard the *Osprey* when it's funded by big oil. But now you won't have to, will you? Whatever coverage you were going to run on *Green World* is off. Skyline's finished. No "Come and fly aboard the *Osprey*" any more. You can walk away. From where I'm standing, I'd say *you* had the best reason to kill Howard.'

Mia couldn't speak, scarcely able to believe what she'd heard. 'Ivy . . . you can't possibly think that—'

'Get back!' Ivy fumbled for the door handle, voice trembling. 'You stay away from me,' she said. 'I didn't do this. I had *nothing* to do with what's happened to Howard. And if you try to tell anyone that I did – the police or any of the other guests – I'll make sure everyone knows that you were up here. Anyone who'll listen. I'll tell them you knew who was funding this thing and that, before Howard died, you were going to plaster it all over *Green World*. See if you can recover from *that*.'

Mia gawped at her. But before she could say anything further, Ivy had thrown open the cabin door and stormed into the corridor, leaving her in stunned silence.

21

As she paced up and down the cabin she shared with Ivy, the fear that Jade had been wrestling with since the discovery of Howard's body was on the brink of becoming overwhelming.

How had Astrid known that Howard was her uncle? Had Ezra told her? Howard certainly wouldn't have. It didn't seem to be a fact of which he had ever been proud. And what was she doing, telling the passengers?

With a tremendous effort she forced herself to take several long, deep breaths. She couldn't simply keep her head down until they made it back to Longyearbyen. After the bizarre display she had just put on, that particular strategy was no longer an option. But blind terror wasn't going to help her determine a new course of action, either.

Calming herself sufficiently that she could think clearly, Jade tried to unpick what had happened in the lounge. She'd panicked. She had already been frightened, and when that writer – Chloé, was it? – had spoken so casually about Howard being her uncle, it had caught her off guard.

Gritting her teeth, she swore at the empty cabin. What if Chloé said something to the others? What if Niamh, or even Ezra, took her to one side and asked her to explain the spectacle she had made of herself? That kind of attention was the last thing she wanted.

Maybe she could play it off. Perhaps she could go to Chloé and say that she was grieving – in shock – and had been startled. She was a decent actress when she needed to be. She could probably pull it off.

Grieving . . . With a start, it occurred to Jade that in the five hours since her uncle's body had been discovered, she hadn't once thought about grieving for him. Now that she had calmed herself long enough to consider it, she wondered . . . would she do so later, when the danger had passed? She had resented Howard for placing her aboard the *Osprey* – for trapping her at the top of the world. But she would never have wanted him dead. As she followed this train of thought, it struck her that she was more concerned about how her mum would take this news. Howard had been her brother. More than that, he had helped to raise her. His death would hit her hard.

Jade felt a sudden rush of guilt. She had already put her mum through so much heartache. She didn't deserve any more.

She shook the thought from her head, eyes straying to the small suitcase that was tucked under her bunk. There was no need for her to feel guilty, she tried to convince herself. She hadn't killed Howard.

But someone had.

Dragging out the case, she flung it open and rummaged inside until her fingertips brushed against something solid. Taking hold of the little object, she lifted it from the case, hearing it rattle as she held it to the light. Hoping to be wrong, she scanned the label, looking for something that she might have overlooked or misunderstood. But there was no denying what she had taken. In her hand – hidden all night in her case – was a small bottle of white sleeping pills.

She shouldn't have taken them. It had been petty. Stupid even. But that didn't matter any more. All that mattered was the question she had been asking herself since her uncle's body had been found. Because if the pills hadn't been in his cabin, how then could he have taken enough of them to remain asleep while he choked on helium?

'Jade?'

With a start, she thrust the bottle back into her case, throwing a T-shirt over it to conceal it from view. She then leapt to her feet, wheeling round to find Gwyn in the doorway.

'Sorry,' he said, taking a sudden step back. 'Didn't mean to frighten you. Why aren't you in the lounge?'

Jade cleared her throat, so shaken by his sudden appearance that she could barely speak. 'I just . . .' She found herself stammering, each word a fresh effort. 'Just needed a minute.'

His eyes strayed towards the suitcase, and for a second

she was terrified that he would ask what she had been doing. But he quickly looked away again, his attention firmly on her.

'I'm glad you're here,' he said. 'I wanted to ask about the starters. Last night.'

The starters? She felt herself frown. What did the starters have to do with anything? Whatever was bothering him, it was clearly important. There was an eagerness in his expression. A determination that, in the short time they'd known each other, she hadn't yet seen.

She closed her eyes, trying to clear her head. 'The meat,' she said. 'The meat in Madison's salad.'

'Who served it, Jade? I need to find out, because I know for a fact that those starters were perfect when I loaded them into the dumbwaiter.'

It was a bizarre question, the urgency in his tone only confusing her even more. She could have understood him investigating this last night, but he knew what had happened to Howard. Why was he so concerned about a ruined salad when they had a dead passenger to deal with?

'I don't . . .' She screwed up her face. 'What does it matter? Someone's dead, and you're thinking about—'

'Please, Jade,' he said. 'Please, just trust me. I promise that it matters.'

Grudgingly she forced her mind back to the moment when she had served the starters. 'I picked up two of the charcuterie boards,' she said. 'But I think . . . I think I can remember seeing Ivy getting to the dumbwaiter first.'

'Ivy?'

'Yeah, she was . . . Wait. She was definitely there first. But I think Niamh was the one who actually picked up the salads.'

'What about Liam?' Gwyn pressed. 'Was he not there, too?'

'Liam? No, he was pouring drinks at the table.'

'You're sure?'

'Positive.'

Gwyn cursed. Jade, meanwhile, was beginning to grow frustrated.

'Is this about your CV?' she demanded. 'Skyline's going under and you're worried you won't get another job if you can't prove someone else ruined those salads?'

Gwyn was about to reply, but first he paused, sweeping a precautionary look into the corridor. When he did speak again, he lowered his voice to a whisper.

'Honestly? Yeah. Before Niamh told us what had happened to Howard, that was my first thought. Jasper said that when my contract here is up, we could talk about him giving me a job, but that'll never happen if he thinks I put *whale meat* in his girlfriend's salad. So, yes. At first I was thinking about work. But now . . .' He took a deep breath. 'Something's happening up here. There's the leak, obviously. And the air con. But there are things going wrong in my kitchen, too. First, there's the salad. Then this morning I wake up to find that the walk-in fridge isn't cold any more.'

'The fridge?'

He nodded eagerly. 'It was warm in there when I got up

to start preparing breakfast. It was set to the correct temperature and it was trying to cool down again, but I'm telling you, that fridge wasn't on during the night. On any other day I'd have said that a fuse probably tripped after I went to bed; the thing must have turned off for a few hours while we were asleep and come back on again before we woke up. But with everything else that's going on up here – the air con, the helium – you have to wonder if it isn't all connected.'

'You think someone caused the leak deliberately,' said Jade. 'And that they messed with the air con and turned off your fridge?'

'I think it's possible. Someone's causing trouble up here. The salad, the air con, the fridge . . . Things are going wrong that shouldn't be. I wouldn't be surprised if it's all being done by the same person, and I sure as hell wouldn't be surprised if they were responsible for the helium leak as well.' He adopted a desperate expression. 'I know it sounds far-fetched, Jade. But there was a pair of gloves this morning in the kitchen bin. Black gloves. The kind I wear while I'm working. Why would someone take a pair of those in the middle of the night, if they weren't up to something dodgy?'

It didn't sound far-fetched at all. Not when the pills Howard had supposedly used to drug himself had, in reality, spent the night in Jade's suitcase. If anything, Gwyn was frightening her. With every word he spoke, her own suspicions that someone could have targeted her uncle deliberately were becoming more and more tangible.

'How can you be sure they weren't yours?' she asked. 'The gloves. You must get through loads of them.'

'I changed the liner before I went to bed. It's the last thing I do every night, so the bin should always be empty when I start work in the morning. But today, of all days, I find a pair of used gloves in there.'

'And why are you asking about Liam?'

'You mean, aside from him being a smug little creep?' Gwyn scowled. 'He left our cabin in the middle of the night. Disappeared somewhere for a good fifteen minutes. I don't know why, but if you ask me I think he messed with the air con, turned off the fridge and set up the leak. I think he took a pair of my gloves to avoid leaving fingerprints while he was at it, then he put them in the kitchen bin when he was done, thinking I wouldn't notice. But it's all gone wrong for him, hasn't it? Because now someone's dead.'

Jade's mind raced. Could Gwyn be right? Could Liam accidentally have killed her uncle? It was a plausible theory. At least it might have been, had it not hinged on Howard drugging himself before going to bed.

For a moment she considering telling Gwyn that she had the pills – telling him it was no simple accident that Howard had remained asleep while his cabin filled with helium. Whether it had been Liam or someone else, it seemed someone aboard the *Osprey* had been so eager for him not to wake that they had taken the matter into their own hands.

The words lingered on her tongue. She had to do

something. She couldn't simply sit on both the pills and all that Gwyn had just shared with her. But the chef was looking for someone to blame and, while she was fond of him, she couldn't predict where his mind would go if she showed him the little bottle. He hadn't even known that Howard was her uncle.

'I need to get back to the lounge,' she said abruptly. 'Before Niamh catches me up here.'

Gwyn nodded. 'You probably should. With everything that's happening, she's wound pretty tight.' His eyes softened. 'You'll tell me, though,' he said, 'won't you? If you hear anything else?'

Jade chewed the corner of her lip, not quite able to force a smile. 'Yeah,' she lied. 'Yeah, I'll tell you.'

22

Sitting on his bed, pillows propped up behind him, Jasper's prevailing thought was what a total waste of time this trip had proven to be.

He could have been anywhere right now. A spa. A resort. Somewhere *hot*. The *Osprey* had at least warmed up to the extent that he no longer needed to wear his coat. But it didn't change the amount of precious time that was now being wasted at the top of the world, with nothing to do, ice in every direction and a dead body just two doors down.

Jasper had never seen a corpse before, and he was finding, on reflection, that he'd been surprisingly unmoved by it. It had been a shock, of course. Seeing the old boy lying there with his waxy skin and his blue lips. But he'd never really cared for Howard. Prior to that weekend they'd only ever met a handful of times, occasionally crossing paths in Ezra's home during the months after Isaac's death. Otherwise, they had barely known each other. The fact that Howard was now dead didn't suddenly make any difference to how Jasper felt about him. Instead, once the captain had assured them there was no chance of their own cabins filling with helium, his chief concern was getting home. He had absolutely no intention of staying for days in Longyearbyen while a police investigation took place. If an officer wanted statements from them all, they could take his before the first flight for the mainland left the tarmac. Anything further could be done over the phone.

'This is fucked up,' said Madison. 'Fucked. Up.'

She'd been going on like this for a while now, pacing back and forth on the short stretch of carpet at the foot of the bed. Jasper had been doing his best to tune her out. Not a difficult task, when she so rarely stopped monologuing to check if he was actually engaged.

'Like . . . he was only two doors down. Two! What if that had been *our* room?' The *Osprey* juddered, and Madison let out a shriek as she nearly tumbled to the floor. As she regained her footing, a determined look broke out on her face. 'We are going to *sue*. I don't care that he's your friend, Jas. By the time we're done, Ezra won't know what's hit him. And if he thinks he's getting another dollar from my family, he can think again. When I tell Dad what's happened up here, he's going to want it all *back*!'

Jasper didn't bother telling Madison there was no chance of her father clawing back whatever money he had put into Skyline Voyages. It did occur to him, having been the one to suggest Skyline as an investment opportunity, that he might no longer be in the old man's good graces. But then wasn't any investment a game of chance? Madison's father was an exceptionally wealthy man. If Howard's death really did mean the end of Skyline Voyages, he had countless other budding ventures to which he could turn his eye. And if he was bitter? If he held Jasper responsible for whatever losses he might incur? Well, worse things had happened. Jasper wasn't keen on the old bastard anyway.

He stood abruptly, prompting Madison to stop in her tracks.

'Where are you going?'

'For a drink.'

'And what about me? I'm not going out there with those people.'

'Stay here then.'

She looked at him as if he'd suggested she take an ice-bath. 'You can't *leave me here*. What if it happens again while you're away? What if more helium gets in here and I don't realise?'

'You'd smell it. Just leave.'

'But what if I don't? What if the filter, like, removes the smell or something?'

Heaving a sigh, Jasper turned away and stepped out into the corridor. Madison threw all manner of curses in his wake, but he didn't stop to hear them, her voice rising to a whine before he closed the door behind him.

Standing in the corridor, he listened to the muffled complaints that still came from inside the cabin. As he did so, he wondered if perhaps it would be time to cut Maddie loose when they made it back to the UK. When they first got together these outbursts had been cute. Sometimes even funny. He'd enjoyed watching her lay into whoever had stoked her wrath, before being the only one who could step in and pacify her. But now, a year into their relationship, the novelty was wearing off. Talking her down was becoming more irritating than gratifying. It was becoming more difficult, too.

Putting the thought from his mind, he walked the short distance to the lounge. With the glass doors humming open, he swept a quick look around. Ezra was sitting with Astrid at the table, hunched over a tablet. Ben was on one of the couches, while Liam, Ivy and Niamh all floated about. The others, he assumed, must be in their cabins.

He went straight to the bar, where Liam came to ask what he might like.

'What's the drink Ezra's so fond of?'

Having clearly expected Jasper to simply need some water – a coffee at a stretch – Liam failed to keep the look of surprise from his face.

'Come on then,' Jasper pressed, 'let's not take all day about it. Ezra didn't build this lovely bar for nothing. If we're stuck up here, someone might as well make the most of it.'

Blatantly uncomfortable, Liam cleared his throat. 'It's an Arctic Collins, sir. I might just need to go upstairs and fetch a lemon from the kitchen. With all that's happened this morning, I don't think the bar's been restocked . . .'

He rummaged behind the bar, Jasper becoming silently

irritated as he watched the young man flounder. A moment later, just as he was thinking about saying not to bother, Liam suddenly produced a lemon.

'Never mind,' he mumbled. 'One left.'

Jasper watched him prepare the drink, ice cubes crackling as he poured out the gin. There was no theatre to it today, every movement stiff and functional. Honestly Liam looked terrible, his skin pale and eyes bloodshot. Jasper wondered if he'd been sick. It would be fair enough, he supposed. Ezra wouldn't have trained them for a scenario like this. All the same, he made a mental note to have a word with his own staff when he was home. If ever a customer died in the restaurant, they were all to keep smiling. As Liam was now demonstrating, it didn't do to bring the mood down further.

The drink prepared, Jasper took a sip, looking out of the windows at the frozen wilderness below them. The North Pole . . . Mia would probably say it was beautiful, but Jasper couldn't see what was so special about it. It certainly wasn't worth dying for.

Hearing footsteps, he turned and saw Ezra approaching the bar. He settled onto the neighbouring bar stool with a sigh.

'Glass of water, please, Liam.'

Jasper raised an eyebrow. 'I'm surprised you aren't having something stronger.'

'Can't do it, mate. Need to keep a clear head.'

Liam poured him a glass, only for the *Osprey* to give a particularly violent bump, causing the water to slop onto the bar. Liam scrambled to clean it up, but Ezra took the cloth off him.

'It's all right,' he said. 'It's OK. Why don't you take a minute?'

Liam shuffled away without a word, leaving Jasper to watch as Ezra abandoned the glass, instead taking a swig of water straight from the bottle.

'Don't suppose there's any point in asking how you're doing.'

Ezra gave a hollow laugh. 'No,' he said. 'I don't suppose there is.' He looked into the distance, eyes widening. 'I can't stop thinking of how it was supposed to be me in that cabin. If I hadn't screwed up the room plan . . . Or if I'd insisted we swap.' He pressed a hand to his eyes, voice catching. 'This isn't going to be the end,' he said, once he'd collected himself. 'We're going to find out how this happened, make whatever repairs are needed and get back in the air. I'll have the guys in Tromsø working day and night, if I need to. We've not come this far just to let those bastards at Airborne steal the lead from us now. It's what Howard would have wanted. It's what my dad would have . . .'

He tailed off again, and in the silence Jasper found himself quietly impressed.

Ezra sighed. 'Have you spoken to Devon at all? I've barely seen him.'

Jasper fought to keep a small smile from his lips. Despite the shitshow that this trip had become, watching Devon make such a fool of himself over dinner had been an undisputed highlight. Ezra's face when he brought up the Normanstone challenge . . . At school, Jasper had never understood why Ezra and Alec kept Devon around. He wasn't clever or cunning. Not cultured or witty. No one could match him on the rugby pitch, but anything that required him to sit behind a desk and use his brain was lost on him. And that *ridiculous* citrus allergy . . . When they'd first met, Jasper had doubted it was even real.

Well, Devon wouldn't be around much longer. Not after the display he'd put on over dinner. In that moment he had shown himself to be exactly what Jasper had always known him to be.

He shook his head. 'From what I've seen, he's been keeping to himself. Comes out for a water or a coffee, then goes back to his cabin. I'd say he's pretty embarrassed. And I'll bet he has a raging hangover.'

'I'm sure.' Ezra looked down at the bar, genuinely upset. 'I can't understand where that came from. I know he'd been drinking. But he sounded so *angry*.'

'He's jealous.'

'Of what? He's got his life in the Alps, his business . . . I thought he was happy. What could Devon have to be jealous of?'

Jasper thought for a moment, wondering how best to play the scenario he had been presented with. He could say nothing. Shrug his shoulders and move the conversation along. Or . . .

'Did you know that Devon's having money troubles?'

Ezra's eyes narrowed. 'What kind of money troubles?'

'I can't say for sure. But yesterday I snuck a look at his phone. He was reading an email. I saw a mention of a hundred and fifty grand and of "reparations", before he realised I was there and put it away. My guess is that the silly fucker got some tourist injured on one of his mountain expeditions and now he's being sued.'

Ezra nodded slowly, turning this new information over. 'It would make sense. When I first asked him to come on this trip, he didn't seem keen. Said he couldn't get away. It wasn't until I offered to pay him a consultant's fee that he agreed.'

'A consultant's fee?'

Ezra gave a small shrug. 'It was the only way to get him up here.'

Devon, you cheap bastard.

They were silent for a long moment, a new thought taking form in Jasper's mind.

'Ezra,' he said cautiously, 'how certain are you that what's happened up here was accidental?'

Ezra frowned. 'It has to be. I mean, we'll need the ground crew to run an investigation before we can explain it in full. But I can't see why someone would do this deliberately.'

'Of course,' said Jasper. 'And I understand it's a worrying thought. But given the financial quandaries that our old pal seems so eager to keep quiet, I can't help wondering how much an outfit like Airborne Expeditions might *pay* to have a saboteur on this trip.'

Ezra stared at him.

'Did Devon know?' Jasper pressed. 'About Airborne? Before he came up here, had you told him there was another company trying to pip you to the post?'

'I'm not sure. I can't . . .' Ezra floundered, pressing a hand to his temple. 'I think I did. When I was explaining what this trip was all about, I'm sure it came up. But you can't honestly think—'

'Why not? If Devon knew about them, he could have easily got in touch.'

'I know, Jas. And you're right. Given the opportunity, I can imagine them tampering with the *Osprey*. But *killing* someone?'

'But Howard wasn't *supposed* to die, was he? They couldn't have known that he would be dosed up on sleeping pills, or that there would be a storm to drop his dressing gown across the bottom of his door. He wasn't even supposed to be in that room. It should have been you. And if it *had* been you, you would have woken up, smelled the helium and got yourself out. No one would have died, but the *Osprey* would, presumably, have been grounded while you investigated the cause of the leak. Long enough, I expect, for Airborne to steal the lead.'

Ezra was silent, deep in thought as he weighed up this possibility. 'Who else have you spoken to about this?'

'No one. It only occurred to me just now.'

Ezra nodded. 'Let's keep it that way. I'll share this with the police when we land.'

'If I were you, I'd confront Devon now—'

'No,' Ezra said sharply. 'I'll keep an eye on him, but

there's nothing to be gained from confronting him up here. We'll all have to speak with the police once we're back on the ground. That'll be the time.'

Before Jasper could protest further, Niamh approached and whispered something in Ezra's ear.

'Sorry, mate,' he said. 'The captain's asked for a word.' He waited for Niamh to move along, then clasped Jasper on the shoulder. 'I appreciate you telling me about this, Jas. We'll deal with it when we're back. I promise.'

23

After their exchange by the glass doors – 'conversation' didn't feel quite the right word – Chloé had been more than a little surprised when Jade asked if they could talk. She was even more so when, instead of speaking in the lounge or in Chloé's cabin, Jade insisted on sneaking her to the upper deck and into the little room she shared with Ivy.

'I need to show you something,' she said, quickly closing the plastic door behind them. 'And before you ask any questions, I need you to let me explain. Because I know what you're going to think, and I promise it isn't what it looks like.'

Now thoroughly confused, Chloé had to admit that Jade was making her nervous. Being on the upper deck wasn't helping. She knew there was no greater risk of a leak up here than in the passengers' quarters. All the same, being a level closer to the vast body of helium above their heads was an uncomfortable thought.

But despite her nerves she didn't argue, watching closely

as Jade pulled a suitcase from under one of the bunks. Taking a deep breath, the young steward reached inside, fetched something out and held it to the light. Chloé stared, her eyes widening at the sight of a small plastic bottle.

'Are those—'

The *Osprey* jolted, causing Jade to grasp the side of the bunk. As she shot out her arm to steady herself, a rattling sound came from the bottle. There was no doubt in Chloé's mind. These were Howard's sleeping pills.

'I take things,' said Jade. 'Little things. Things that don't matter. A lot of the time I couldn't even tell you why. I don't *keep* anything. A therapist told me once that it's about power. She said I feel small, and that taking stuff gives me a sense of control.'

Chloé nodded at the bottle. 'Is that why you took those?'

Jade seemed to struggle for an answer. 'I wasn't going to take anything up here. I really wasn't. But Howard said something to me yesterday. Something that . . . well, that really wound me up. So I went into his cabin while you were all having dinner and I took them. I was going to put them back this morning, try to play with his head after he'd spent a whole night looking for them. I only wanted to *annoy* him. But when they found him dead . . .'

Chloé nodded, understanding. Had Howard still been alive, Jade could perhaps have snuck into his cabin while they were having breakfast. If someone caught her, she could pretend to be doing some housekeeping. But now, the risk was too great.

'What did Howard say to you? What was so bad that you wanted to upset him?'

Jade's lip curled. 'He was rubbing it in my face that he'd got me this job. Told me I should be more grateful and that he'd done me this huge favour. He didn't go so far as to actually say it, but I knew what he was suggesting – that if I screw it up here, nobody else will want me.'

Chloé's mind raced at a mile a minute. She felt as if she should apologise, both for the loss of Jade's uncle and for how she had pried in the lounge. But it was clear from Jade's tone that there was no love lost between her and Howard.

'Do you believe me?' Jade asked, the fear clear in her voice.

Chloé nodded.

'And you know what this means,' she pressed. 'You get it, don't you?'

Chloé nodded a second time. She knew exactly what it meant. Howard needed to have been drugged to remain asleep while his cabin filled with helium. But if his sleeping pills had spent the entire night hidden in Jade's case, it was impossible that he could have done it himself.

'Could Howard have had some spare pills?' she asked. 'Another bottle he could have used when he found that one missing?'

Jade shook her head. 'If he did, he hid them well. I ended up having to rummage through his suitcase just to find these.'

'And does anyone else know that you have them?'

'I don't think so. But there's something else.' Jade's expression became even more uncertain. 'Gwyn came to see me. About half an hour ago.'

'The chef?'

'That's right. He doesn't think the helium leak was an accident. He says that someone turned off his fridge during the night and put that bit of charcuterie in Madison's salad, and he thinks the same person messed with the air con and set up the leak.'

'Does he have any idea who?'

'He thinks it's Liam. They share the room next door. He says that Liam got up during the night and left the cabin for fifteen minutes.' Jade swallowed back a lump. 'He said as well that he found a pair of gloves in the kitchen bin – the kind he wears while he's preparing food.'

Chloé knew which gloves Gwyn meant. He had been wearing a pair when Astrid had taken her and Ben to the kitchen during their tour of the upper deck.

'How can he be sure they weren't his? He must get through several pairs a day. It's surely not as if he could keep track of them all.'

'I asked him the same thing. He says that he changed the bin liner before going to bed, so it should have been empty when he got up this morning. Instead he found a pair of gloves in there.'

Chloé was silent, taking a moment to catch up. 'Do you think he could be right?' she said. 'About Liam?'

Jade scowled. 'I mean, Liam's a creep. He was bragging to Ivy yesterday about how he'd watched Niamh type in the code to her safe, like he was hoping it would impress her or something. Not that it's much of a code. Zero-eight-zero-five. If Niamh can't even be bothered to think of four different numbers, I'd say she *deserves* to have her safe broken into. But can I see him doing *this*? I don't know. For one thing, Liam doesn't have a staff keycard. He had to borrow Ivy's just to help with the housekeeping, because he's gone and left his in Tromsø. Without that, he can't get into any of the cabins, into the electronics bay . . . But if he really did go wandering about in the middle of the night, then he was clearly up to something.'

'Could that have been a cover story?' asked Chloé. 'Reduce the chance of coming under suspicion by having you guys believe he's forgotten his card?'

'I think you're giving him too much credit,' said Jade. 'If Liam's smart enough to plan ahead like that, I'd be surprised. But I guess . . . maybe?' She screwed her eyes shut. 'I can't think why, though. Why would Liam drug my uncle? Why would he want him dead?'

'It could have been two people,' said Chloé. 'Perhaps Liam set up the leak and someone else drugged Howard. They might have had no idea what the other was doing. It could still have been an accident.'

'That still doesn't explain *why*. Why else would they want him drugged? Did they want him to miss something? Were they hoping to break into his cabin while he was asleep? I didn't see anything in there that your average thief would bother stealing.'

For a while Chloé said nothing, turning over in her

mind everything Jade had shared. 'Why are you telling me all this?' she asked. 'Why not one of the others?'

Jade put the bottle back in her case, carefully covering it with a T-shirt. 'The only other people who knew Howard was my uncle were Niamh, Ezra and Astrid. Niamh and Ezra don't like me much. I thought . . . well, to be honest, I was worried they wouldn't believe me. That they might think *I* had killed him, and that I was only telling them about the pills as some kind of cover story.'

'What about Astrid? She seems nice. A little kooky, perhaps. But nice all the same. I'm sure she would help you.'

Jade pulled a face. 'Astrid's proven, with you, that she can't keep anything to herself. If I told her, I reckon within five minutes Ezra would know it, too. But you . . .' She paused, searching for the right words. 'You already know that Howard's my uncle. When you came to ask if I was all right, you actually seemed to care. And you're a journalist. I thought you might know what to do about this. How to make sense of it all. That's what you hear about journalists doing, isn't it? They investigate things.'

Chloé hesitated. 'I'm glad you told me,' she said. 'And I promise that I believe you. But, Jade, I'm a travel writer. Now that this trip's gone up in smoke, I'm not even a journalist. I'm just a blogger again. That said,' seeing Jade's dismay, she continued quickly, 'I will do my best to help you with this. I think you're right to keep it quiet while we're stuck up here. I don't see what we can do about it right now, and we won't be helping anyone if we cause a panic. But in a few hours, when we land, you need to tell the police. I'll come with you, if you like. We can explain it together.'

At the mention of the police, Chloé saw panic in Jade's eyes. But after thinking for a long moment, she gave a single nod. She clearly wasn't happy, but having a plan at least seemed to settle her nerves.

'Come on,' said Chloé. 'We should get back to—'

Before she could finish her sentence, the cabin door swung open.

'*What's going on?*'

Seeing alarm erupt on Jade's face, Chloé turned to find Niamh standing in the doorway.

24

In ten years as a steward on the Mediterranean, the most traumatic event Niamh had witnessed was a doctor being called out to the yacht when the owner's new girlfriend suffered a severe allergic reaction to a piece of shellfish. Coming in at a close second had been the night when a drunk guest was sent back to shore for getting handsy with a member of the crew.

Ten years. Two incidents. So to have learned that during her first weekend as chief steward a passenger – one of *her* passengers – had lost his life had been little short of horrifying.

After briefing the others, Niamh had shut herself in her office, tears stinging the corners of her eyes. The sight of Howard's body would be forever burned into her mind, blue lips parted, as she searched frantically for a pulse that she knew wasn't there.

Inevitably, once the initial shock had passed, the grubby thought had occurred to her that this could be the escape she so desperately wanted. While she might have caught herself daydreaming about it, she hadn't ever seriously considered breaking her contract with Skyline Voyages. No matter how miserable the prospect of three years aboard the *Osprey* made her, she prided herself on her professionalism. She also knew that if she were to leave simply because she hadn't enjoyed an assignment, she would never be given a decent posting again. This, however . . .

Ezra was adamant that Skyline Voyages would survive. With a thorough investigation and some repairs when they returned to Tromsø, he was convinced the *Osprey* would be airworthy again in no time. They had to keep going, he'd told her. It's what Howard would have wanted. Even if he was correct, though, and Skyline Voyages did pull through, surely nobody would blame Niamh for walking away. Not when the aircraft itself had killed someone – killed its owner, no less – during its very first outing. If anything, she imagined it would look strange if she *stayed*.

But she couldn't even take comfort in that – in the thought that she might no longer have to spend the next three years of her life up here. Because however much she resented them, she took her duties seriously. And while she knew there was nothing she could have done to save Howard, she still felt as if she had failed.

In the hours that had since passed, she had done her best to bury her guilt. She urged herself that there was nothing she could have done. In the absence of a way to somehow help Howard, all she could do now was maintain her professionalism. Continue being the stalwart leader her team needed.

Not that they were making it easy.

Since his screw-up with the salads, Gwyn had been awful, skulking around the kitchen like a vengeful phantom. Liam and Ivy, meanwhile, had been rendered nervous wrecks by the discovery of Howard's body. As for Jade . . . Having just lost her uncle, Niamh knew she might need to be treated more gently than the others. She wasn't a monster, after all. But if there was one thing she couldn't accept, it was guests being brought unannounced to the upper deck – least of all an inquisitive reporter.

'So, you see,' Chloé concluded, 'I noticed that Jade was looking distressed in the lounge. I asked if she was OK, and when she got upset I suggested we talk up here, away from the others.'

Standing together in her tiny office, Niamh chewed her lip as she mulled this over. 'Well,' she said in a level tone, 'that's very kind of you.'

She knew she wasn't being told the truth. Or at least not the entire truth. She could see it in the way Chloé so unwaveringly held her gaze, and in the way Jade's eyes stayed glued to the floor. But there was nothing to be gained from grilling the young steward on what they had actually been doing. With Chloé now apparently watching over her, the risk of causing a scene was too great.

'Yes,' she continued, 'very kind. But if Jade could take you back to the lounge now, we really shouldn't have guests on this deck.'

'Of course.' Chloé adopted an expression of what Niamh

suspected was faux concern. 'I'm sorry, I didn't mean to break any rules.' She didn't move, though. Instead her eyes twitched to the corner of the cabin. 'What's that for?'

Following her line of sight, Niamh's mood took a turn for the worse as she settled on the balloon. She should have burst it. The moment Madison turned it down, she should have popped it and stuffed it in a bin. But, ever the attentive host, she had worried about the noise frightening one of the passengers, resolving instead to tuck it away in the corner of her office.

'It was for another guest.'

'Jasper and Madison?' Chloé asked. 'It's their one-year anniversary, right?'

'That's right. Mr Berry had asked Ezra to have a balloon and some champagne waiting in the cabin, but they decided they'd rather not have it. Not enough space.'

'And how did you inflate it? Did you do it up here? Or back in Tromsø?'

Niamh could hear the undertone in Chloé's voice. She was trying her best to sound casual – disinterested even – but there was an eagerness lurking beneath the surface. It was just a balloon. What was there to be so interested in?

She should ask again for Jade to take Chloé away. Take her back to the lounge and keep her there. But after ten years of being told that guests must have whatever they desired, she was compelled to put on a smile and answer the question.

'I blew it up on the flight over. Ezra hadn't had the

chance to choose which balloon he preferred until after we'd taken off.'

She saw Chloé's eyes probe the room, eventually coming to rest on the little canister under her desk.

'Jade.' Eager to bring this conversation to an end, Niamh leapt in before their guest could ask another question. 'Would you please take Chloé back downstairs? And if you don't mind, we'll have no more guests on the upper deck.'

Jade nodded and, without a word, led Chloé back into the corridor, closing the office door behind them.

What a mess, Niamh thought, letting out a sigh as she sat at her desk. What a complete and utter train-wreck. She dropped her head into her hands. Of course, it had all been a mess already. Between her team's hopelessness, Ezra behaving as if he was completely unaware of why he'd hired her and the total shambles into which their first dinner service had descended, even before Howard *died* there had been plenty to feel down about. Had they even known that he was taking sleeping pills?

Niamh froze. Had they known? It had been more of a rhetorical question. But now that she thought about it, Niamh couldn't remember seeing any mention of the pills in the waivers each passenger had been required to complete before coming aboard.

Reaching under the desk, she hurriedly typed in the code to the safe. She had to know. For the sake of her own guilt, she had to confirm if this was something she could have foreseen – could have prevented.

There were two shelves inside the safe, and from the top she drew out a plastic folder. Niamh was now in such a hurry that she didn't even pause to scowl at the vape she had confiscated from Ivy. Placing the folder on the desk, she turned frantically through the pages until she found Howard's. She cast her eye over it, breezing past allergies and existing health conditions until she reached the section on medication.

Nothing. There was no mention of any sleeping pills.

She had hoped that this result might come as a relief. That she would be able to convince herself Howard's death wasn't her fault. Instead, she gritted her teeth. How was she *ever* supposed to have done her job properly if not even the owner of the company could fill out a waiver properly? The odds had been stacked against her before they'd ever left the ground.

Slapping the folder shut, she went to put it back in the safe. But before she could, she stopped.

She and the other stewards each had a master keycard, to be used when they needed to enter a guest's cabin. On the lower shelf of the safe was a spare, kept in the event of an emergency. No one should have touched it since they left Tromsø. Niamh certainly hadn't, and she was the only one who knew the code to the safe. And yet, as she looked at it now, she was certain the keycard was not in the same position as when she had last seen it.

She stared at it, trying to make sure.

Yes. She knew every inch of this office. Sharing a cabin with Freja, it was the only space on the airship that felt like hers. The last time she had opened this safe, she was certain the keycard had been face-up, with a Skyline Voyages logo on display. With her affinity for neatness and order, it would have bothered her to see it any other way. But now, as Niamh looked into the safe, she could clearly see that it was face-down.

25

In an effort to determine how, exactly, the leak that had filled his employer's cabin with helium could have occurred, Captain Schäfer had been inspecting the electronics bay for well over thirty minutes.

He would soon need to return to the cockpit and insist that Freja take a few hours' rest. She would undoubtedly argue that she was fine to continue, despite having piloted the *Osprey* now for well over fourteen hours. But with no idea of what the next few days would hold – how long they would be kept in the sky – he needed both of his pilots to be alert. They were still a considerable distance from Longyearbyen, where the passengers would disembark, and from there they would need to return the airship to Tromsø. Schäfer doubted their departure to the mainland would be immediate, though.

A bureaucratic nightmare seemed to be brewing over the radio, the small police force in Longyearbyen insisting that its officers be allowed to board the *Osprey*, conduct an inspection and take statements from everyone present. That made sense, Schäfer supposed. Longyearbyen was the closest settlement, and it was where the guests had all come aboard. He could understand why the local police would be reluctant to hand the proceedings over to their counterparts in Tromsø.

But the investigation taking place in Longyearbyen presented two problems, the first of which was that there was nowhere for Howard's body to be kept. The town's graveyard had been taken out of commission in the 1950s, with permafrost preventing any bodies that were buried from decomposing, and death on the island had been forbidden ever since. Schäfer wasn't even sure if the town's hospital had a morgue, leaving him with no idea of quite what could be done about an airship dropping out of the sky with a corpse on board.

The second problem – and the one that was giving the captain such cause for concern – was that there was nowhere for an airship to be tethered. If the police in Longyearbyen did insist that the *Osprey* stayed put while they conducted their investigation, it would have to be kept in the air, leaving Schäfer, Freja and Jakob with no choice but to pilot it around the clock until they were given permission to leave. An airship was designed to stay aloft for days – even weeks – at a time. If some kind of agreement couldn't be reached with the police, they might soon find themselves putting that claim to the test.

Whatever happened, Schäfer needed to keep both of his pilots well-rested. They had a long return journey ahead, and he couldn't have either of them overcome with exhaustion before they even made it back to Longyearbyen.

But first he had to reach a conclusion on why cabins aboard his airship were being allowed to fill with helium.

'Captain.'

Turning to face the voice, he saw Ezra standing sheepishly in the doorway. Schäfer could understand why he looked so uncomfortable. Their last conversation, in the corridor outside Howard's cabin, hadn't been a pretty one.

'I shouldn't have let him take that cabin,' Ezra had wailed. 'I should have insisted we swap.'

Schäfer remembered feeling confused. 'You couldn't have known this would happen,' he had said.

But Ezra had been inconsolable. 'We should have delayed. I should never have let us take off before the air-con unit had been repaired.'

At this point Schäfer had felt his sympathy turn to fury. He jabbed a finger at the door. 'You knew that the system in this cabin was faulty? You knew this could happen and you didn't tell me?'

'I didn't know *this* could happen! I thought the worst we'd have to deal with was a few problems with the temperature.'

Schäfer had turned to Niamh, scarcely believing what he was hearing. 'Were *you* aware of this?'

'I found out yesterday afternoon, when Howard called me down to complain about his air conditioning. I'm so sorry, captain. I had no idea that *you* didn't even—'

'And are any of the others faulty?'

For several moments none of them had answered. At last Astrid spoke up, her voice breaking. 'It's just this one. I'm working with the ground crew in Tromsø to get it repaired.' She looked down at the ground. 'I'm sorry, captain. It didn't seem worth troubling you.'

Wasn't worth troubling him . . . How was he supposed to pilot an aircraft when details like this were being kept from him? The simple answer was that he couldn't. And going forward, he wouldn't. He had taken this role out of respect for Isaac, one of the finest pilots he had ever worked with. But once the passengers had been safely returned to Longyearbyen, and the *Osprey* to Tromsø, he would be tendering his resignation.

Still standing in the doorway to the electronics bay, Ezra cleared his throat. 'You asked to see me.'

'That's right, sir.' Even in his presently furious state, Schäfer stood up straight, a decades-long career compelling him to clasp his hands behind his back. 'I've been inspecting the equipment and I may have an explanation for the leak in Mr Barnes's cabin.'

Ezra's eyes widened. 'Well, that's . . . that's good to hear. Should I fetch Niamh? And Astrid maybe?'

'Not yet, sir. It's only a theory for now. An imperfect one, at that. But short of an act of God, I can see only one way the helium aboard this airship could have made its way into a cabin, and it's a three-step process that requires substantial specialist knowledge.'

Ezra paused, the relief on his face turning to concern.

'A *process*? Hold on now. You're talking about sabotage? Someone doing this deliberately?'

'I'm afraid so.' Schäfer's eyes passed over the instruments. 'First, the helium filter inside that cabin would need to be compromised. Second, the alerts that should sound in the cockpit would need to be disabled. And finally, an opening of some kind would need to be created somewhere in the climate-control system.'

'An opening?' Ezra repeated.

'A cracked pipe perhaps. Or, at the very least, one that isn't airtight. This would be the most crucial part. Because while the filters and the alerts in the cockpit are there as fail-safes, the simple truth is that there should be no way for the helium ever to make it into the system. Clearly all three of these things have happened. And it seems to me that only someone with both sufficient access to the *Osprey* and specialist knowledge of its infrastructure could achieve that.' He looked Ezra in the eye. 'This is why I asked to speak with you, sir. I was hoping you could tell me if there's anyone in the ground crew who you have reason – any reason whatsoever – not to trust.'

Ezra pressed both hands to his face. 'I don't know. I suppose there must be, but I can't imagine who.' He gave a sigh. 'Jasper's just suggested to me that someone might have been paid to do this by Airborne Expeditions. He thinks it could be one of the other guests.'

Schäfer grimaced. 'I could see Airborne wanting to organise this. They wouldn't have known that the person in that cabin was taking sleeping pills. They'd have had no idea that such a leak might prove fatal. But I struggle to imagine one of the guests being their trigger man. For one thing, we know that the filter in Howard's cabin was broken before we left Tromsø. As for the alert system . . .' Schäfer motioned towards one of the consoles. 'There's no evidence to suggest it's been tampered with in here. Which means something must have been done inside the envelope to the sensors themselves. And then there's whatever opening has been created in the climate-control system to allow the helium inside.'

He stepped into the corridor, indicating a hatch in the ceiling. 'In theory, someone could have climbed through there and done both of those things while we've been in the air. But again, I struggle to see how. Not only would they need to know exactly what they were doing, but they would need a staff keycard – none of the guests' cards would unlock that hatch. And even if someone *did* get up there unnoticed, they would need to take the oxygen mask to breathe inside the envelope. We know that hasn't happened, though, because when I used the mask this morning to assess the helium levels inside the cabin, the tank was completely full.'

Ezra nodded, his expression grim as he stared at the hatch. 'I understand. And we're ruling out the idea of it being the storm, as well?'

'We'll need a thorough assessment from the ground crew to rule it out definitively. But again I would say it's highly unlikely. Howard's filter might have been damaged already when we left Tromsø, but we would still be relying on the storm jostling the airship so violently that it rendered all of the helium sensors inside the envelope useless and shook something loose in the climate-control system. If you ask me, all of the evidence points towards someone setting this up on the ground, before we even took off. That said, I do think this morning's on-board temperature suggests that someone up here has been causing trouble.'

Schäfer returned to the electronics bay, where he pointed towards a small screen displaying two numbers. 'This is where we set the ambient temperature. The figure on the left is the temperature we've set it to. The figure on the right is the actual temperature. When I came in here this morning, while the airship was still very cold, the figure on the right – the *actual* temperature – was considerably lower than we would like. But the figure on the left – the *designated* temperature – was exactly as it should be. And all the while the airship was steadily warming back up.'

'What does that mean?'

'It means one of two things. Either a mechanical fault occurred during the night, causing the climate-control system to misinterpret the designated ambient temperature, before inexplicably correcting itself just as we all woke up. Or someone snuck in here during the night and lowered it manually, only to return several hours later and reset it.'

'Why would someone do that?'

'My best guess is that they're trying to fake a fault. Give the impression that the system malfunctioned.'

'And could that have been Airborne Expeditions, too?'

'I think it would make sense. A helium leak, a suspected problem with the on-board temperature . . . If they're trying to ground us long enough that they can start operating first, I'd say they're going the right way about it. With someone in Tromsø and someone else in the air, who knows what else they could have tampered with?'

Ezra stared at the little screen. 'Let's say someone *has* been messing around with this during the night. Is there no way they could have accidentally allowed helium into the climate-control system?'

'None that I'm aware of,' said Schäfer, 'unless someone on the ground has done something extremely clever that would facilitate it. Which, I suppose, is possible. But we won't know until an investigation has taken place.'

Ezra sighed. 'Thank you for showing me all of this. And . . . I'm sorry. For not telling you about the filter in Howard's cabin before we set out. That was a mistake. One that I . . . well, one that I don't expect I'll ever be able to make up for.'

The captain nodded stiffly. 'I appreciate the apology, sir, but I'm afraid it doesn't change what's happened. Out of respect for your father, I'll see the *Osprey* back to Tromsø and I'll offer any assistance that I can to the investigation. But that will be the end of my affiliation with Skyline Voyages. You'll have my resignation as soon as we've landed.'

Ezra nodded. If he was surprised by Schäfer's decision, he didn't show it. Heaving a sigh, he swept an unhappy glance across the controls, as if he might somehow spot a blinking light or a flashing warning message that would explain what was happening to his airship.

'I'm sorry,' said Schäfer. 'I'm sure this must be very difficult.'

'We'll pull it back. Put out a good statement. Get the ground crew to give this place a thorough sweep. Maybe we'll even organise another press trip next year. By the time we start operating, this will all be just a bad memory.'

Schäfer frowned. He had been talking about Howard, rather than the damage to the company. Perhaps Ezra wasn't ready to engage with it. He had certainly been badly affected in the minutes after the body was discovered. Focusing on the *Osprey* might be a way of distracting himself.

The floor shook beneath their feet, forcing Ezra to grip the door handle to stay upright.

'You get back down to the lounge, sir,' said Schäfer. 'It'll be more comfortable there. If there are any other developments, I'll be sure to let you know.'

26

'Chloé,' Ben hissed. 'Chloé!'

The glass doors to the lounge slid shut behind him, sealing them both in the corridor. Coming stubbornly to a halt, he stared at her, bemused.

'What are we doing?' he asked. 'Seriously, what's wrong?'

Pausing at her cabin door, Chloé turned back and gave him a desperate look. 'Please just come and sit with me,' she said. 'I need to talk to someone and I don't want the others to hear.'

He didn't look convinced, but at the sound of faint footsteps in the stairwell, he didn't argue. Jogging to catch her up, he was suddenly in such a hurry that as he passed Howard's door he caught the belt of the dressing gown with his foot, lifting it clean away from the robe.

Chloé felt a spark of panic. 'Put it back,' she whispered. 'Quick! Just chuck it!'

Doing as he was told, Ben snatched the belt from the ground, balling it up and dropping it on top of the robe.

He then cleared the remaining distance between them and ducked into the cabin.

Closing the door, Chloé instructed him to sit on the bed, waiting until she'd heard whoever had been on the stairwell pass by. She checked the time on her phone. They would have to speak quickly. Aware of the other guests' eyes following them as she led him from the lounge, she knew that someone would ask what they had been doing if they were away for too long.

'What I'm about to tell you needs to stay between us.'

'Of course.'

'I mean it, Ben. I need a second opinion before I share any of this with the police. But I need it to stay between us, and I *need* you to keep an open mind.'

Ben still looked unsure, but eventually he nodded. 'All right,' he said. 'Yeah. I can do that.'

Chloé took a deep breath, then described all she had learned on the upper deck, from the pills in Jade's case and the discovery that Howard had been Jade's uncle, to the canister of helium in Niamh's office and the pair of gloves that Gwyn had found in the kitchen bin. When, finally, she came to an end, Ben heaved a sigh.

'It's the pills that worry me most,' said Chloé. 'I was thinking before that if someone caused the leak deliberately, they couldn't have known Howard was taking them. They wanted only to damage the airship and were expecting that whoever was in the affected cabin would notice and leave.' She looked at Ben pleadingly. 'I know you think I'm barking up the wrong tree, but you must see that—'

'I do. If the pills were hidden under Jade's bed, Howard couldn't have taken them himself.' Ben shook his head. 'God,' he murmured, 'I can see why you wanted to talk this over.'

'I think someone drugged him at dinner.'

Ben looked up at her incredulously.

'We know it was the helium that killed him,' she pressed. 'The captain said that his lips turning blue was proof of that. And we know that if he hadn't been dosed up on sleeping pills – or at least on *something* – he wouldn't have slept through it. But if his pills were in Jade's case, the only way he could have been dosed up at all is if someone else drugged him.'

'I guess that makes sense,' Ben admitted. 'But d'you really think someone could have drugged him at the table? In full view of seven other people? How would you manage that without any of us seeing? Without Howard *himself* seeing?'

'I don't know. But he didn't seem at all affected while we were eating. If he'd been given such a significant dose of something earlier in the afternoon, surely we would have seen him getting sluggish at some point?'

'It could have been done *after* dinner,' said Ben. 'We all have water in our cabins. Maybe someone spiked *that* and he drank it before going to bed.'

Chloé thought about this, trying to remember if the water bottle in Howard's cabin had been empty when they peered through the door that morning. It was no use. She had been too distracted by the sight of Howard himself to notice much else.

'It's possible,' she said. 'Although you'd need a way into his cabin. None of our keycards open his door. It would either have to be done by one of the stewards or, at the very least, with one of their cards. But I can't imagine any of them doing it, and I can't see how you would steal a card without being caught.'

'It would surely be easier, though, to steal a staff keycard than to drug someone in a room full of witnesses.' Ben pressed his hands to his face. 'I can't believe we're actually considering this.'

'You think I'm wrong?'

'No,' he said quickly. 'No, I don't think that. If the pills Jade showed you really were Howard's, then I agree there must be something going on. But you're talking about *murder* . . .' He exhaled heavily. 'All right. If it'll help put your mind at ease, let's talk it through. This canister in Niamh's office – I suppose you're thinking someone could have used it to fake the leak. Put it in Howard's cabin, opened it up and let it fill the room.'

'I think it needs to be considered.'

'How big was it? The canister. What sort of size?'

Chloé held up her hands, positioning them around a foot apart.

Ben shook his head. 'No way. I got something that size for a stag weekend a couple of years ago. It was meant to fill ten balloons and it barely managed that. I'd be amazed if you could get enough helium out of it to fill a room, let alone for long enough that someone might asphyxiate.'

'I still think we should consider it. Maybe you just had a faulty canister?'

'OK. How about the scent? Captain Schäfer said they gave the *Osprey*'s helium an artificial scent as a safety measure. That's what we all smelled when Ezra opened Howard's door. That sweet, sickly kind of smell; the cabin reeked of it. But the canister Niamh bought to fill Jasper's balloon won't have been given the same treatment. So if *that* helium was used, what did we all smell?'

Chloé bit her lip. He made an irritatingly good point.

'Could the scent have been added in some other way?' she asked.

'I suppose so. If you put down a diffuser or something. But I don't see how someone would actually do it without us realising. I mean, I was a little distracted by the body, but I didn't see anything in Howard's cabin that would make the place smell. Did you?'

Chloé was silent.

'Besides,' Ben continued, 'there's another problem with that theory. Two, in fact.' He held up a finger. 'The first is that you would presumably need to be inside the cabin with the canister. You'd need to put it in there, and when you were . . .' He tailed off, trying to choose the right word. 'When you were *finished*, you would need to remove it. If the helium being released was enough to kill Howard, it would surely be enough to kill whoever was in the room with him, too.'

'Not true,' Chloé cut in. 'You could open the canister, leave it in the cabin and come back for it later.'

Ben shook his head. 'That doesn't work, either. Because now we come to the second problem with this scenario, which is the dressing gown. I know we've talked about this already, but I still don't see how you would get the dressing gown flat against the bottom of the door from outside the room.'

Chloé turned his theory over in her mind, looking for holes. 'Fine,' she said. 'The canister doesn't work. But can we at least give some real thought to how someone might have drugged Howard over dinner?'

'Again,' said Ben, 'I just don't see how. If – and I do mean *if* – someone spiked him, I think it must have been with the water bottle in his cabin. There's no way you could slip him a load of crushed sleeping pills over the dinner table without anyone noticing.'

'It might not have been done at the table. Someone managed to get a piece of *whale* into Madison's salad without her noticing. Maybe something was put into his food before it was served.'

'Maybe,' Ben agreed. 'But Madison didn't actually *eat* her salad. The only reason we know about the whale is because someone spotted it on bloody Instagram. Howard, on the other hand, ate pretty much everything he was given. He would have noticed.'

'His drink, then. What if he drank something that had been spiked? You hear it happening in bars all the time.'

Ben grimaced. 'I don't see how that would work, either. All of the glasses were empty when we went to the table, and we all poured from the same bottles of water and wine. I guess it's possible there could have been something in his glass when we sat down, but wouldn't we have seen that? Assuming we *are* talking about some kind of crushed sleeping pills, would you not notice that there was a layer of powder waiting at the bottom of your glass?'

Chloé's eyes fell to the floor. 'You think I'm going mad, don't you?'

'No. I think it's totally reasonable to consider this stuff, especially after Jade came clean to you about those pills. But I do think there's one theory we haven't considered. One that would explain pretty much everything.' He looked her in the eye. 'What if the pills Jade took from Howard's room weren't the only ones he had with him? If he had another stash, he might have taken *those* before he went to bed, and we're right back to him dying in an accidental helium leak.'

'Jade's convinced they were the only ones,' Chloé fired back at him. 'And besides, what about the gloves? Gwyn seems pretty certain someone took a pair of his nitrile gloves during the night. Surely the only reason you'd do that is if you were up to no good and didn't want to leave any fingerprints.'

Ben frowned. 'I'm not convinced by the gloves. I mean . . . If Gwyn wears them every day, I don't see how he can be so sure they weren't just a pair of his. And if you were using them to hurt someone, why would you put them in a bin where they might be noticed? I get that you can't exactly throw them out of the window while we're up here, but wouldn't you hang on to them until you could get rid of them?'

'Jade says that Gwyn changes the bin liner at the end of the night,' said Chloé. 'So it should have been empty when he started work this morning. As for why you'd put them in the bin, holding on to them until we get back to Longyearbyen is surely too great a risk. If you were caught with them, how would you explain that? The kitchen bin seems the perfect place to get rid of them. As you say, Gwyn must put several pairs in there every day. Whoever took them must have banked – clearly, mistakenly – on him not noticing that there was one more pair.'

For a long while neither of them spoke.

'Look,' said Ben, 'I get that it's frightening. And I don't think it's wrong of you to question this stuff. But we're only going to be stuck up here for a few more hours. Once we're back in Longyearbyen the police will search this place. They'll find out what caused the leak, and I'd bet any amount of money that they'll find a second bottle of pills in Howard's room.'

'And if they don't?'

'Then I guess they'll need to consider the possibility of him being spiked. But honestly, Chloé, if that were the case . . . how would they investigate it? It's not as if there's any CCTV up here.'

Feeling despondent, Chloé sat down on the bed. Before she could sink further into despair, though, a sudden thought struck her. 'No,' she said. 'There isn't CCTV. But we might have something just as good.'

27

Sitting on her bunk, head in her hands, Ivy was so frightened that it was all she could do not to be sick.

What had she been thinking? Threatening Mia and then storming out in a blaze of fury . . . *What* had she thought that would achieve? The answer, of course, was that she hadn't been thinking. She had panicked, acting on pure instinct.

The whale meat . . . She had known it was a mistake, but she hadn't been able to help herself. When the starters were sent down in the dumbwaiter and she opened the hatch to see the charcuterie boards arranged neatly inside, for a few seconds she had simply stood and stared. It had been more than revulsion that she'd felt. Having been so convinced that Mia would be on her side about Skyline Voyages, she had been completely and utterly dismayed. And when the moment came that she laid eyes on the little slivers of black meat, she had been filled with an overwhelming sense of powerlessness.

She couldn't recall making a conscious decision to put

the meat in Mia's salad. All she could remember was looking at the boards, picturing the vast body of helium above their heads and feeling a pressure build so suddenly inside her that she thought she might scream if she didn't find some way to release it. Then, independently of the rest of her body, she had watched as her hand shot out, snatched up one of the pieces between forefinger and thumb and tucked it beneath the leaves of the nearest salad.

The sense of relief – of the pressure being eased – had been immediate. But she didn't have the chance to enjoy it for long. Appearing at her side, Niamh had thrust her hands into the dumbwaiter, scooping up two of the plates.

'Don't just stand there,' she hissed. 'Get these served.'

Relief was instantly replaced with vivid terror as Ivy saw that Niamh had collected the salads. Heart leaping into her throat, she tried to call after her – to tell her to wait. But it was too late. Niamh was already making her way around the table, leaving Ivy with nothing to do but watch as she set down the tainted salad not in front of Mia, but Madison instead.

Staring, wide-eyed, as Madison inspected her plate, Ivy had waited for the meat to be found. It took an agonisingly long time. Upon receiving her starter, the American's first reaction had been to wrinkle her nose, then to raise her phone and take several pictures of it from a variety of angles. But as the others began to eat, she didn't join them.

Realising that Madison didn't plan on *eating* the salad, Ivy allowed herself to feel a small flicker of hope, and when Niamh instructed them to clear the plates she bolted towards the table, ensuring she made it to Madison first. As she loaded the plate into the dumbwaiter, she plucked the meat from beneath the leaves, depositing it onto one of the now-empty charcuterie boards.

By the time Madison noticed it in her pictures, Ivy had known she was safe. If anything, she had been satisfied. With the blame being immediately assigned to Gwyn, she was in the clear. And with the revelation that Skyline Voyages had received funding from oil barons sending Mia storming from the table, Ivy felt she had achieved her goal. While the evening's events hadn't played out as she had intended, what mattered was that the *Osprey* would no longer be featured on *Green World*. As a result of her actions, half a million Instagram followers wouldn't be duped into believing what was going on up here was good, and when she went to bed a few hours later it had been with a sense of satisfaction.

The discovery of Howard's body had changed all that. Ivy had no particular care for Howard himself. If anything, once Captain Schäfer had assured them they were safe, her first thought was that this might be a good thing. After all, his death would come as a more significant blow to Skyline Voyages than anything she could have achieved. The fact that he had been killed by his own airship even lent the situation some poetic justice.

But Mia had promptly put an end to that particular train of thought.

She could see how it must look. Ivy had insisted on a private discussion, spouting about the evils of helium and whale meat. It shouldn't have come as a surprise that Mia had deduced she was the one to tamper with Madison's salad. Just as it stood to reason that she would also assume Ivy might have been responsible for the helium leak. If their roles were reversed, Ivy expected she would harbour exactly the same suspicions.

She took a deep, shuddering breath.

Mia thought she was a killer. And what had she done about it? Panicked and made threats, before storming off in a rage. How long would it be until Mia shared those suspicions with the other passengers? And how long would it take her, once they returned to Longyearbyen, to speak to the police? All Ivy had as her defence was Captain Schäfer's insistence that a leak shouldn't be possible. And yet it had happened. Howard was dead, his room full of the sweetly scented helium.

'Ivy . . .'

Lost in her thoughts, she jumped at the sound of a voice inside her cabin, looking up to see Niamh poking her head around the door.

'I'm glad you're up here,' she said. 'Could I have a quick word?'

28

Having returned to the lounge, Chloé had been sitting at the dining table for nearly an hour, staring at her laptop as she watched the GoPro footage she had recorded during dinner.

So far, she had concluded that there was nothing to be gleaned from the food. Nobody at the table touched anything Howard ate, and if Gwyn or one of the stewards had added something to it, they had done so before it was served. Of course she couldn't rule out this possibility, considering that it seemed to be exactly what had happened with Madison's salad. But with no way of testing it from the footage alone, she instead watched what Howard drank.

She wrote off the idea of something having been in the wine. Howard didn't touch a drop all evening, presumably wary of mixing alcohol with his sleeping pills. Nor was there any chance of his water being spiked, with the bottles of glacier water being shared by everyone else at the table. She wondered about the possibility of someone adding something to his water after it had been poured, but this proved fruitless, too. The camera offered a clear view, and while various people had refilled his glass throughout the evening – she'd even refilled it herself after they toasted Isaac – no one had interfered with it. She considered whether there could have been something waiting in the bottom of his glass when they sat down. With the little wooden plaques marking each of their places, the culprit would have known exactly which one to target. But she let this theory go as well. Ben was right. Even through the frosted glass, Howard would surely have noticed a layer of powder sitting on the bottom.

The one drink he consumed that Chloé couldn't verify was the whisky they had been served at the end of the evening. Liam had been right in his suggested positioning of the GoPro; by putting it on the corner of the bar, she had an unobstructed view of the table, but this also meant she couldn't see him pour them out. Her first glimpse didn't come until he served them, making his way around the table with all nine glasses on a tray.

Given Gwyn's account of Liam acting suspiciously during the night, her heart beat more quickly at the thought of how easy it would have been for the bartender to add something to Howard's measure. After all, he'd poured and then served it himself. Likewise, he was the one who suggested Chloé set up her GoPro so that he wouldn't be in view behind the bar. But her hopes – if that was the right word – were dashed when she saw Howard take a single cursory sip, only to quickly wash it down with the glass of water she poured for him. Again, presumably mindful of mixing alcohol with his pills, Howard let the remainder of his whisky sit completely untouched. Chloé was no expert, but if Liam had spiked it, she would have been surprised if the small sip Howard had taken was enough to render him so heavily unconscious that he wouldn't stir while his cabin filled with helium.

Admitting defeat, she snapped the laptop shut. She felt dreadful, the rocking of the *Osprey* leaving her queasy after focusing so intently on the screen. But it was more than that. It had been uncomfortable seeing Howard moving around so casually in the recording, oblivious to the fact that his death was just hours away. The excellent quality of the footage was salt in the wound. With the table so beautifully laid and the coral-coloured light seeping in through the windows, Chloé was reminded of how confident she'd been that her time aboard the *Osprey* marked the beginning of a new chapter. The culmination of all her efforts these past three years. Instead she was going home to corporate copywriting work. To a single bed in her friend's spare room. At the same time she was also filled with guilt, remembering that while she was grieving a career opportunity, a member of their party had lost his life.

Eager for a distraction, she reached for her phone. It was nearly six o'clock, meaning they had a little over six hours left until they returned to Longyearbyen. There were also messages from her mum and from Ellie, both asking how the trip was going. She would need to respond at some point, but she didn't yet have the heart to type out a reply.

Letting out a sigh, she put the phone down on the table and pressed her hands to her eyes. She imagined that she was back home. Not in Ellie's flat, but in Scotland with her parents. It wasn't until she heard someone sitting down in the seat beside her that she looked again.

'Sorry,' said Mia. 'Can I sit with you?'

'Of course.' Sitting up straight, Chloé slid the laptop to one side. 'You doing OK?'

Mia didn't answer immediately. There was a solemn look about her, all of the life that she had exuded during their first day of the trip now gone. 'I think . . .' she said at last. 'Oh, God, I can't believe I'm saying this. But I'm really worried Ivy might have had something to do with what's happening up here.'

Chloé fought to keep her expression neutral. She was eager to hear more, but Mia was clearly in a fragile state. If she pounced on her, there was a good chance it would only rattle her even further.

'She took me aside yesterday afternoon,' Mia continued. 'Turns out she's a budding eco-warrior who joined Skyline because she thought it was going to help save the planet. But now she's got it in her head that helium's as bad for the environment as jet fuel, and that Ezra's lying to us all by using it.'

'What did she want you to do about it?'

'She seemed to think Ezra had tricked me into coming up here. I think she was expecting that I'd thank her for telling me, and then I'd refuse to feature Skyline on *Green World*. But I told her no. I've done my research. I know the value and the pitfalls of using helium.' Mia shook her head. 'She was gutted. You could see it in her face. Then she asked if I knew that they were serving whale at dinner, and if I wasn't opposed to *that*.' Mia looked Chloé in the eye. 'I'm not imagining it, am I? For a slice of whale meat to turn up in Madison's salad an hour later . . . And then for there to be a helium leak.'

'It'd be one hell of a coincidence,' Chloé agreed. 'But do you really think she would go so far?'

'I'm convinced Ivy put the whale in the salad. To be honest, I think it was meant for me, but the plates got mixed up somehow and Madison ended up with it instead. I think Ivy was hoping I would eat it – or at the very least *find* it – and then be so upset that I refused to cover Skyline. As for the leak . . .' Mia tailed off, gathering her thoughts. 'I don't know how she would go about that. Especially when the captain seems to think it's impossible. But I can't stop thinking about it. She comes to me ranting about the evils of Skyline using helium and then, when I don't give her the answer she's after, the owner of the company is killed *by* that helium.'

Chloé turned this over in her mind. She could see why Mia was so shaken. 'I think you're right about the whale meat,' she said. 'If the food last night was anything to go by, Gwyn seems too good a chef for it to have been an accident. And I agree it seems way too much of a coincidence for it to have happened after Ivy came to speak with you. As for Howard . . .'

She paused, thinking of the gloves Gwyn had found.

Ivy would have known there were gloves in the kitchen for her to take, just as she would have had access to Howard's food before it reached the table. If she had really wanted to sabotage the *Osprey*, it would surely occur to her that she shouldn't leave fingerprints. But how would she do it? As Mia had said, the captain seemed to believe it couldn't be done. And would Ivy really feel strongly enough about stopping Skyline that she would murder someone?

'Have you discussed any of this with her since last night?'

Mia nodded. 'I took her to one side after we . . .' She paused again. 'After we *found* Howard. I told her I wasn't accusing her of anything, but that if she knew something about what had happened, she should tell someone.'

'And how did she take that?'

'Not well.' Mia's expression darkened. 'I told you yesterday that *Green World* has had a tough year. We got caught up in a scandal, all to do with a new clothing manufacturer called Halo. They were operating in South-East Asia, supposedly providing an ethical alternative to the sweatshops that supply a lot of the big brands. The workers were being treated fairly, the materials were being sourced responsibly and the clothes themselves were really good. We did our research. We asked for pictures of the working conditions, spoke over Zoom with the suppliers and some of the workers. Everything seemed legit. So we covered them on the channel. A load of other outlets did too. But then . . .'

She faltered. Chloé listened attentively, hanging on every word.

'Then it all came out,' Mia continued. 'Some undercover job revealed that everything we'd been given was fake. All of the pictures we'd been sent had been doctored. The "workers" we spoke to were actors. It was awful.'

'But surely your followers understood. Especially if you weren't the only ones caught out.'

'Some did. But it raised questions about whether anything else we put out could be trusted. Our social following took a hit, several of our advertisers dropped us – it got so bad we had to let one of our team go. Couldn't afford to keep everyone on.'

'That's why you were so worried last night,' said Chloé. 'When it came out that Skyline had received investment from oil tycoons.'

Mia nodded. 'I might have overreacted. I understand you can't always choose where your investment comes from. But our content needs to be completely clean. I can't risk us getting hit with another Halo.' Tears appeared in the corner of her eyes. 'When I asked Ivy if she knew anything about what had happened to Howard, she thought I was accusing her of murdering him. That I must think *she'd* done it. She stormed out, but before she went, she said that if I tried to accuse her of anything else, she would out me for having been on the *Osprey*.'

Mia wiped her eyes with the back of her hand. 'Sorry. I don't mean to burden you with all of this. I'm probably . . . I don't know. It's probably all messing with my head, isn't it? Being trapped up here, all of that helium sitting right above us. I know Ezra and the captain say we don't need to worry. That what happened in Howard's cabin can't happen anywhere else. But it's hard to believe them, when his body's just out there.'

She looked towards the glass doors, staring into the corridor. 'Do you remember the glaciers we saw? Outside Longyearbyen?'

'Of course.'

'They're melting. Some of them have been here for thousands of years. But do a Google search. Look at them seven or maybe eight years ago and you'll see that they're shrinking.' She raised a hand, shielding her eyes. 'I only want to do some good. That's all I've ever wanted. And now . . .'

Chloé took her hand. She had no idea what to say. She wasn't sure there was anything she *could* say. They sat in silence, Mia's shoulders heaving as she gave in to quiet sobs.

Several minutes later the glass doors opened, Devon trudging into the lounge.

'Man alive,' Jasper announced from the couches. 'Look who's deigned to grace us with his presence. Run out of water in your cabin, have you?'

Devon didn't reply, scowling as he made his way straight to the bar. Chloé knew that Jasper was only poking fun at him, but it did look as if Devon might be struggling with a hangover. Slumping against the bar, he asked Liam for a glass of water, which he drained almost straight away.

'Don't suppose you've bothered speaking to Ezra yet,' Jasper pressed. 'Not planning to apologise for making such a spectacle of yourself last night?'

Devon didn't reply. Instead he poured a second glass of water, which this time he began to sip.

'I'll take that as a no,' said Jasper. 'You know how highly Ezra thought of his dad. If I'd come out with the shit you spewed over dinner, I expect I'd be feeling pretty ashamed of myself right now. I'd even . . . well, I don't know. I suppose I'd be trying to make some kind of *reparations*.'

Chloé saw Devon look sharply in Jasper's direction, his eyes bulging. Still, though, he said nothing. After a moment of tense silence, he lifted his glass and the bottle of glacier water from the bar and began to stride towards the door.

'Brilliant,' continued Jasper. 'Just walk away. That'll make everything better. That'll solve *all* your problems, won't it?'

This seemed to be one jibe too many. Passing the couches, Devon snapped, turning on his heel and advancing on Jasper.

'Listen, you smarmy little shit. I don't know what you've heard, but if you don't—'

'Hey!' Leaping up from the opposite couch, Ben threw himself between the two men. 'That's enough,' he called out, holding Devon at bay. 'That's enough!'

Devon leered at Jasper over Ben's shoulder, the photographer forming a steadfast barrier.

'I know that things are tense,' said Ben. 'We're all frightened and we're all desperate to get home. But we can't lose our cool while we're stuck up here. Keep it together for a few more hours. For all I care, once we're back on the ground you two can agree never to see each other again. But right now you have to *chill out*.'

The lounge fell into an uncomfortable silence as they waited to see how Devon and Jasper would respond. After what felt like a painfully long time, Devon relented, muttering something under his breath and turning towards the doors. Before he could leave, though, Mia called after him.

'Was it true?' she asked. 'What you said last night . . . Were those really Isaac's last words to Ezra?'

Pausing in his tracks, Devon looked back over his shoulder. 'Yeah,' he said quietly. 'Yeah, it was true.'

'And was that . . .' For a second, Mia looked pained. 'That can't have been how Isaac spoke to him all the time, can it? Ezra described him so affectionately. He wouldn't have given Howard that photo, wouldn't have done all of *this*,' she waved an arm around the lounge, 'in Isaac's name if that was always how he treated him.'

Devon thought for a little while. When he finally replied, he did so slowly. Cautiously. 'That was the only time I actually met Isaac. But I can easily believe it wasn't the only time he spoke to Ezra in that way.'

'What about you, Jasper?' Mia pressed. 'Did you spend much time with him?'

'I met Isaac once or twice. And yeah, he was tough. But Ezra wasn't the only kid in that school whose old man was an arsehole. You just got on with it. And if you're trying to suggest that Isaac was *abusive*—'

'No,' Devon cut him off. 'No, I'm not saying that.'

'Then what *are* you saying?'

Devon seemed to think again about leaving, his eyes straying towards the corridor. Instead he sighed, sinking onto the couch. Ben sat down next to him, clearly primed to leap up again if needed.

'Look,' said Devon, 'Ezra always spoke fondly of Isaac. The guy was his hero. But I never heard him speak about Isaac treating him with any fondness. It was always *Dad's done this* or *Dad's going to this place*. Ezra spoke about him like a celebrity. Like someone he was obsessed with from afar, rather than someone he actually knew.'

'I never heard any of that,' said Jasper. 'All I ever saw was Ezra picking fights he couldn't win.'

'That's because you didn't share a dorm with him. I used to hear it every bloody night.'

Jasper shook his head, and Chloé thought she caught him rolling his eyes.

'Who did Ezra fight?' she asked.

'Everyone,' said Jasper. 'He couldn't stand being the scrawniest kid in the school. If you so much as looked at him in a way he didn't like, he'd take a swing at you.'

'And the fact he never won these fights didn't put him off?'

'Well, he had something of a protector. Didn't he, Devon?' Jasper's eyes flicked towards the opposite couch. 'You were always stepping in and defending him. Alec and I could never understand why.'

Devon shrugged. 'I felt sorry for him. Hearing Ezra go

on about Isaac every evening, and then seeing how hard he would push himself every day . . . It made a bit more sense after I'd overheard Isaac on the day of the challenge. But even before that, with the way he'd get himself pummelled on the rugby pitch, or would throw a punch at a boy twice his size for giving him a dirty look – I think I knew there was something going on. I couldn't just let him get his head kicked in.'

'That was kind of you,' said Mia.

'It was bloody stupid,' said Jasper. 'If you'd left Ezra to it – let him get roughed up a couple of times – he'd soon have piped down.'

Devon seemed to have nothing to say to this, taking another sip of his water.

'I can't understand why you would want to please someone like that so badly,' said Chloé.

Devon grimaced. 'Try to put yourself in Ezra's shoes. Isaac's father – Ezra's grandfather – came from money, but he lost it all on the stock market and drank himself to death when Isaac was a teenager. The way Ezra used to tell it, Isaac then raises himself up from nothing to become one of the youngest airline pilots ever to qualify. He starts his own cargo carrier just before he turns thirty. He travels the world with Howard, has ideas like *this*.' Devon flicked a glance at the lounge. 'In another life he'd have been rubbing shoulders with Richard Branson. With a CV like that, you can easily see why he'd have high expectations of his only son.'

'And why Ezra would be so eager to make him proud,' Mia added.

'But did the teachers not care?' asked Chloé. 'At this school of yours. Could they not see that Ezra was . . . I don't know. That he was *struggling*?'

Jasper snorted. 'A school like that didn't exactly pride itself on having open conversations about mental well-being. People hear the words "boarding school" and they picture white bow ties and cricket in the sunshine. But that place was *hard*. We're talking cold porridge for breakfast, frost inside the windows during the winter. If they could have got away with *caning*, I reckon they probably would have tried. It wasn't somewhere you sent your kid if you were concerned about them being happy.'

Chloé mulled this over, even the choice of Ezra's school painting a clearer picture of his relationship with his father. She thought she could understand how he must feel. But as she looked around the lounge – saw the lengths to which he'd gone to prove himself Isaac's successor – she couldn't help but feel saddened. She thought of her own little family unit, trying to imagine one of her parents speaking to her in the way Devon had described. It wasn't just heartbreaking. It was unfathomable. Her thoughts turned back to the Normanstone challenge and, as she pictured Isaac telling Ezra how ashamed he was, she found this time that her sorrow turned to anger.

'How did Isaac die?' She addressed the room as a whole, any prior reluctance to voice this question now gone. 'I know that he and Howard were travelling to the North Pole. But how did it happen?'

Jasper looked at Devon. 'You're probably best qualified to answer that one. Our resident mountaineer.'

Devon winced. 'It was a group of them skiing to the Pole. For most of the trek the ice is supposed to be over six feet thick. But at some point their guide must have led them onto a patch that wasn't stable. Maybe the snow made it look safer than it actually was. Maybe the guide wasn't any good. It doesn't matter. All that matters is that the ice gave way, the line connecting Isaac to the rest of the group failed and his gear dragged him down into the water.'

'But how did the line fail?' Chloé pressed. 'Isn't the whole point of having one that it *doesn't* fail?'

Devon's expression darkened. 'Accidents happen. Sometimes equipment just gives out.'

'You would know,' Jasper murmured.

Devon's nostrils flared, and as the two of them locked eyes, Chloé was convinced she might be about to see another confrontation. Ben clearly thought the same thing, tensing in preparation to leap between them again. But Devon seemed eventually to think better of it. His shoulders slumped, and with a scowl he let his gaze drop to the floor.

'That's an awful way to go,' said Chloé. 'It must have been tough for Ezra.'

'He was in a bad way,' Devon agreed. 'For the best part of three months he barely ate, barely slept. Barely spoke a word. Then Howard told him about Skyline Voyages.' Devon shook his head. 'I can remember it even now. After twenty years. He sat Ezra and his mum down in the kitchen and told them that he and Isaac had come up with the idea during their trip. I think he might have been asking for their blessing, or something to that effect.'

'He didn't ask Ezra to help him then?'

'He hardly needed to. If anything, Howard was trying to convince him to cool his jets. Ezra was only seventeen, remember. Howard was telling him not to rush into anything. Said he should study something sensible at uni. Take some time to figure out what he wanted to do. But the moment he brought it up, Ezra was on board. Skyline became his North Star. His whole world. After that conversation, Howard drew up the plans that he and Isaac had discussed in the days before he died, and Ezra decided that as soon as he was old enough he was going to help make it happen.'

'And now this has happened.' It was Mia who spoke up this time, but no one answered. Not even Jasper had a comment to make.

'Were Ezra and Howard close?' asked Chloé. 'Before Skyline?'

Devon's brow furrowed. 'I don't think so. I remember him talking in our dorm about Isaac and Howard's trips around the world together. But Howard was always Isaac's friend, rather than anything to Ezra. I suppose that changed after Isaac died, though. Howard was at the house all the time, checking in on them both. Seeing how they were doing.'

'Alec and I thought he wanted a crack at Ezra's mum,' said Jasper.

'Bollocks,' Devon snapped at him. 'Isaac's death hit Howard *hard*. I remember a day when we were both visiting. I went upstairs to the bathroom, and at the end of the landing I saw that the door to Isaac's study was open. Howard was sitting at the desk, head in his hands. The guy was distraught.'

Jasper shook his head. 'If you say so,' he murmured.

'What was he doing in the study?' asked Ben.

Devon gave a little shrug. 'He helped Ezra's mum sell the cargo airline that Isaac had set up. I think he might have been helping with some of the legal stuff that needed dealing with, too. The will and the house. That sort of thing. He spent hours in there, going through Isaac's documents.'

'And why did he wait?' asked Chloé. 'You say that Howard didn't mention Skyline Voyages until two – nearly three – months after he'd come back from the Pole. It sounds like he must have had plenty of opportunity if he was at the house so often. So why didn't he say anything sooner?'

Devon frowned. 'I expect they had a lot on their minds. The funeral, the airline . . . He probably didn't have a chance to think about it until after things had started to settle down. Maybe he was in two minds about doing it at all. Isaac was his friend; they were going to do it together. It might have taken Howard that time just to decide that he was going to attempt it on his own.'

Chloé supposed this made sense. She pictured the scene Devon had described: Howard sitting bereft in Isaac's office, head in his hands.

At that moment there was movement in the corridor. Following Devon's gaze, Chloé saw through the glass doors that Captain Schäfer was putting on the oxygen mask, getting ready to test the helium in Howard's cabin again. Niamh and Ezra were there, too, watching stoically as Schäfer opened the door and disappeared inside.

'Everything OK?' asked Mia.

Devon was staring, brow furrowed.

'Devon?'

He didn't reply, rising silently from the couch.

'Where are you going *now*?' Jasper protested.

Devon shot him a look. 'You wanted me to apologise, didn't you?'

Jasper seemed puzzled, but before he could say anything more, Devon had gone out into the corridor, the glass doors closing behind him. Chloé saw Ezra tense, but he stayed where he was, listening for a minute as Devon spoke. She wished someone would stand closer to the doors, so that they would slide open and she could hear what was being said. But it was no good. A moment later Ezra ushered Devon into his cabin.

'Jasper,' said Ben, 'what did you mean? That comment to Devon, about Isaac's safety line failing: *You would know*. What were you talking about?'

'Ah . . .' Jasper clasped his hands in his lap, tilting his

head to hide a small grin. 'I really shouldn't say. It isn't my place to gossip about Devon's business.'

'But I get the sense you're going to do it anyway.' Mia fixed him with a hard look, which only seemed to amuse him even more.

'I don't know all the details,' he said. 'But I'm fairly certain there must have been an accident of some kind, involving one of the tourists Devon takes on these trips into the mountains.'

'What makes you say that?' asked Chloé.

Jasper looked her straight in the eye, having to chew the corner of his lip to keep his grin from growing any wider. 'Devon's being sued,' he said. 'To the tune of one hundred and fifty thousand pounds.'

29

As Niamh closed the office door, sealing them inside, Liam felt his palms begin to sweat.

'I'll make this brief,' she said. 'I don't want to keep you away from the lounge, but we need to have a word about your keycard.'

'My keycard?'

'That's right. See . . . I've been speaking with Ivy. And she seems to think you left it in Tromsø.'

Fighting to keep a straight face, Liam cursed inside his head. Why the *hell* would Ivy tell her that? Fully aware of where this question must be leading, he clenched his jaw. Keep it together, he reminded himself. *Just keep it together*.

'Yeah,' he said. 'Yeah, that's right. I'm really sorry. It won't happen—'

'I don't suppose,' Niamh continued, 'that you've taken the spare from the safe at any point. Only it's been moved since yesterday morning.'

His heart beginning to beat a little quicker, Liam's eyes strayed towards the safe nestled beneath the desk. He remembered how nervous he'd been. Even in the middle of the night, well aware that the others were all asleep, he'd thrown hurried glances over his shoulder as he typed in the code and snatched up the card.

'No,' he said, hoping he sounded more convincing than he felt. 'I haven't touched it. Even if I wanted to, I wouldn't know the code.'

'That's what I thought. But it's occurred to me that the last time I opened the safe, you were there.' Niamh looked him straight in the eye. 'You remember, don't you? I brought you in here to give you the balloon for Mr Berry's cabin. Before you left I had to lock some paperwork away. I can't help but wonder if perhaps you saw me typing in the code and then borrowed the card to hide the fact you'd forgotten yours.'

Cursing again inside his head, Liam fought to keep his expression as neutral as possible. He needed to tell the most convincing lie of his life. Better than any he had ever used to charm his way through an interview or tempt a girl back to his cabin. More effective than any attempt to skip a shift or impress an important guest. Depending on how well he delivered them, his next words could determine whether Niamh believed that he had played a role in a man's death.

'I do remember,' he said, carefully layering some confusion in his voice, 'but I didn't *need* the spare. It was Ivy who told you I'd forgotten my card, right? She only knew about it because I borrowed hers to finish making up the cabins before we picked up the guests. Aside from that, I haven't needed one.'

That had been good, he thought to himself. Over the years he'd found that the trick to telling a perfect lie was to mix it with the truth. Of course he'd seen Niamh typing in the code to the safe, and he had absolutely taken advantage of that during the night to steal the spare card. But it was also true that he had borrowed Ivy's to do some housekeeping before the passengers came aboard. Niamh would surely know that – Ivy would presumably have told her. With a bit of luck, it would help to convince her of the rest of his story.

Heart thundering against his ribs, he watched Niamh's face, scanning for any sign that she might doubt him.

'Listen very carefully,' she said. 'It's all right if you took it. But I need to know. Because *someone* has, and I'm sure I don't need to tell you that as well as the guests' cabins, the staff keycards open the door to the electronics bay.'

Liam felt a lump rise in his throat. Swallowing it back down, he forced himself to look her in the eye. 'Sorry,' he said. 'I don't know what to tell you. But if I hear anything from one of the others, I'll be sure to let you know.'

Niamh's eyes narrowed. Did she believe him? He couldn't tell.

Finally she sighed. 'Fine,' she said. 'Get yourself back to the lounge, please.'

Stepping back into the corridor, Liam closed the office door behind him and made his way to the bathroom as quickly as he could without running. Locking himself inside, he turned on the tap and splashed water on his face. It was freezing, so cold that it made him gasp. It soaked into his shirt and dripped onto the floor, his skin turning red as he stared into the mirror. He didn't care. With his entire body trembling, he took a long, slow breath. Then another. Then, when he was just about certain that he wasn't going to have a panic attack, he darted across the corridor to the cabin he shared with Gwyn, where he hurriedly towelled dry his face and hair. Changing out of his sodden shirt, he wasn't quite calm, but he at least felt a little steadier.

His shaky tranquillity didn't last long. As he was about to leave, Gwyn barged into the cabin, a determined expression on his face. Panicking, Liam tried to slip past him, but the chef blocked his path.

'I have to get back—'

'I don't care.' Gwyn shoved him into the centre of the cabin, closing the door to cut off his escape. 'Last night,' he said, 'when you got up and went wandering about. Where did you go?'

Liam felt his palms begin to itch, his pulse rising again. He thought the bastard had been asleep. He'd been sure . . .

He clenched his fists, thinking about whether he could scurry past and make a run for it. He'd never be able to. Not with the door closed and Gwyn planted squarely in front of it.

'What's your problem?' he demanded. 'Am I not allowed to go to the bog?'

Gwyn scowled at him. 'The bathroom's right across the corridor, idiot. If that was where you went, I'd have heard you *flushing*.' He took a step closer, towering over Liam.

'D'you want to know what I think? I think you went to turn off my fridge. And at the crack of dawn this morning you turned it back on.'

'Are you serious?' Liam tried to laugh the accusation away, but it came out all wrong, strangled and weak. 'You spend too much time alone in that—'

'What about the whale meat?' Gwyn pressed. 'In Madison's salad. Was that you as well? Jade seems to think it couldn't have been. Says you weren't anywhere near the dumbwaiter when I sent them down. But I'm not so convinced. I reckon a sneaky little guy like you could make it work.'

At this, Liam was able to summon a morsel of genuine defiance. 'You're off your rocker, mate. I haven't messed with your fridge, and I sure as shit didn't touch your bloody salads. Now get out of my way or I'll shout for Niamh.'

He thought Gwyn might refuse, but after a long pause the chef stepped aside. Without a second's hesitation, Liam swept from the little room. Almost immediately, however, he stopped, the sound of hurried footsteps echoing towards him. Listening as the footsteps faded away, he realised that someone was descending the stairwell, making a frantic dash for the lower deck.

Gwyn heard it too, coming to join him in the corridor. At first the chef looked confused. Then an expression of pure fury spread across his face. Following his gaze, Liam saw what had caught his attention. It was the kitchen door, gently swaying on its hinges.

30

As he sat alone on the leather couch, Jasper's mood was growing vicious. He'd had more than enough of this now and, with every passing minute, was becoming increasingly eager to be back on the ground.

He looked around the lounge, taking in Chloé and Mia at the table, and Astrid and Ben on the other couch. He was sick of the sight of them. Of their worried faces and the nervous tones in which they insisted on speaking, as if it would somehow make their situation better. With every shudder of the *Osprey* or scrap of inane chatter, he could feel himself becoming more irritable, the sensation of being trapped clinging to his skin like a set of wet clothes that he couldn't remove. Even the stewards looked terrible. It was Jade and Ivy who were on hand, Liam having been taken upstairs for a word with Niamh. Ivy, in particular, looked as if she might break down at any moment, flicking anxious little glances towards Mia and Chloé.

He couldn't even go back to his cabin for some privacy.

It had been a good couple of hours since he'd left Maddie in there alone, and he knew that every minute he stayed away would only be stoking her wrath further. Even now he could feel his phone buzzing in his pocket. She had been messaging him incessantly, demanding in increasingly unambiguous terms that he come back. Jasper hadn't bothered to read the last few messages, but he could feel them coming through, the time between each one growing shorter and shorter.

And all the while, to think that Devon had really gone to apologise . . .

Jasper couldn't quite believe it. When he had suggested it, he had only been trying to get a reaction. To get under Devon's skin. He hadn't thought it would actually happen. But Devon and Ezra had been gone now for fifteen minutes – whatever they were talking about, they must really be getting into it. The situation only irritated him further. He'd enjoyed seeing Devon slip up over dinner. Inadvertently helping him make amends was considerably less satisfying.

Feeling his phone buzz again in his pocket, he swore under his breath. It wasn't that the thought of facing off with Maddie frightened him. It was more that, after a couple of hours spent thinking about breaking things off once they'd made it back home, he simply didn't want to deal with the tantrum she was brewing. He took a breath, trying to keep his frustration from rising. They still had some distance to cover before they returned to Longyearbyen, with nothing to be seen through the windows but water and ice in every direction. He couldn't let his temper get the better of him now.

Turning his mind back to the conversation that was currently taking place in Ezra's cabin, he tried to imagine what the two of them might be discussing. Perhaps it wasn't an apology that was taking them so long. Perhaps Ezra was grilling Devon about his financial difficulties, demanding to know whether he'd been recruited as a saboteur by Airborne Expeditions.

He dismissed the thought as quickly as it had arrived. When he'd suggested this idea, Jasper had only half-believed it himself. If he was completely honest, he didn't think Devon was smart enough to pull off something like that. On the other hand, accidentally killing someone while attempting a harmless bit of sabotage seemed exactly the sort of bumble that only Devon would be capable of. Perhaps it really had been him.

As if on cue, he heard the glass doors part and twisted in his seat to see Devon returning to the lounge. He waited for Ezra to come through too, but there was no sign of him. For whatever reason, he had stayed behind.

Jasper didn't move, watching Devon intently. He didn't look as if Ezra had just put him in his place. If anything, as he seated himself at the bar he appeared pretty pleased with himself. Jasper tried to look away. To put it out of his mind. But his curiosity quickly became too powerful to ignore. Could the smug bastard really have made amends? He had to know.

Raising himself from the couch, he turned towards the

glass doors, almost barging straight into Liam. God, he looked in a sorry state, too. Brushing past the pale-faced bartender, Jasper went straight to the end of the corridor and knocked on Ezra's door. When no answer came, he tried again. Still there was only silence.

In the bathroom, Jasper supposed. Or maybe on another of his many Zoom calls with the office in Tromsø. Growing ever more frustrated, he went back into the lounge, where he saw that Liam had taken up his post again behind the bar and was pouring Devon a glass of glacier water.

What the hell had been said in that cabin? He tried again to put the thought out of his mind, but as his eyes lingered on Devon, his need to know became overpowering.

Striding towards the bar, he leaned in close so that he could keep his voice low. 'You were gone a while,' he said. 'What were the two of you talking about?'

Devon's eyes narrowed. 'I was apologising. Exactly as you suggested. Or are you going to tell me now that I shouldn't have?'

Before Jasper could answer, the doors opened once more. Hoping for Ezra, his heart sank when he saw that it was Madison instead.

'You!' Glaring at him, she stormed across the lounge. 'Why the *fuck* aren't you looking at your phone? I know you have it.'

'Not now, Maddie.'

'Don't tell me *not now*. Why aren't you coming back to

the room? You know I don't want to be out here. You've been gone for *hours*.'

'Maddie, will you shut up!'

Her mouth fell open in a silent gasp, but Jasper didn't pause to placate her. Instead he turned straight back to Devon, hissing through gritted teeth.

'I'm on to you, Dev. I saw your phone yesterday. A hundred and fifty grand? What did you do? Let some tourist fall down a mountain?'

This prompted a reaction. Devon rose to his feet, towering over Jasper. Behind the bar, Liam looked terrified at the prospect of a fight breaking out, but Jasper was undeterred.

'You want to know what I think?' he pressed. 'I think if our friends in Dubai have had something to do with what's happened up here, then your door should be the first Ezra knocks on.'

'Boys!' This time, it *was* Ezra. Calling out to them, he hurried across the lounge, carrying his phone in one hand and a glass of water in the other. Setting them down on the bar, he gripped each of their shoulders. 'What's going on?'

'You tell me,' said Devon. 'This little shit's just come over and accused me of being *bribed*.'

'Look,' Ezra said sternly, 'I know that emotions are running high. Everyone's frightened. But let's all calm down. We still have a few hours left before we're back. We can't afford to—'

'Will you stop looking at me!' Turning to face the voice, Jasper saw that it was Ivy who had spoken. Appearing close to tears, she seemed to be addressing Mia and Chloé. 'Stop it,' she wailed. 'Will you just *stop it*!'

'Ivy . . .' said Mia, 'no one's looking at you.'

'Yes, you are. I've seen you. You're *staring* at me. And *she's* been staring at me, too!' Ivy shot a look at Chloé. 'I haven't done anything! You think I killed him, but I haven't *done anything*!'

Silence fell, the entire group so perplexed by this outburst that Jasper momentarily forgot his quarrel with Devon. The ceasefire didn't last long, though. Because now it was Gwyn who came barging into the lounge.

'Who's been in my kitchen?' he demanded. When no one replied, he adopted a fierce expression. 'I know someone's been in there. I heard you running down the stairwell a few minutes ago. Liam heard it, too, so you might as well come clean.'

Jasper stared at him, taking in the chef's wild eyes and trembling fists. Bloody hell, he thought to himself. To think he'd considered giving this lunatic a job.

'Fine,' Gwyn spat. 'I can't see what you've done yet. Or what you've taken. But I will. I'll work it out and, when I do, you'll—'

'Enough!' Ezra raised his voice, silencing the chef in an instant, then strode into the centre of the lounge. 'All of you. *Enough*. I know you're frightened. I am, too, and I'm so, so sorry to have put you all in this position. But we need to remain calm. We have to *band together*.' He sighed, running a hand through his hair. 'Gwyn. I don't know what you heard up there, but no one has been in your kitchen. And Ivy, I'm certain no one thinks you're responsible for what's happened to Howard. As for you two . . .' He turned to the bar, fixing Jasper and Devon with a desperate, pleading expression. 'You're my oldest friends. I know you don't always see eye to eye. But could you, please, for the next few hours . . .'

He tailed off, confusion spreading across his face. For a second Jasper thought he was looking at *him*. Then he heard it. Beside him, Devon was starting to make rasping noises.

'Dev . . .' Ezra took a tentative step towards him. 'Dev, what are you . . . ?'

But Devon didn't answer. It didn't seem as if he could. Jasper watched as his chest began to heave, his eyes bulging.

'Dev,' Ezra repeated, fear building in his voice. 'Devon, what's happening?'

Devon tried to answer him, but no words came. He reached with one hand for his throat, while with the other he dropped his glass to the ground. Jasper watched as it landed with a soft thump, the last few drops of water staining the carpet.

'Jesus Christ . . .' Ezra wheeled on the spot, turning towards the bar. 'Liam! What was in that drink?'

Liam shook his head, staring at Devon in total disbelief.

'He can't breathe,' said Mia. 'He can't breathe!'

She was right. Jasper could hear small, desperate noises escaping from Devon's throat, his lips still parted. His eyes were now like golf balls, his whole body convulsing as he fought to draw breath. He took a single step away from the bar before dropping to one knee, gripping the dining table to steady himself.

'Liam!' Ezra roared. 'What did you put in his drink?'

Liam couldn't answer, leaving them all to watch as Devon's face turned red. Then, at last, his struggle ceased. A final strangled noise gurgled in the back of his throat and he fell silent, tipping forward onto the carpet.

31

Chloé's second day aboard the *Osprey* now marked two morbid first experiences. In Howard, she had seen her first corpse. And in Devon, she'd had her first brush with death itself.

On the rare occasion she had ever pictured someone dying, it had been like in a film. Quick. Clean. Devon's death had been neither of those things. From the look in his eyes, it was clear that he had been afraid and in a great deal of pain.

The moment he hit the floor, Madison let out a scream that quickly became a sob. Jade went running to the upper deck in search of Niamh and Captain Schäfer, while Ezra fell to his knees, rolling Devon onto his back as he searched for an EpiPen. Finding only a keycard, he sprinted to Devon's cabin, returning a minute later with a small black pouch. There was a brief, frantic discussion of how to correctly use the pen, before Niamh swiped it from Ezra's hand and jabbed it into Devon's thigh. But by the time it had finally been administered, they could all see that it was too late.

Chloé didn't say anything. She was so taken aback by the horrific spectacle of Devon's death that she could barely think. She went to stand with Ben and Mia, both of whom were watching, stricken-faced. Chloé couldn't even look. Devon's expression, wild and frantic, was burned into her mind. The choking sounds he'd made during his final moments filled her ears on a loop.

After Niamh had spent several fruitless minutes attempting to resuscitate him, it was reluctantly agreed that Devon was beyond help. Lifting him carefully from the ground, Ezra, Jasper, Ben and Schäfer carried him to his cabin. Not a word was spoken while they were away. The group fell into sombre silence, the only sound the howling of the wind outside.

Desperate to be away, but with no desire to go back to the cramped confines of her cabin, Chloé went to the window. The ice was becoming sparser now. As they put the Pole further and further behind them, the white mosaic had become a tumultuous sea, chunks of ice cast adrift like craggy white islands. Staring down on the freezing water, with the skies around them grey and angry, she yearned to be home, so despondent that she didn't even care any more about her doomed feature. As she thought of Howard and Devon – even Isaac Day, lost beneath the ice – she wished more than ever to be back in London's hustle and bustle, or with her parents in Scotland. She thought of the tree in their front garden and how any day now it would turn golden, the leaves falling gently onto her mum's old Renault Clio. The thought of the car was, bizarrely, a small source of comfort. It had needed replacing for years – in truth, it was barely roadworthy – but her mum refused to get rid of it. It was old and French, she would say. Just like her. And if she could keep going, so could the Renault.

But what first came as a comforting memory quickly caused Chloé's heart to sink even further. Because she wasn't going home. Far from it. While they might have only a few hours left aboard the *Osprey*, the fact of the matter was that they were going to Longyearbyen. And with a police investigation awaiting them – an investigation into not one, but now two suspicious deaths – who could say when they would be allowed to leave?

Feeling herself sink even deeper into despair, she took out her phone. She wanted to call home. She wanted a sample of her dad's endless, unwavering optimism, or to hear her mum chirping, *C'est trop beau pour être vrai*. But of course she couldn't. Even if there had been a signal, what would she say? How could she possibly explain what had happened since they last spoke?

In a final bid to shut out the *Osprey*, she put the phone away and pressed the heels of her hands to her eyes, applying pressure until little white spots began to appear in the darkness. She pictured the Renault, forcing herself not to think of the helium that lingered like a spectre above their heads. And there she stayed until those who had carried Devon's body returned solemnly to the lounge.

'How did it even happen?' Madison broke the silence. 'Devon was just there. He was . . .'

She tailed off, having to fight back another sob. In

answer to her question, Ezra went straight behind the bar, where Chloé watched him glare at the surfaces. His eyes darting back and forth, he scowled, failing to find whatever he was searching for. Then he ducked out of sight, emerging a moment later with a small plastic bin.

Liam, who since the moment Devon keeled over had been sitting silently at the table, watched this inspection with a mixture of fear and puzzlement. But when Ezra, his expression grave, reached into the bin and withdrew half of a freshly squeezed lemon, terror broke out across the young bartender's face.

'No!' he cried, springing to his feet. 'I haven't touched that!'

'It's behind *your* bar, Liam,' said Ezra. 'And I assume it was you who poured Devon the water he'd been drinking.'

'I don't care,' Liam's voice rose. 'I didn't put that in his drink!' He was backing away, eyes fixed on the lemon. 'I didn't do it,' he stammered. 'I didn't do it!'

'Liam—'

'I didn't kill them!'

The room fell silent, with each of them, it seemed to Chloé, reaching exactly the same realisation at once.

'Him,' Liam said quickly. 'I didn't kill *him*.'

But the damage was done. 'That's not what you said,' Jasper spat at him. 'You said *them*. Why would you say *them* when Ezra only asked you about Devon?'

Liam, so visibly terrified that he could barely form a sentence, stammered something about being confused.

About making a mistake. But looking around the group, Chloé could see the doubt on each of their faces.

'Liam,' Ezra's voice was firm, eyes blazing, 'if you know anything about what happened to Howard – anything at all – you have to tell us.'

The lounge was dead-silent, everyone waiting as Liam's lips quivered. After a few moments had passed with no sign of a reply, Ezra held up the lemon.

'Listen to me. This was an accident. I don't think anyone here believes you would give it to Devon deliberately. But you're going to have to talk to the police. That's a fact. There's no escaping it. And if it comes out later that you know something about Howard which you haven't shared, I expect it'll be considerably more difficult to persuade them that *this*,' again he brandished the lemon, 'really was an honest mistake.'

For what felt to Chloé like an eternity, they watched as Liam stared at the lemon. Then, just as she became convinced that he was too petrified to say anything more, he burst into tears.

'Oh, God,' he stuttered. '*Oh my God . . .*'

Ezra crossed the lounge, stony-faced, and took the seat beside him. If Liam noticed, he didn't show it. He wept for several minutes, hands pressed to his face. When, finally, he'd gained enough self-control to speak, he looked up at Ezra with wet, bloodshot eyes.

'I didn't know what I was doing,' he said. 'Please believe me. I didn't know . . .'

'What have you done, Liam?' Ezra glared at him,

waiting for the young bartender to reply. When no answer came, his voice rose, causing Chloé to jump so violently she gave an involuntary whimper. '*What have you done?*'

Flinching, Liam screwed his eyes shut, drawing a deep breath. 'I've . . . I've been messing around with things up here. During the night. I've been . . .' He tailed off.

'What things, Liam? What have you tampered with?'

'Some of the blackout blinds. In the cabins. I did those after we set out from Tromsø. And then during the night I turned off the walk-in fridge. Made Gwyn think it wasn't working properly. And I . . .' He swallowed back a lump. 'I messed with the air conditioning.'

Ezra threw a glance at Schäfer. Chloé could see what was passing between them. It was on all their minds: Liam had interfered with the climate-control system.

Ezra leaned forward another inch in his seat. 'Why? Why have you done this?'

Terrified, Liam braced himself, then said, 'Because Airborne Expeditions are going to pay me for it.'

Chloé looked around the lounge. She could see in everyone's faces, serious and sombre, that this revelation frightened them as much as it did her.

'We can't do this here,' said Captain Schäfer. 'We should take him—'

'They wanted to pull ahead.' Liam cut across him, his voice becoming frantic. 'They wanted you to think the *Osprey* wasn't working properly. Wanted to ground it long enough for them to start operating first. But I think . . .'

He looked wildly at Ezra. 'Well, that doesn't make sense, does it? The fridge, the blinds, the air conditioning – I didn't think about it at the time. The money was too good, and it's not as if any of it was going to . . .' He paused. 'Was going to *hurt* someone. But thinking about it now, those things surely wouldn't ground the *Osprey* for long enough. A helium leak, though? That would do it.' He took a shuddering breath. 'I think they must have someone else. In Tromsø. Someone who set things up so that when I messed with the temperature, it let the helium in.' Tears beaded in the corner of his eyes again. 'I'm sorry,' he said. 'I'm so sorry. I didn't think – I had no idea it would . . .'

He began once again to sob uncontrollably, shoulders heaving. The rest of them watched, hanging on every morbid word.

When, finally, Liam's sobbing subsided, Captain Schäfer addressed him. Unlike Ezra, he made no attempt to soften his tone. 'Do you have any proof?' he asked sharply. 'Messages? Emails?'

Liam flinched again, then shook his head. 'Everything was done by text message. It all came from a withheld number. The last one was yesterday morning, about twenty minutes before we picked you up.'

Schäfer looked to Ezra. 'It's unlikely, but if we give those messages to the police there's a chance they might be able to trace—'

'No.' Liam interrupted him. 'No, I've . . . I've deleted them. All of them.'

Schäfer's nostrils flared. 'So how can you even be sure that they were who they said they were? Anyone texting you from a withheld number could say that they were from Airborne Expeditions.'

Liam looked confused. 'I guess so. But who else would want to sabotage Skyline Voyages?' He closed his eyes. 'The things they knew . . . About how the *Osprey* works, where I would need to go. They knew exactly what was going to happen. They said that if the airship was freezing but the settings in the electronics bay were all correct, then it would look like the climate-control system had glitched during the night.' He shook his head. 'They've *got* to have someone in Tromsø, right? To know those things. They've *got* to.'

At this, Chloé found herself frowning, something about what Liam had just said snagging on her mind. Before she could consider it, though, Ezra pounced on him again.

'What about payment? You said they'd paid you to do this. A good forensic accountant might be able to trace that.'

Liam's eyes dropped to the ground. 'They were going to pay after we got back to Tromsø.'

Ezra's shoulders sank and, across the lounge, Jasper snorted.

'Idiot,' he said. 'You're never going to see a penny.'

The group fell silent, the realisation sinking in that there really might be no way to trace whoever Liam had been in touch with.

'So you *did* take the spare keycard.' Chloé turned to face Niamh, who looked accusingly at Liam.

'Keycard?' Schäfer's eyes narrowed. 'What keycard?'

'Each of the stewards has a master card,' Niamh explained. 'With one spare kept in the office, locked inside the safe. I was *convinced* this morning that someone had touched it during the night.'

'How can you be so sure?' asked Ezra.

'It has a Skyline Voyages logo on one side. I've got into the habit of keeping it face-up, with the logo on show, and when I last went into the safe, yesterday morning, that's how it was. But today it's face-down.' She glared at Liam, who looked like he might be sick. 'You needed a staff keycard to get into the electronics bay, but you'd left yours in Tromsø. So you watched me type in the combination and took the spare during the night.'

Liam gave a small nod, unable to meet her eye.

'And what about Devon?' It was Jasper who spoke up this time. 'He's dead now too.'

'I didn't do that.' Liam's eyes flew wide, terror taking him again. 'I *didn't*. I would know it!'

'Liam . . .' Ezra silenced him with a single word, eyes boring into him with as much hatred as Chloé thought she had ever seen. '*You* gave him that glass of water. That lemon was in the bin behind *your* bar.'

'But I didn't—'

'You're a *mess*. We can all see it. You probably did it without even noticing.'

This time Liam said nothing, his gaze sinking to the floor.

'Captain,' Ezra said sharply. 'How long until we return to Longyearbyen?'

'A little over three hours.'

Ezra nodded, rounding once more on Liam. 'You're going to stay here. Right here. Where we can all watch you. In the meantime, captain, may I suggest you radio the ground crew and have them relay to the police everything that's happened? I want them ready to meet us the minute we land.'

Monday 15 September 2025

After the flight

32

In the early hours of Monday morning, a little after midnight, the *Osprey* returned to Longyearbyen.

The remaining leg of the journey was spent largely in silence, no one having the spirit to attempt conversation. Sitting at the top of the dining table, expression vacant and hands tightly clasped, Liam seemed almost not to notice that they were there. Chloé imagined he must be bracing himself for the police questioning that he would soon receive, rehearsing his explanation for his actions during the night.

For the last hour or two they drifted around the lounge, slumped on the couches and sitting at the table. As they passed over the northernmost coast of Svalbard and began making their way over the Spitsbergen National Park, no one looked for bears. No one even commented on the herd of reindeer that at one point massed beneath them.

Mercifully the storm began at last to ease, the *Osprey* steadying beneath their feet. Chloé found that she had grown so used to the airship's rocking and churning that it felt strange not having to constantly right herself. But the weather wasn't through with them yet. With an hour left of their journey, snow began to fall. It came down lightly at first, but grew heavier by the minute. By the time they reached the landing site, it was coming down so determinedly that, even in the hazy light that substituted for nightfall, Chloé could barely make out the mountains flanking them.

Joining the others by the windows, she watched as the pilots lowered the *Osprey* into the same valley from which they had taken off just thirty-six hours earlier. As the ground came up to meet them, she saw a hive of activity. The ground crew who had seen them off moved frantically around, guiding the *Osprey* in to land, while a black four-by-four sporting flashing blue lights stood a short distance away. Immediately Chloé knew it must be a police vehicle. The same coach that had brought them from the hotel also waited nearby, parked at the point where the road came to an end.

Once the *Osprey* had touched down with a slight bump, Nora, the member of the ground crew who had ushered them aboard, swept into the lounge. Flanked by a pair of police officers, she began calling out instructions for disembarking. Her voice seemed impossibly loud, the first to be heard inside the lounge in nearly three hours.

Liam left first, accompanying the police officers without resistance. Still standing at the window, Chloé watched as he was loaded into the back of the car. The rest of them were then instructed to gather their belongings from their cabins and make their way onto the coach. Liam's statement would be taken straight away, while the others would each be required to give theirs in the morning. When Madison asked how long they would need to stay in Longyearbyen, Nora couldn't answer. All she would say was that they would be escorted at some point to the town's tiny shopping mall, where any additional clothes they might need would be paid for by Skyline Voyages. Chloé's heart sank, realising that they might be staying much longer than she had dared to hope.

Zipping her laptop and GoPro into her rucksack, when it was her turn to be ushered down the little ladder, Chloé was so desperate to be free – to be away from the bodies, and to no longer have the helium suspended above her head – that she practically threw herself through the door. The cold struck her immediately, prickling her skin and forcing the breath from her lungs. Snow crunched beneath her feet, and within seconds she could feel it settling in her hair. She didn't care. If she was honest, she barely even noticed. The relief that she felt at being away from the *Osprey* was more powerful than anything the elements could throw at her.

Two more members of the ground crew beckoned her forward. Chloé was certain that more of them had rifles slung over their shoulders than on the morning they'd left, although she didn't stop to ponder this, hurrying instead towards the sanctuary of the coach.

No one spoke as they settled into their seats. Chloé didn't even express her surprise at seeing Gwyn and the remaining stewards join them a few moments later. It seemed the local police wanted to speak to them as well, before allowing them to return to Tromsø.

Once everyone was aboard, the engine rumbled into life and they began to roll forward. As they went, Chloé took one last look at the *Osprey*. She couldn't say if it was exhaustion, the thought of Howard and Devon still on board or the sheer distance that still remained between herself and home, but the sight of it prompted a sudden surge of emotion. Grounded, with vehicles and men moving frantically around as it strained against the propellers in an effort to return to the sky . . . in the end it was too much. With tears threatening to form in the corners of her eyes, she had to look away.

They trundled silently back into Longyearbyen. At that time of night not even the huskies, which had barked and yapped as they left the town nearly two days earlier, seemed interested in them. Sheltering from the snow, they all stayed tucked inside their kennels as the coach passed by.

Chloé struggled to make sense of the scene outside. The street lights lining the roads were all on, and yet it was undeniably light. The kind of dusky light that, back home, she would have expected at daybreak on a grey winter's morning. Her mind drifted to the memory of a lock-in that she and Ellie had once attended, walking back to their student halls as the darkness lifted. She felt like she had been robbed of several hours, her mind refusing to believe that it could really be the middle of the night.

Arriving at the hotel, she felt a strange sense of déjà vu

as they waited in reception to be allocated rooms. Within a few minutes, though, keycards had been handed out, and after Ezra had announced that they would reconvene first thing in the morning to be escorted to the police station the group dispersed. Having been pointed by the receptionist towards a flight of stairs, Chloé followed Mia and Ben into a narrow corridor.

'You down here as well?' asked Ben.

Chloé nodded, looking at the number on her card. 'Room . . .' She gave the smallest, hollowest laugh, prompting Ben to raise an eyebrow. 'It's 207. Same room I was given when we first arrived.'

They reached Mia's room first and then Chloé's.

'Sleep well, guys,' said Ben.

'Sleep . . .' Mia murmured. 'As if any of us are going to sleep tonight.'

No more words were said between them. Instead, as Mia disappeared inside, Chloé exchanged a stiff nod with Ben, watching for a few seconds as he continued down the corridor.

Inside her room, she dumped her rucksack on the floor and went straight to the window, eager to close the blackout curtains. But before she could, she paused. On the lawn outside the back of the hotel – now covered with a thick white carpet of snow – she saw a couple of residents from the town. They were dressed in heavy winter gear, their phones pointed towards the sky while a pair of huskies scampered around their feet. Following their line of sight, Chloé realised that they were looking up at the

Osprey, watching as it traced slow, miserable circles over the valley.

She wondered why it wasn't carrying on to the mainland, where it could be tethered in Tromsø. Were the weather conditions to blame? Maybe Schäfer was waiting for the snowfall to ease. Or perhaps it was a matter of jurisdiction. Chloé had no idea whose responsibility it would be to investigate a crime committed while airborne above the North Pole, but the police who had been there to meet them were presumably based in Longyearbyen. Maybe they weren't yet allowing Schäfer to take the *Osprey* back to Tromsø and effectively fly away with their crime scene.

Whipping the curtains closed, Chloé toppled backwards onto the bed. She was completely drained, yearning for sleep, but her mind refused to allow it. It wasn't simply that the midnight sun was playing havoc with her sense of time, or the homesickness that sat like a weight on her chest. It was that, despite her best efforts, she couldn't stop picturing Howard's and Devon's bodies. And in the fleeting moments when she did manage to divert her attention to something else, the only place her mind would go was to the two questions that still didn't make sense.

The first was how exactly Liam had managed to put lemon juice in Devon's drink. He was a good bartender. A great one even. And while he had accepted the conclusion that he'd been so distracted – so overwhelmed – by having accidentally killed Howard that he had managed to pour Devon the lethal dose of citrus, Chloé struggled to see it.

And the second was who had drugged Howard. Because

regardless of Liam's confession – regardless of whether he really had been duped by Airborne Expeditions into filling Howard's cabin with helium – the fact remained that his pills were in Jade's suitcase. There was simply no way he could have taken them himself.

Together, these two problems led inevitably to a third. Because for Liam to have been set up would mean that another member of their party must be guilty. One of the people with whom she had just spent the past two days would need to have had a reason to kill both Howard and Devon. And for the life of her, she couldn't think of what that reason would be.

Screwing her eyes shut, she forced the questions from her mind. They weren't hers to answer any more, if they ever had been. Her imagination was running away with her. Liam had confessed, and at that very moment he was giving his statement to the police. In the morning Chloé would need to give hers. If she could just *sleep* . . .

After half an hour of trying to silence her thoughts, she turned on the TV, hoping for a distraction. This quickly proved useless. With the only English-speaking channel available being BBC World News, her mind simply drifted back to Liam and the pills.

Finally she fetched her laptop from her rucksack, sat upright on the bed and plugged in her GoPro. She needed to see the footage again. She needed to see, with her own eyes, that there was no way Howard's food or drink could have been spiked. Perhaps then she would be able to let it go – and finally get some rest.

Sinking into her pillows, she hit play, letting the footage run from the beginning. She watched as the starters were placed on the table, and then the main course and the desserts. Just as before, she saw no way that anything Howard ate or drank could have been tampered with. The thought still lingered that Liam could have added something to his food out of shot, but there was nothing she could do with that theory, beyond sharing it with the police when she gave her statement. Likewise, it was still possible that Liam had spiked Howard's whisky before he served it, but again she dismissed that idea. He had confessed to so much after Devon's demise: to being in touch with Airborne Expeditions and tampering with the climate-control system . . . If he had given Howard something to make him sleep, would he not have admitted that, too?

She knew that she should close the footage down. It wasn't helping. But as she watched Ezra hurry from the lounge, so eager to present Howard with the photo in his cabin, she let it play on, watching out of morbid curiosity.

With her eyes glued to the screen, she sighed as he returned to the table, the parcel clutched in his hand. Little did he know, Chloé thought to herself, that in a few hours' time he would have lost both of the men in that photograph. The journey that Howard and Isaac had started all those years ago . . . It seemed Ezra was destined to finish it alone.

She watched for a few seconds more as Ezra handed over the parcel and seated himself at the table.

Then she stopped.

Her heart leaping into her throat, she leaned forward over the laptop. Could she have seen . . . ? Surely not. *Surely* . . .

With a quivering hand, she rewound a few seconds and watched it again. Then, to be sure, she rewound it once more, watching for a third time. It didn't matter how many times she let the footage run, there was no denying what she'd seen.

Putting the laptop to one side, she sat bolt upright, suddenly feeling sick at the ramifications of what she'd stumbled upon. Liam was innocent. Someone had drugged Howard, but it hadn't been him. And with this footage, Chloé had inadvertently captured video evidence of the true culprit.

She began to pace around the room, turning her new theory over in her mind as she analysed it from every possible angle. She had the sensation of tugging on a ball of yarn, the tightly wound spool unravelling in her hands.

Howard's killer had been in front of them and they hadn't seen it. Because why would they? Of all the people aboard the *Osprey*, why would this person ever have crossed their minds?

Finally Chloé forced herself to stop, working hard to slow her racing thoughts. She had to share this with someone. The police would need to see it, of course, but she had to be sure. She had to know first that she wasn't leaping to a mistaken conclusion, exchanging one innocent party for another. The question was who. Who could she trust?

Heart pounding, she scrambled for her phone.

33

Half an hour later, Chloé sat in the corner of the hotel restaurant, laptop and GoPro on the table in front of her.

It was a glamorous space, with soft lighting and gleaming crockery. Floor-to-ceiling glass offered a spectacular view of the fjord and the mountains, while a raised pedestal in the middle of the room meant that the tables furthest away could still enjoy it. Even the bar, well stocked with an impressive selection of wines and spirits, had been built at a slight angle, so that no patrons would have to sit with their backs to the windows.

Chloé suspected the looming wilderness on the other side of the glass might have something to do with it, but the place felt cavernous as she sat there alone. When she and Ben had come for breakfast, just hours before they boarded the *Osprey*, it had been full of fellow diners, all tilting their chairs to take in the scenery. At nearly half-past two in the morning her only companion was a cuddly polar bear from the hotel gift shop. Seated at the bar, its paws were wrapped around an empty Martini glass.

She glanced at her phone, looking for something from Ben – an explanation as to why he hadn't shown up yet. But there was nothing.

Are you up? she had messaged him from her room.

The reply had come within a few minutes: Yep. Just FaceTiming Alec.

Can I come and see you? Chloé had then asked. Need to show you something.

There had been another pause. When Ben's response eventually came, it read: Restaurant. 10 minutes.

With his ten minutes now long-since up, Chloé fidgeted nervously, watching through the enormous windows as the snow continued to fall. Every few seconds her eyes flicked towards the door. 'Come on,' she murmured, leg bouncing under the table. '*Come on.*'

Finally there was movement. A figure appeared at the door. Not Ben, though. It was Ezra.

Chloé froze, watching as he swept a quick look around the restaurant. Seeing that the place was otherwise empty, he gave a satisfied nod and began to stride towards her.

'Chloé,' he called out wearily, 'what's this all about then?'

She swallowed back a lump. 'Nothing,' she said. 'I was just waiting for Ben.'

'I know. I was with him when you messaged. We were FaceTiming Alec together, filling him in on everything that's happened. They still had a few things to discuss, so I said I'd come see what was troubling you.'

Chloé hurried to her feet, snatching the laptop and the GoPro from the table. 'I need to leave.'

'But I thought you had something to talk about. Surely you can share whatever you had for Ben with me instead?'

'I made a mistake,' she said, fighting to keep her voice level. 'I'm sorry, Ezra, but there's no point in me showing you. I'd only be wasting your time.'

'Sit down, Chloé.'

'I really shouldn't—'

'*Sit down.*'

His tone invited no argument. Chloé looked frantically around, but there was no one she could call out to. No one to help her.

'Now,' said Ezra, taking the seat across from her. 'Open your laptop. And show me whatever you were going to show Ben.'

Her hand beginning to shake, Chloé opened the laptop. She thought desperately for something she could show Ezra instead – some cover story that she could invent. But again she cursed herself. In her haste to show Ben what she'd found, the shot in question was already waiting when the screen lit up.

'This is it?' said Ezra.

'No.' Reaching for the mousepad, Chloé tried to close the footage down. 'No, this is something else. Just something I was working on while I waited.'

Ezra caught her wrist. 'You weren't working on anything, Chloé. When I came in you were staring at the door. Waiting. Now show it to me.'

Terror gripping her, Chloé pressed play, Ezra's hand

still clamped around her wrist. The footage began to move, Saturday's dinner playing out on the screen.

Ezra leaned forward a fraction. 'You were filming . . .'

'For my Instagram.'

'And why were you so eager to show this to Ben?'

His tone was confused. Curious even. But Chloé could hear something else. Something infinitely more menacing, lurking below the surface. He looked her in the eye, and she could see that he knew what she had come here to say.

She thought about running. About snatching up her laptop and bolting for the door. But with her back to the window, she would have to make it past him before she could escape, and she could see that he wasn't going to let her leave without a fight. If he managed to catch her – tackle her to the ground – she would never be able to overpower him. Right now, they were talking. And until she could devise a way to escape, that was all she had. She had to keep him talking.

His question rang in her ears. *And why were you so eager to show this to Ben?*

She took a deep breath, knowing that once she spoke these words there would be no taking them back.

'Because it wasn't Liam. He didn't fill Howard's cabin with helium, and he didn't put lemon juice in Devon's water. It was you.'

34

Neither of them spoke. The laptop screen suddenly forgotten, Ezra stared at her, eyes wide with disbelief.

'Chloé,' he said, 'I don't know what you think you've seen in this footage, but you can't possibly believe that I could . . . That I would ever . . .' When she didn't reply, his expression hardened. 'If you're going to make an accusation like that, you'd better have some evidence.'

Chloé swallowed back a lump, hoping that when she spoke, the tremor in her voice wouldn't be too noticeable. It didn't matter either way, she told herself. They both knew that this conversation was for show. He was testing her, seeing how much she knew. That was all right, though. Ezra wasn't going to let her leave, but any moment now Ben would arrive. He would finish FaceTiming Alec and then join them in the restaurant, at which point she would scream for him to help her. If she tried to run now, Ezra would overpower her, but he couldn't subdue Ben and certainly not both of them at once. Until he came, she just had to keep Ezra at bay. And she could think of no better way to hold his attention than to lay out everything she had managed to piece together in her room.

'Devon worked it out too,' she said. 'Didn't he? That's why he had to die. He had the answer.'

She took a long breath, aware of how closely Ezra was watching her.

'Liam is plenty of things,' she continued. 'Many of them not good. But he *is* a good bartender. Too good to give lemon juice to a man he knew was allergic to citrus. On the *Osprey* we all bought into the idea that he was distracted. He thought he'd killed Howard – accidentally, of course – so he believed he was off his game. But I can't imagine he would be so distracted as to give Devon a drink that might kill him. If anything, with Howard on his mind, I expect he'd be even more careful. That begs the question of why, though. Why would someone kill Devon? Why set Liam up? And the answer that makes the most sense is that Devon had worked it out. He knew what had actually happened to Howard.'

'We all know what happened to Howard,' said Ezra. 'The helium leak—'

'No,' said Chloé. 'Howard was killed by helium, there's no denying that. As Captain Schäfer said when we found his body, the blue lips confirmed it. But there wasn't a leak.'

She paused to swallow back a lump that had formed in her throat. Her mouth was dry, heart pounding in her ears.

'There's something my mum likes to say: *C'est trop beau pour être vrai*. It means too good to be true – and that's exactly what the leak in Howard's cabin was. We all believed it was real, even though Captain Schäfer told us it shouldn't be possible, because we were convinced we had seen it. We saw the body, we smelled that sickly-sweet scent when you opened the cabin door . . . But I think Devon realised the truth. He saw what had actually happened, and you killed him to keep him quiet.

'The question is: how? How had Devon seen through it? We all looked into Howard's cabin, and we all saw exactly the same thing. And yet from that one glance he somehow deduced how the leak had been faked. The answer, I think, hinges on Devon being unique in two distinct ways. The first was that he had spent twenty years leading mountaineering trips into the Alps, and the second was that he suffered from a severe allergy.'

Ezra gave a short, bullet-like laugh. 'You think that by just *looking* at Howard's cabin, Devon was able to see how a helium leak could have been faked. And you think he worked this out because of his *citrus allergy*?'

'I do. On Saturday night, when we all sat down for dinner, you announced to the table that the staff were aware of a couple of allergies among the group. You didn't say what they were or, for that matter, who suffered from them, but we know that one was Devon's. So it stands to reason that he would be the most likely of us to recognise the other. And I think that's exactly what he did. At some point, he concluded that the red skin around Howard's mouth wasn't a by-product of the helium. It was an allergic reaction. One that, over the course of twenty years in the mountains, he'd probably come across before.'

'A reaction to *what*?'

'To rubber. One of the excursions Devon offered to his clientele was high-altitude climbing. I'm sure I don't need to tell you that hiking above a certain threshold requires an oxygen tank, with a rubber mask covering the mouth and nose. A mask very similar to the one Captain Schäfer wore when he assessed the helium levels in Howard's cabin.'

For the first time since he'd sat down, a flicker of fear passed over Ezra's face.

'This afternoon,' Chloé continued, 'I spent a few minutes inside Niamh's office. She said that Jasper had asked for there to be something special in his and Madison's cabin to mark their anniversary, so you instructed her to source a balloon. She brought it with her aboard the *Osprey* and, crucially, she brought a small canister of helium to inflate it.'

Chloé paused for a second. Ezra was staring at her, hanging on her every word.

'Here's what I think happened. In the middle of the night, while we were all asleep, you went to the upper deck. You put on a pair of Gwyn's nitrile gloves from the kitchen, to avoid leaving fingerprints, and you went to the office, where you took the spare keycard from Niamh's safe.'

'*Liam* took the keycard,' Ezra cut in. 'He admitted it to us all. He'd seen Niamh typing in the combination and he took it so that he could fiddle with the climate-control system.'

'He did,' Chloé agreed. 'But that doesn't mean he was the only one. He had it for a grand total of fifteen minutes, and was in such a hurry to get rid of it that he didn't even stop to make sure it was in the same position as when he found it. So I think you both took it, at different points during the night and for different purposes. As for the combination . . . Jade told me it was zero-eight-zero-five. I didn't catch it at the time, but now that I have, it's obvious. You even showed it to us – you dated the picture you gave to Howard. Zero-eight-zero-five. As in *August 2005.* It's the month Howard and your dad went on their trip to the North Pole. The month your dad died, and when all of this began. I can't believe that's a coincidence. So yes, Liam might have seen Niamh typing the code in, but I'd bet it was *you* who gave her that combination in the first place.

'The point is – you took the keycard. You also took Niamh's canister of helium and . . .' Chloé hesitated, the thought of what she was about to describe making her feel sick. 'And the face-mask from the oxygen tank. You then used the keycard to enter Howard's cabin. Once inside, you put the oxygen mask – now attached to the helium canister – over Howard's mouth and nose. He reacted to it, causing the rash we saw around his mouth, but he didn't resist. Not while he was under the influence of a heavy dose of sleeping pills. Once Howard was dead, you left something in there. A diffuser of some kind, which you left running to ensure the cabin would smell sweet, like the helium from the airship.'

'This is ridiculous,' said Ezra. 'If there had been something like that in the cabin, we would all have seen it when we found Howard's body.'

'We might have done,' said Chloé. 'Had you not insisted on being the first inside. I think you barged in ahead of anyone else so that you could hide it inside your Skyline Voyages puffer jacket. That thing easily looked thick enough to conceal a small object, and no one thought twice about you wearing it while the *Osprey* was so cold. Then, when Captain Schäfer tried to usher us back into the lounge, you went straight to your *own* cabin, where we heard you being sick through the door. But we didn't see you, of course. What you were really doing, I expect, was faking some pretty convincing retching noises while you stashed whatever you'd used to create the scent. That's why the cabin didn't smell when the captain inspected it later. We assumed that the filter had kicked in again, and that whatever helium had been trapped inside the cabin overnight had escaped when we opened the door. The truth is that you'd removed whatever you left in there to give it that scent in the first place.

'But planting the diffuser wasn't the last thing you did before leaving Howard's cabin. To truly sell the idea of the leak, you needed the cabin to appear airtight. So you came up with the idea of Howard's dressing gown being flat against the bottom of his door after you'd left. That one really had me stumped. As Ben kept asking me: how could you press the dressing gown flat against the door from outside the room? But I understand now how you did it. You used the belt.'

Ezra didn't respond to this, but Chloé was sure she saw a slight twitch in the corner of his eye.

'Here's what I think you did,' she said. 'While you were still inside the cabin, you positioned the dressing gown as close to the door as you could manage, and you threaded one end of the belt underneath, into the corridor. You then left the cabin and used it to tug the robe flat against the door. You probably then stashed the belt in your cabin, to get rid of with the diffuser. But when the captain held on to the robe and used it to plug the gap under the door from the outside, I think you must have changed your mind. You couldn't risk being seen crouching down and threading the belt back through the loops on the robe. But a loose belt is probably less likely to arouse suspicion than a missing one, so I think you fetched it from your cabin later on and dropped it on top of the robe. The only problem *there* was that the corridor is so narrow I saw Ben catch it with his foot while he was walking past. If the belt had been threaded through the loops, as one might typically expect it to be, he'd have taken the whole robe with him. Instead, it came clean away.

'With Howard dead, the diffuser in place and the dressing gown flat against the door, you must then have gone back to the upper deck, where you returned the oxygen mask, the helium canister and the master keycard to the office. The last thing you did was put your gloves in the kitchen bin, which probably seemed safer than trying to hide them in your cabin. After all, Gwyn must get through several pairs of them every day. He was hardly going to notice one more. The mistake you made *there* was hiring two very competent people. Because Niamh noticed that the keycard in the safe wasn't as she'd left it the day before; and Gwyn, having changed the liner in the kitchen bin before going to bed, saw a pair of used gloves in the morning that shouldn't have been there.'

'It's an impressive story,' said Ezra. 'It's just a shame you can't prove any of it.'

'Perhaps not all of it,' Chloé agreed. 'But I can prove you were the one who gave Howard the large dose of sleeping pills that kept him drugged while you killed him.'

'Howard dosed *himself* up on those pills.'

Chloé didn't reply. Instead she reached for the laptop, rewinding the footage to the moment Ezra left the table. 'It's the glasses,' she said.

'What glasses?'

'The water glasses. You leave after the desserts to fetch Howard's photo from your cabin, and you take your glass with you.'

'So?'

'So I didn't think anything of it at the time. I don't suppose any of us did. We assumed you were so excited by the thought of giving Howard the photo that you didn't stop to put it down before you left. But look at what happens when you come back.'

As if on cue, Ezra returned in the video to the lounge.

'You set the glass down on the table. Because Howard is left-handed, and is seated to your right, you naturally set the glass right beside his.'

Ezra stared at the screen, watching as he placed his glass mere inches from Howard's.

'You then take a bottle of water . . .' Chloé could hear her voice beginning to tremble as the crucial moment edged closer. 'And while Howard is busy unwrapping the photo, the rest of us all watching to see what you'd given him, you refill both of your glasses. You immediately take a sip, but you don't take it from *your* glass.'

They both watched as, on the screen, Ezra did exactly as Chloé described. Without question, he took Howard's glass, instead of the one he had brought back from his cabin. Then, rather than returning it to the spot from which he'd lifted it, he transferred it from his right hand to his left and set it down on his opposite side, leaving the glass he had just placed for Howard standing alone.

'Would you look at that,' said Ezra. 'I didn't even realise.' He looked up from the screen, meeting Chloé's eye. 'It was an honest mistake. Look at how close the two glasses were. I was distracted . . . I picked up the wrong one.' He frowned, seeing that Chloé wasn't convinced. 'What is it that you think's happened here? Why is this bothering you so much?'

She took another breath, trying to stifle her rising fear. 'When I realised what had happened with the glasses, it occurred to me that perhaps it wasn't an accident that you took yours with you when you left the table. Instead, maybe fetching the picture was exactly the excuse you needed to visit your cabin and exchange your glass for another that you'd prepared ahead of time.'

'Prepared . . . prepared *how*?' Ezra looked at her sternly. 'Listen to me very carefully, Chloé. I can understand being upset by what's happened this weekend. I can even understand wanting to make sense of it, but this . . . This is absurd. More than that, it's exceptionally inappropriate. The *Osprey* will be inspected when it returns to Tromsø. Liam has confessed to sabotaging the trip on behalf of Airborne Expeditions. Howard dosed himself with those pills, and I made an honest mistake with the water glasses. It was a tragic accident.'

'Liam was never in touch with Airborne Expeditions,' Chloé replied. 'He believes he was, because he can't see why anyone else would want to sabotage the *Osprey*. But he has no proof that whoever he spoke to was really from Airborne. He never saw anyone. He never heard a voice. All he had were text messages from an unknown number.'

'So who was he talking to, if not Airborne?'

'You. I think it was you the entire time. You knew that there shouldn't be any way for the helium to accidentally enter the climate-control system. But if someone were to interfere with the system at the exact time Howard was killed, it becomes a whole lot easier to believe that that's what happened. So you approached Liam via an unknown number. You pretended to be from Airborne Expeditions and you offered money to carry out what he thought was a little harmless sabotage. When Howard's body was found, Liam reached the same conclusion we did. The climate-control system had filled with helium at the same time as he'd been fiddling with it. He *believed* he had killed Howard. And after Devon died too, and Liam was on the brink of a breakdown, you drew a confession out of him, with all of us there to witness it.'

'What about the other things Liam said he'd messed with? The fridge? The blackout blinds?'

'A cover story, so as not to frighten him off. You couldn't have him thinking he was involved in a deliberate attempt to get helium into the climate-control system. If he thought that's what you wanted, I don't think he would ever have agreed to it.'

Ezra scoffed. 'This is *ridiculous*.'

'Is it? Liam told us his last message from Airborne came just before the *Osprey* picked us up on Saturday morning. As we were leaving the hotel, you sent a text message. Told us all that if we needed to do the same, we should do it before we left Longyearbyen . . . And then there's the bit that Liam remembered. He said that when he asked what his instructions would achieve, he was told that the climate-control system would appear to have glitched during the night. Those were your words. When you gathered us all in the lounge, just before we found Howard's body, you said that the climate-control system appeared to have *glitched* during the night. You didn't say malfunctioned. You didn't say it had gone rogue. You said that it had glitched.'

'Oh, come on . . .' said Ezra. 'You're basing all that on a *word*? How can you even *remember* something like—'

'I'm a writer,' Chloé cut across him. 'I'm good with words.' She chewed her lip for a moment, trying to keep her fear at bay for a little longer. 'As for the sleeping pills . . . Howard didn't dose himself. He couldn't have done. Because he didn't have his pills. They were in Jade's suitcase.'

This, she could see, caught Ezra off guard. For the first time, he appeared genuinely uneasy.

'She stole them,' Chloé went on, her confidence bolstered by how alarmed he looked. 'While we were all having dinner. Howard had upset her on Saturday afternoon, and Jade wanted a way to get back at him. She has them even now. So there's no way Howard could have dosed himself, which means someone else must have drugged him.'

She looked towards the laptop screen. 'I've watched this footage *a lot*. No one touches Howard's food. He doesn't have any wine, he barely sips his whisky when we all toast Isaac and he drinks water from bottles shared by several other people. That glass, though . . .'

Ezra had turned sheet-white, his eyes glued to the screen. As the footage continued to roll, Chloé thought back to the Winter Mojito Liam had made for her, the chopped mint clinging to the inside of the glass as the drink went down.

'You couldn't have a layer of crushed pills sitting at the bottom of the glass,' she continued. 'Howard would be too likely to notice. But just a few minutes after we first boarded the *Osprey*, you said that you'd chosen the frosted glasses personally. You told us you'd done it for the ambience. Frosted glasses for a frosty place. Only I don't think that's true. I think the *real* reason you wanted them to be frosted was so that you could coat the inside of one with powder. You swapped that glass with Howard's, and he drank from it to wash down the whisky you insisted we all have. In the process he washed down the crushed pills that would keep him asleep while he was murdered. I'll bet you even drew up the seating plan yourself, to ensure that you could make the swap. You did have those wooden place settings carved in Longyearbyen. You even had one made for me, with only a couple of days' notice. That's a bit much, wouldn't you say? At the time I was flattered, but now I'll bet it was all so that you could be completely sure you were sitting on Howard's left.'

Ezra didn't speak. He didn't even move. Chloé's heart, meanwhile, pounded in her ears. Where was Ben? How much longer could he and Alec possibly need to talk?

A new possibility crossed her mind, causing her blood to run cold. Perhaps he wasn't coming. Perhaps Ezra had told him not to. Now that it had occurred to her, she could picture it clearly. Ezra telling Ben that he would see what was troubling Chloé, and that he need only worry about joining them if they called for him.

'Why didn't Devon say anything?' Ezra demanded. 'If he knew this was how Howard had been killed – managed to work all of this out from a rash – why didn't he tell the captain? Tell *me*?'

Chloé clasped her hands together under the table to keep them from trembling.

Keep talking, she urged herself. *You have to keep him talking*.

'I don't think he can have worked out *everything*. He can't have known about the gloves. But he saw the oxygen mask when Captain Schäfer went to investigate the cabin. He would have known that there might be a canister of helium somewhere on board, too, because Liam had first put the balloon in his cabin instead of Jasper and Madison's. So I think it's fair to assume that, once Devon had started thinking about the rash around Howard's mouth as an allergic reaction, as opposed to a side-effect of the helium, he deduced from those two pieces of information how Howard might have been killed.

'Now if I were Devon, my next questions would be how a killer could have entered Howard's cabin, and why it would smell sweet if there wasn't actually a leak. He can't have known about the spare staff keycard in the safe, given that *we* didn't even know about it until after he had died. But I think he could have reached the same conclusion I did about the scent: that something must have been placed in the cabin overnight and then removed when Howard's body was found. And following that deduction, I think Devon must have remembered that you were the first person inside. You removed whatever gave off the scent, and therefore you must have been the one to kill Howard.

'And he *did* come to speak with you. The two of you went into your cabin, supposedly so that Devon could apologise for the way he had spoken about your dad over dinner. And when did that happen? Just after he'd seen the captain putting on the oxygen mask to carry out another check of Howard's cabin. I think that's when he worked out what had caused the rash, and I think that's what the two of you went away to discuss.

'If I had to guess, I would say that he probably tried to blackmail you. Jasper told us that Devon was having money troubles – that he was being sued by a client who had been injured on one of his excursions. He must have seen an opportunity to cash in, realising that he could ask you for money in exchange for his silence. He looked pretty pleased with himself when he came back into the lounge. Given that he didn't immediately come out of that cabin and share his theory with the rest of us, I reckon you probably agreed to it. Then, when Ivy and Gwyn had their outbursts, you took advantage of the commotion to spike Devon's drink with lemon juice.'

'Liam,' said Ezra. 'It was *Liam* who put lemon juice in Devon's drink. We found the bloody thing in his bin!'

'*You* found it,' said Chloé. 'Or at least it looked like you did. I think it was you who Gwyn had just heard in his kitchen, when he came barging into the lounge. After your conversation with Devon, you ran up there and took a lemon. You then went into your cabin and squeezed that lemon into a glass of water – the glass you were carrying when you came to break up the fight that was about to start between Jasper and Devon. Then, with Ivy and Gwyn causing a distraction, you must have quickly swapped your glass with Devon's.'

She nodded at the laptop screen. 'We've already seen you do it once. It would be the exact same trick. And once Devon was dead, you went behind the bar, where you appeared to find the squeezed lemon in the bin. Again, we'll never prove it, but I think you probably had it hidden in your pocket, ready to take out and pretend you'd just found it.

'It was even you who searched Devon for an EpiPen, after he'd fallen to the ground. When it seemed he wasn't carrying one, you went running to his cabin, to look there instead. I wouldn't be remotely surprised if you *had* found one in Devon's pocket, and if the frantic dash to search his cabin was just a ruse to keep it away from him for another minute or two – make sure the job was done.'

For a long while Ezra was silent. When at last he spoke, Chloé couldn't help but notice something different in his voice. He wasn't angry. He wasn't even frightened. He sounded distressed – desperate even.

'Why would I do this?' he insisted. 'My company, my guests, my dad's legacy . . . I had more to lose up there than anyone else.'

Bracing herself, Chloé took a long breath, nails digging into her palms as she clenched her fists beneath the table. 'Your dad's legacy is precisely why,' she said. 'I think Howard killed him.'

35

Any hope that Chloé had harboured of Ben coming to the restaurant was now gone. There was no way he and Alec could still be talking. Too much time had passed. Clearly, upon volunteering to see what Chloé wanted, Ezra had said something to keep him from joining them.

She tried to think of a way she could signal to him, but her phone was in the pocket of her jeans and there was no way she could fetch it out to place a call – let alone send a message – without Ezra stopping her. No help was coming. In the middle of the night, in one of the most remote places on Earth, she couldn't even rely on a stranger wandering into the restaurant. If she was going to get away, she would have to do it herself.

From the wild look in Ezra's eye, she could see that with her last bombshell – the revelation that Howard had killed his father – she still had his attention. That was good. As long as he was still sitting and listening, she had time to think of a way out.

'Last year,' she said, 'when your mum died, Astrid went

with you to the UK, so that she could help clear out the family home. She said that while the two of you were up in the loft, sorting through your mum's things, you found a box of your dad's handwritten notes. Astrid thought they weren't anything important, to have sat up there for all those years. But when you saw them, she said you looked as if you'd seen a ghost. Those were her words. She thought you were just shocked to see something that Isaac had written personally, but I think she was wrong. Looking back on all that's happened, I think you must have found something *extremely* important.

'After Isaac died, Howard would regularly come to your house, to check on how you and your mum were holding up. Devon, Jasper and Alec would often be there too, keeping you company. Before he came to speak with you – to *apologise* for his behaviour over dinner – Devon described a day when he'd seen Howard sitting in Isaac's study. He told us Howard spent a lot of time in there, going through your dad's documents as he helped your mum sell Isaac's cargo airline. On this day, though, he looked devastated, head in his hands, and naturally Devon believed that he was looking at a man in mourning. Howard had lost his best friend. Perhaps he even had survivor's guilt. But I don't think that's what Devon saw. I think what Howard had actually been doing in the study – what he had been doing every time he came to check on you and your mum – was searching for the notes that you came upon in the loft. And, unable to find them, he was going out of his mind with stress. Because those notes were the reason he had committed murder. Those notes, I believe, were your dad's plans for Skyline Voyages.

'The only person whose word we have to go on that he and Isaac dreamed up Skyline Voyages together, during their trip to the North Pole, is Howard's. But how likely does that really sound? Howard told us on Saturday that Isaac had wanted to go on their trip to the Pole for *years*. Clearly the place had been on his mind for a long time. Likewise, we know it was Isaac who had the entrepreneurial flair to found a cargo airline of his own. Howard was just along for the ride.

'Isaac had already planned out Skyline Voyages, and he only *shared* the idea with Howard during their trip to the Pole. Then, when the ice gave way beneath him, Howard saw an opportunity. The safety line didn't fail. Howard cut him loose, so that he could find Isaac's plans and claim Skyline for himself.'

Chloé pictured the scene Devon had described. She imagined the ice cracking beneath their feet. She imagined Isaac, dressed in winter survival gear, disappearing into the water. Even the thought of it made her shudder. A cold white death-trap just waiting to happen.

'Devon must have worked a little of this out, too. He can't have known about the notes in your mum's loft. But given his line of work, he *would* have known how unlikely it would be for the kind of safety lines that Isaac and Howard were using to fail. He also knew better than anyone quite how much Isaac meant to you. Once he was turned on to the idea of you murdering Howard, I can't imagine it would be much of a leap for him to assume that Howard let your dad die.

'As for Howard himself, he must have found *something* of Isaac's plans during all those visits to you and your mum. The fact that Skyline Voyages exists suggests that after three months of searching your house – three months that Devon thought he'd spent grieving, and helping your mum with everything Isaac left behind – he'd found enough in the study to get started. And that's when he sat you and your mum down to tell you about it.

'The way Devon told that story yesterday afternoon, it sounded as if Howard was trying to give you hope. Reassure you that Isaac's legacy was going to live on. But I can't help wondering if it was really as innocent as that. Now I'm thinking: what if Howard felt he had to test the water before he claimed Isaac's ideas as his own? That's why he spoke to you and your mum. Not to get your blessing, but to see your reaction. Once he'd got hold of as much of Isaac's preliminary work as he could find, he wanted to see that neither of you had ever heard of Skyline Voyages. And he got what he needed, didn't he? Isaac had clearly never spoken to you about Skyline. Howard could claim it.

'But he ended up with a good deal more than he bargained for, because he also got *you*. You saw Skyline as an opportunity to live up to your dad's legend, and you were determined to seize it. Devon said that Howard even tried to talk you out of it. He encouraged you to go to university. Follow your own passions. But you were too far gone. You were going to help Howard build Skyline Voyages whether he liked it or not. And that's exactly what you did. Or at least it's what you did until last year, when you stumbled on some of Isaac's plans in the loft and you realised what had happened. You realised that the story of Howard and your dad coming up with Skyline together had been a lie. You realised that Howard killed him for it. And you realised that for nearly twenty years you'd helped him build the company that should have been your dad's.'

For what felt like an eternity, they sat in complete silence. Then, at last, Ezra sighed. 'Let me see your phone,' he said.

Chloé frowned.

'It's all right. I'm not going to take it. But if we're going to continue this conversation, I need to be sure I'm not being recorded.'

Without a word, Chloé took her phone from her pocket and held it out.

'You show me,' he said.

Doing as she was told, Chloé unlocked the phone and found the voice recorder app. She held it up so that he could see it wasn't running.

Ezra nodded, satisfied. 'Set it down on the table where I can see it.'

Chloé did as instructed. She was terrified, feeling like she was looking into the eyes of the polar bear she had seen watching over the baggage carousel at the airport. An apex predator that could end her life as naturally as it could walk or breathe. Only the killer before her wasn't stuffed. It was very much alive. More than that, it had her cornered.

'You took such a risk . . .' she said. 'You must have known – if anyone suspected you it would be the end of Skyline. The end of Isaac's dream. You'd have destroyed the company before it had even begun.' She took a deep breath. 'Tell me something. Just one thing. Airborne Expeditions . . . They're going to pull ahead now. While the *Osprey*'s grounded and the crew is trying to repair a leak they can't find, Airborne are surely going to be the first to start operating. Why would you do that to yourself? To Isaac's legacy?'

A small smile touched the corners of Ezra's mouth. 'Liam willingly confessed to a room full of people that Airborne paid him to make this happen. He's probably confessing it to the police as we speak. Do you not think *they* are going to be investigated? Grounded, even, while those allegations are dealt with?'

'But the *Osprey*—'

'The *Osprey* doesn't need an investigation. Captain Schäfer has identified exactly what needs to be done. We need to install a new air filter in Howard's cabin, new helium sensors in the envelope and new piping in the climate-control system. All of which, if we move at speed, can be done in a matter of weeks.'

'But the passengers,' said Chloé. 'Surely no one's going to want to fly with you after this.'

'Of course they will. Once the work's been completed,

we'll conduct a thorough, independent safety test, which we'll pass with flying colours because, as you've so eloquently explained, there was never anything wrong in the first place. We'll have a few cancellations, undoubtedly. But we're fully booked for nearly three years. Any empty cabins will be filled soon enough. And with a successful safety demonstration and a few smooth flights under our belts, no one's going to care for long about what happened this weekend.' He looked at her with puppy-dog eyes. 'Airborne Expeditions won't pull ahead. We'll be up and running again before you know it. *It's what Howard would have wanted.*'

He clasped his hands on the table, any hint of the warmth he'd shown these past few days gone. 'Now here's where we stand, Chloé. You've put me in a tricky spot, but I think we can reach an understanding. So let me tell you what's going to happen. You're going to give me that laptop and that GoPro. And you're going to tell me how much money it'll take to keep you quiet.'

Chloé's heart pounded in her ears. She couldn't let him take her gear. Not when it contained the only proof of Liam's innocence. And yet she was certain this was an offer she wouldn't be permitted to turn down. One way or another, Ezra was leaving this restaurant with her footage.

She scrambled for a way out. She could make a run for it, she thought. Snatch up the laptop and the GoPro, dash into the lobby and scream for help. Someone would surely hear her . . .

But with her back to the window, she would need to get

past Ezra. If she was too slow, he might tackle her to the ground and take the laptop anyway. She needed to be clever. She needed him to *let* her stand. Let her leave the restaurant.

'How do I know you can pay?' she asked, frantically cobbling together a plan in her mind. 'If we do make a deal. How can I know you'll honour it?'

'You know what we're charging to fly on the *Osprey*,' Ezra replied. 'It'll take some creative accounting. But with two more routes opening in the next few years . . . you know that I can do it.'

She nodded, doing her best to look as if she were considering it. 'Ten million,' she said. 'I want ten million pounds.' She forced herself to meet Ezra's eye, heart pounding so violently against her ribs that it hurt.

He nodded. 'Done.'

'Just like that?'

'Just like that.'

He reached across the table for the laptop. Before he could take it, though, Chloé laid a protective hand on top of it.

'But we have to go to my room,' she said. 'I've copied the footage to my hard drive. If you're taking this, you should take that as well.'

Ezra raised an eyebrow. 'You'd better not be trying something here, Chloé.'

'I'm not. It's a habit I've got into, backing up my footage so there's no chance of losing any. If we're doing this, and I'm accepting your money, I don't want you coming after me later because you've found out I might still have a copy somewhere. I can't imagine that would go down well.'

For what felt like an agonisingly long time, Ezra watched her. 'No,' he said. 'I don't suppose it would.' He tightened his grip on the laptop. 'Fine. Lead the way. But I'm keeping this.'

Chloé tried to protest, but he yanked the laptop away from her.

'Look,' he said sternly, 'if you're telling the truth, there's no need for you to keep it. But if you're not . . .'

Chloé nodded. Cursing how quickly her poor excuse for a plan had begun to unravel, she relinquished her grip on the laptop.

As they rose to their feet, her mind began to whir. She walked ahead. Behind her, Ezra cradled the laptop and GoPro under his arm, his free hand resting on her elbow to keep her from going too fast. Making a run for it, once they were clear of the restaurant, wasn't an option any more. Not while Ezra had the footage. Nor was screaming for help. Even if someone were close enough to hear her, with Ezra only inches away, he would see what she was about to do and clap a hand over her mouth before she'd even managed to cry out.

Feeling so frightened that she thought she might be sick, Chloé found a new thought creeping into her mind. Ten million pounds was an unfathomable amount of money for Ezra to just give her. What if he only agreed to it to keep her quiet until he could arrange for her to disappear permanently? After all, that was exactly what he had done to Devon.

They passed through the hotel reception, Chloé hoping desperately that there would be someone at the desk. Her heart sank when she saw that it was unattended. At nearly three in the morning, she supposed she should expect nothing less. The night porter was probably in the back somewhere, filing paperwork or making a coffee.

Descending to the lower storey, Chloé fought the urge to panic. Halfway down the corridor was her room. Once inside, she estimated that she could spend perhaps a minute pretending to search for a hard drive that didn't exist. And when Ezra realised he was being played, what then? Even with the element of surprise, she doubted she could wrestle the laptop from his hands. But trying to flee and leave him with the footage wasn't an option, either. Not when she would be effectively condemning Liam to being sentenced as a murderer.

With one last idea as to how she might escape, she came to a halt at the door, so frightened now that she could barely think straight. As she slid her keycard into the lock, the light above the handle glowed red. Hands trembling, she took out the card and slowly reinserted it. Again the light glowed red.

She felt Ezra tense behind her, his grip on her arm tightening. 'What's going on?'

'I don't know.' Chloé could hear the fear in her voice. 'My card . . . it isn't working.'

She inserted the card a third time. When the light

glowed red once more, she grasped the handle and shook it, the sound of rattling plastic now filling the corridor.

'Chloé, if you're trying something here . . .'

'I'm not! I swear. My card, it isn't—'

Before she could finish, the door opened, and Chloé breathed a sigh of relief as she looked into Mia's eyes.

The following moments seemed to play out in slow motion. As Chloé saw the confusion on Mia's face, she felt Ezra immediately release his grip on her arm. She imagined his eyes widening, mouth falling open as he realised he had been tricked.

With the time for pretence now over, Chloé raised her voice. 'It's him!' she screamed. '*It's him*!'

Before Mia could react, Ezra gave Chloé a sharp shove in the small of her back and she went tumbling into the room. Taking Mia down with her, they both landed heavily on the floor.

'Chloé . . .' Mia groaned. 'What's happening?'

But Chloé was barely listening. Scrambling to her feet, she saw through the open door that Ezra had fled. 'We have to stop him,' she said. 'We have to get that laptop back.'

Mia seemed no less confused, but Chloé didn't stop to explain any further. She had hurt her leg in the fall, her knee throbbing as she clambered to her feet. She carried on all the same, stumbling through the door just in time to see Ezra bolting down the corridor.

A few doors down, Ben appeared. 'What the hell's going on?'

Again Chloé didn't stop to explain. Wincing, she began to run as best she could down the corridor. With each step her knee complained more fervently, but she forced herself to keep moving. All that mattered was the footage.

At the top of the staircase she saw Ezra standing by the reception desk. He was panting, unsure of where to go. At the sight of Chloé pursuing him, with Ben and Mia in tow, he scowled, before flying outside into the car park.

Chloé followed. The snow came down harder than ever, to the extent that it was difficult even to see a few yards ahead. But she could just about make out Ezra. He was standing in the middle of the car park, wheeling around on the spot, with the laptop still clutched under his arm as he tried to find his bearings.

Away to her right, Chloé heard a voice calling out. Turning to face it, she squinted, managing to see three men in police uniforms running towards them through the snow. Two of them, she noticed, carried rifles.

'Get inside!' they called out. 'Get back into the hotel!'

Ezra didn't move. He stood frozen in the middle of the car park, looking from Chloé to the advancing officers. Then came a sound, quiet at first, but growing louder with each passing second. It was a soft thumping noise, coming from somewhere above them. At first Chloé thought it might be the *Osprey*, its propellers whirring as it flew over the hotel. But she soon realised what she was hearing. A helicopter. And it wasn't simply growing louder. It was growing closer.

This was too much for Ezra. The panic in his expression turning to outright fear, he took one last look at the approaching officers and then bolted.

'Stop,' one of the officers called out. 'Stop right there!'

But Ezra wasn't listening. He didn't even pause to see where he was going. Fear had so completely overcome him that he simply ran into the snowstorm. A moment later the helicopter passed over the roof of the hotel, flying straight over Chloé's head.

'It's going after him,' said Ben, holding up a hand to shield his face from the snow.

Chloé shook her head. The helicopter couldn't be hunting Ezra down – the pilot had no reason to. And yet it did seem to be following him. She watched as the chopper gave chase. Then, when it reached a point where it must have caught up to Ezra, it sailed clean over him, continuing towards the edge of town.

Chloé watched it go, struck by a sudden, terrifying thought. She pictured all the extra rifles she'd seen being carried by the ground crew as the *Osprey* landed. And she recalled her conversation with Astrid, thinking about the use of helicopters to frighten away bears that ventured too close to the settlement.

Coming to a halt, the police officers steered them roughly towards the hotel.

'Inside,' one of them commanded. 'Back inside. Now.'

'Are you going after him?' Chloé asked.

'Too dangerous,' the officer replied. 'We'll search for him when the air-team says it's safe.'

'But he doesn't know where he's going. He's going to get himself killed!'

'And if any of us go after him, he'll get us killed, too. His best chance now is that the helicopter watches over him until the snow has cleared.'

The officer took Chloé by the arm, but she wriggled free, hurrying to edge of the car park.

'Ezra!' she bellowed into the thick white void. '*Ezra*!'

But it was no use. Swallowed up by the snow, Ezra was gone.

36

It was another two hours before the blizzard let up. When the sky finally cleared, a pale sun shone over Longyearbyen, illuminating the town in a clean white light. Chloé had never seen snow like it. The brightly coloured Norwegian cabins popped against their newly covered surroundings, while the fjord looked the most startling shade of blue. Even the mountains that surrounded the town were unrecognisable, covered from their peaks to the ground with what could easily have been a layer of thick fondant icing.

They didn't see Ezra again. After they had been ushered back into the hotel, Chloé, Ben and Mia were taken to the restaurant. A receptionist emerged from an office and brought them hot drinks, while two police officers explained that during their time away, the bear that Astrid had mentioned on Friday had been sighted twice more in the local area. A safety warning had been issued to the locals, but this hadn't been seen aboard the *Osprey*.

Around an hour after they had been shown into the

restaurant, a call came through to one of the officers. He answered it in Norwegian, then mournfully told Chloé and Ben that while the bear had been shepherded away, it hadn't been until after Ezra had come face to face with it on the edge of the town.

As she heard that Ezra's body was in the process of being recovered, along with her laptop and GoPro, Chloé struggled to determine how she felt. She wanted to hate him, and as she thought of Howard and Devon – thought of the way Ezra had threatened *her* in this very restaurant – on some level she did. But she also pictured the scene Devon had described of the Normanstone challenge. She thought of Isaac Day's final words to his son and, before she could stop herself, she felt a small measure of sympathy for him. For the bereaved boy who, all these years later, had gone to such terrible lengths for the approval of his long-gone hero.

For the next couple of hours Chloé relayed what she'd seen in her footage and had learned from speaking with Ezra. The two officers listened intently, departing only when the hotel's other guests began to arrive for breakfast. Before they left, they encouraged all three of them to get some rest, reminding them that when they were ready, they would need to make a formal statement at the police station.

Chloé knew they must look exhausted. She certainly felt it, having been awake now for nearly twenty-four hours. She doubted she would be able to sleep, though. While her body was groaning for rest, she was still wired after her confrontation with Ezra. The perpetual daylight that had shone on them all night wasn't helping, either. Her phone said that it was almost seven o'clock when the officers left, but she could just as easily have believed it was the middle of the afternoon.

Mia left straight away, going back to her room the moment the officers had gone. Ben, meanwhile, stayed seated. He hadn't said a word while Chloé described what had happened with Ezra, sitting the entire time in subdued silence. Now that they were alone, he cleared his throat.

'That was smart,' he said quietly. 'Going to Mia's door like that.'

Chloé looked down at the table, too drained to take any satisfaction from his appraisal. 'I thought it was worth a shot,' she said. 'After you'd said goodnight, and Mia told us she wasn't going to be sleeping . . . although I was terrified I'd get the wrong room. Or that she might have nodded off after all. Or that she just wouldn't answer.' She met Ben's eye. 'I did think about going to yours. But Ezra knew which room you were in. He would have realised what I was doing.'

Ben pressed his hands to his face. 'I'm sorry,' he said. 'I'm so, so sorry. When Ezra offered to go and meet you, so that I could keep speaking to Alec . . .' He tailed off. 'I just . . . I don't know what to say, Chloé. I'll never be able to tell you how sorry I am.'

'You couldn't have known,' she said. 'We all thought it was Liam. And it's not as if I'd said in my message why I wanted to see you.'

'I know,' he said. 'But even so.'

Chloé tried to think of something she could say that might help. Nothing came to mind. Instead she reached across the table and took his hand. Not a word was said between them. It didn't need to be.

The restaurant was becoming busy now, the sound of cheerful chatter rising as eager explorers in mountaineering gear browsed the breakfast buffet. Others went straight to the windows, looking up and pointing at the *Osprey* as it continued to hover over the valley. Chloé was actively trying *not* to look at it. Instead she watched a lone reindeer that had found its way to the patch of lawn outside the hotel. It kicked at the snow with one hoof, creating a hole from which it then fetched a mouthful of green grass. On any other day the sight would have brought her pure joy. But in that moment she was too dazed to appreciate it.

Their fellow passengers from the *Osprey* were starting to drift into the restaurant, too. Madison came first, seating herself at a table in the corner, where she occupied herself with her phone. Jasper came a few minutes later, but rather than joining Madison, he went straight to a table on the opposite side of the room. Chloé wondered what conversations might have been had between the two of them in the hours since disembarking from the *Osprey*. She decided it would be best not to know.

Ivy, Niamh and Jade came shortly after, still dressed in their stewards' uniforms. Now that their duties aboard the airship no longer applied, they too seemed keen to keep to themselves. That said, Jade did meet Chloé's eye across the restaurant and they exchanged a small smile. Gwyn was there as well, trailing behind. He paused at the door, murmuring something to Jade before making his way to Jasper's table. Jasper looked up quizzically at the chef's arrival, before motioning for him to sit down.

Astrid came later, and while Chloé wondered if she and Ben should invite her to join them, she looked perfectly happy taking a table to herself. Looking contentedly out of the window, she'd adopted yet another new jumper, this time bearing a smiling walrus in a scarf and bobble hat.

'Chloé,' Ben said suddenly. 'Look.' He pointed towards the sky. The *Osprey* was moving, no longer floating idly above the town, but drifting away over the fjord. 'They must be sending it back to the mainland.'

Chloé didn't reply. She was glad to see it go. To no longer have it literally hanging over them. And yet she felt tears beading in the corners of her eyes. After all it wasn't simply the *Osprey* she was watching disappear. Her big break – the opportunity that she had wanted so desperately . . . It had all come crashing down around her.

A Norwegian voice rang out across the restaurant, a woman in a waterproof jacket and a thick pair of leggings hurrying over to their table. Seemingly oblivious to their presence, she gazed out of the window, an expression of sheer wonderment on her face. She wasn't looking up at the *Osprey*, though, leading Chloé to assume she must be watching the reindeer. She wished the woman would back up a little. Sure, it was a novel sight. But there would be plenty more where that one came from.

But just as she was starting to become irritated, her weariness getting the better of her, Chloé realised that it wasn't the reindeer that had caught their visitor's attention, either. She was squinting at the fjord, trying to pick out something in the distance.

She called something over her shoulder, speaking again in Norwegian. In response, a man at her own table came bustling over, holding out a pair of binoculars. The woman snatched them from his hands and began frantically scanning the distant landscape.

Her frustration forgotten, Chloé was now curious. She wasn't the only one. Others were gathering at the window, straining their eyes to pick out whatever it was she had seen. A couple beside them must have managed it, as they gave a sudden cry of delight, murmuring excitedly to each other.

Finally noticing that she was standing in front of Chloé and Ben's table, the woman looked suddenly sheepish. 'Sorry,' she said, holding out the binoculars. 'Here. Look.'

Ben took them and held them to his eyes. At first he didn't react, combing the view for whatever she'd seen. Then his face lit up in a broad grin.

He passed the binoculars to Chloé. 'There,' he said, pointing. 'On the other side of the fjord. It's just tracing the edge of the water.'

Chloé raised the binoculars, the landscape snapping into clear focus. But she couldn't find anything of note.

'Look at the ridge,' said Ben. 'Between those two mountains. It's about to pass by, walking from right to left.'

Chloé did as instructed, and finally she saw it. White against the snow-covered mountains, she had no idea how anyone could have seen it without the binoculars, but she was glad that the woman had. The bear was padding along the edge of the fjord, head swaying as it sniffed at the ground with a dark muzzle. Chloé was aware that her mouth was hanging open, but she didn't care. She stared at the creature, then gasped as a small white cub came bounding into view.

The cub ran ahead a few paces, before turning to see why its mother had stopped. Chloé, too, was beginning to wonder. It was only as the mother raised her head, looking into the sky, that Chloé realised what had caught her attention. It was the *Osprey*. She was watching as it floated past, moving purposefully down the valley.

For a moment the bear stood where she was, her black eyes fixed on the airship. Then she resumed her course. Rejoining the cub, she began once more to pace beside the water, leaving Longyearbyen behind as they made their way into the wilderness.

Three months later

At a roadside bar, a few miles from Havana's José Martí Airport, Chloé took a swig from a bottle of lager.

With their driver nowhere to be seen when they touched down at the airport, the trip wasn't off to the smoothest of starts. That was OK, though. Chloé knew that the best adventures rarely went to plan. The driver, having realised his mistake, was on his way and, while they waited, she was content to sit in the sun, listen to the music that crackled from a nearby radio and take pictures of the passing traffic. She had read all about Cuba's classic cars, a result of a 1950s ban on foreign-made imports, but it was a joy to see them in person. Already, in the twenty minutes they had been waiting, she had amassed a colourful bank of pictures and video footage for her Instagram.

Just as she was about to capture a particularly fetching '55 Chevy, her phone began to vibrate in her hand. Alec was attempting to reach her via video call.

The moment she answered she saw the irritation in his face, his London office providing an elegant backdrop.

'Was that bloody driver really not waiting at the airport?'

Chloé couldn't help but smile. While it had taken some time, she was growing accustomed to Alec's apparent aversion to a friendly greeting. Ben insisted it was a good thing. If he didn't say hello, it was a sure sign that you were in the circle of trust.

'Should be here any minute,' she said. 'It's not a problem, though. We're getting some brilliant pictures of all the vintage cars.'

'Is Ben there?'

Chloé flipped the phone round, so that Alec could see him. Seated across the plastic table, Ben was busy inspecting his camera.

After they'd returned from Svalbard, Chloé had wondered if she and Ben might have seen the last of each other. As she'd expected, upon hearing what had happened Alec immediately cancelled the feature. Between Howard's death and Ezra's unmasking as his killer, he'd made it clear that not a word on the *Osprey* would be printed in his magazine. It really did seem as if Chloé's time writing for *Condé Nast Traveller* was over before it had even begun. As for Ben, he would have other assignments to set out on, other writers to work with.

She would have been lying if she said the thought didn't leave her despondent. Of the few good things that had come from her time in the Arctic, the friendship she'd struck up with Ben was undoubtedly the best. So she had been pleasantly surprised to find that he was just as eager to stay in touch. They messaged once or twice a week and even met a couple of times for drinks. On both occasions he insisted that he had been waxing lyrical to Alec about how well she had conducted herself aboard the *Osprey*. Chloé believed him, but she was also well aware that this trip to Cuba – her first official assignment for *Condé Nast Traveller* – was more of an apology for all Ezra had put them through than a sign that Alec valued Ben's opinion.

After the *Osprey* departed, they had been required to spend three more days in Longyearbyen, while the local police took their statements. With her laptop and GoPro having lain for some time in the snow before they could safely be recovered, Chloé had been terrified that her footage would be lost. But while the laptop had been damaged, the GoPro was made of sturdier stuff. The footage she had captured was damning – doubly so when Jade admitted to having taken Howard's pills, with no sign of any others in his cabin. A few days later a team member from Skyline Voyages' head office in Tromsø was even able to provide an email, showing that Ezra had personally insisted on the *Osprey*'s water glasses being frosted. But Chloé had still been required to recount everything she and Ezra discussed in the restaurant, going over their conversation again and again as she did her best to repeat it verbatim, for the record.

She had been allowed, under close supervision, to call home and explain the situation. It had taken a gargantuan effort to convince her parents not to book an immediate flight to Longyearbyen. They were satisfied only when the investigating officer took the phone and confirmed that Chloé was being questioned purely as a witness, rather than as a suspect. But that hadn't stopped them travelling from Glasgow to Gatwick on the day she flew home, so that they could meet her at Arrivals.

The media, in the meantime, had been going wild, with Chloé finding on the day she finally came home that the *Osprey* was still on the cover of three different newspapers. A short statement had been issued by Skyline Voyages, announcing that the company was no longer accepting bookings and that its operations had been put on hold until further notice. Likewise, it was mentioned that Howard, Devon and Ezra's bodies were being returned to the UK. But it was the drama of the case, with the airship over the North Pole, the use of helium, the framing of an innocent man and the revelation that Ezra Day himself had been responsible for it all that fuelled the frenzy. The small matter of Ezra's own death at the paws of a polar bear didn't hinder the story, either. Inside the tabloids there were double-page spreads containing headshots and descriptions of everyone who had been on board, with Chloé's own image ripped from her Instagram.

For a week it was all the papers wanted to talk about. Then, just as it looked as if they were beginning to run out of new details to print, things got really out of hand.

Chloé couldn't say how the press got hold of this particular detail, but she was woken one Tuesday morning to the sound of Ellie knocking urgently on her door. It wasn't until a phone was thrust into her hand, and she could see the story herself, that she realised what had happened. Somehow it had become known that the piece of evidence that had unmasked Ezra Day as Howard's killer was a snippet of footage shot on an old GoPro by a twenty-seven-year-old travel blogger. A blogger who had only been invited in the first place to fill in for an unexpected dropout.

Chloé was badgered incessantly on social media by reporters begging her for comment. She was even contacted by the host of a true-crime podcast, asking if she would make a guest appearance to discuss what had happened. Within a few days it became so intense that she'd had to turn her phone off. And on the day she turned it back on, she received a call from Alec.

He had got straight to business, gingerly telling her that the magazine was planning a feature on a new boutique hotel in Cuba, and that if she would like a second chance to prove herself, he would be happy to send her. She would be there for a week, with Ben going as her photographer.

'The offer still stands,' he said curtly. 'Same as last time. Do a good job and we might have more work for you.' He paused at that point to clear his throat, and Chloé could hear from his tone that he was distinctly uncomfortable. 'I feel we probably owe it to you, after everything you went through up on that airship. Take on this job and I hope you'll consider us even.'

As with their first conversation, when Alec had called to offer her his place aboard the *Osprey*, Chloé had been so bowled over by this idea that it took her a moment to process. She recovered quickly, though, and, having pulled herself together, eagerly accepted.

As for the others, she hadn't heard a great deal. Although Liam was held by the police in Longyearbyen for a few more days of questioning, the footage from Chloé's GoPro ensured that the charges against him were dropped, at which point she heard that he had been allowed to return to the UK. She had emailed Jade a couple of times, learning that she was applying for jobs at hotels in London, and that Gwyn – bizarrely – was now cheffing in one of Jasper's restaurants. Jade also revealed that Chloé's suspicions in the hotel restaurant – that Jasper and Madison had split up – had been correct, with a series of fresh modelling shots on Madison's Instagram suggesting that she had returned to the US. Mia looked to be hard at work again at *Green World*, while a quick look at Niamh's LinkedIn profile showed that she had returned to the superyacht recruitment agency where she had worked for nine years before joining Skyline Voyages.

Chloé often wondered about them all. She doubted any of them would forget the experience they had shared at the top of the world. But it seemed as if life was simply carrying on.

'I've just had a very long and apologetic email from the hotel,' Alec continued. 'I've told them a dozen bloody times that it's *you* they should be speaking to, but the message doesn't seem to be getting through. Did they really not say *anything* to you? Didn't try to message while you were on the flight or something?'

Ben shook his head. 'Nope. Must be an honest screw-up. It's all good, though. As Chloé says, we're getting some great stuff with all the vintage motors that keep passing by.'

Before Alec could protest further, a black people carrier skidded to a halt beside the bar, with the name of their hotel printed onto tinted windows. A harassed-looking man stepped out. 'Señor Rhodes,' he called out to them. 'Señorita Campbell?'

'We'll have to call you back, Alec,' said Chloé. 'The driver's here.'

'So he should be. Right, have a good time. Let me know if you run into any more problems. And for God's sake bring me back something good.'

Promising him that they would, Chloé ended the call and put the phone in her rucksack. Beside her, Ben was stowing his camera in its case.

He shot her a grin. 'Ready to go?'

She drained what remained of her beer. Then, gathering up her things, she rose to her feet, unable to withhold a smile of her own. 'Ready.'

Acknowledgements

As ever, I have several friends, family and team members to thank for keeping me going during the writing of this book.

First, thank you to agent extraordinaire Harry Illingworth for all that you do. I'm incredibly fortunate to have you in my corner, and am looking forward to convening somewhere very soon for a celebratory pint.

Thank you to Emily Griffin, Rachel Imrie and Joanna Taylor for trusting me with a premise that felt completely bonkers. I don't suppose any of you will have expected me to suggest an airship over the North Pole for my next idea, but from the moment I suggested it you've been completely on board with me taking a swing. Thank you as well for your editing prowess, and for providing the perspective needed to take my early ramblings and mould them into something coherent. As always, I wouldn't be half as proud of this book were it not for your insight and talent.

Thank you to Sam Rees-Williams and Hana Sparkes for all you do to publicise my books. Whether it's a London tube poster or a line-up of incredible live events, I'm constantly in awe of the effort and creativity you put into presenting these stories to the world.

Thank you to Rob Orme, one of my best friends, for coming with me to Svalbard while I was researching this book. At one point, it looked as if I might be making the trip alone. But I should have known, when I tentatively messaged a few different friends to ask if anyone might come with me, that Rob's answer would be an immediate yes. It's a week that I look back on as one of the best of my life, and I couldn't wish for a better friend to have shared it with.

On the subject of Svalbard, I would highly recommend that anyone who is interested in learning more about this extraordinary place looks up Cecilia Blomdahl, whose brilliant YouTube and Instagram content proved an invaluable source of insight and inspiration. For similar reasons, *Visit Svalbard* was also among my most-visited Instagram channels during the writing of this book. Both are well worth checking out, but for those who are particularly intrigued, trust me when I say that there's no substitute for visiting Svalbard yourself. If you have the chance, just go. You can thank me when you get back.

A shoutout as well to my former clients at Goodyear UK, who generously gave me the opportunity to fly on the Goodyear Blimp in May 2022. To spend an hour aboard an airship in flight was an experience I'll never forget, and one that would ultimately prove invaluable to the writing of this book.

Thank you to Andrew Plygawko and Luke Maw, not

only two of my best mates but also two of the smartest guys I know, for chatting to me about some of the various ways one might identify a room that has been full of helium. I wish I could somehow have found a way to work the digital clock into the story, but the suggestion of scented gas was pivotal in its own right.

Four books into my career, it seems more than appropriate to give an extra special thank you to my readers. To everyone who has bought a book, come to an event or said something nice on social media . . . The support you've shown me these last few years has been little short of astonishing. On a similar note, thank you to all of the incredible booksellers who have championed my writing. Whether it be by recommending my books, putting them in shop windows, organising reading groups . . . None of this would be happening if it weren't for you, and I'm eternally grateful to each and every one of you.

Finally, thank you to my wife Hayley for putting up with me for yet another book. Your patience and confidence in me have been as unwavering as ever. Perhaps even more so, having been pregnant with our first child during the gargantuan process of editing this book. I tend to sign these things off by saying that I hope I'm making you proud. I suppose I need to update that now, and speak to both you and the newest arrival of our little family. All of this – every word I write and every story I dream up – is for the two of you.